DEFINING THE PROBLEM

Moscow was no more.

In one atomic instant had disappeared not only the city itself, but a rich cultural tradition and the intellectual and political leadership of the land. Yet most of the uniformed men sitting around the conference table had not yet fully grasped the implications of the sudden disappearance of the hub of Mother Russia.

But the Deputy Minister of Defense, who had by grudging common consent become Acting Premier, was a career army officer and only too ready to seize the military option as the best means of asserting and consolidating his new power. And the target was not only obvious but vulnerable.

"The Republic of Texas," intoned Acting Premier Luchenko. "We shall crush it underfoot as if it were a cockroach."

By Daniel da Cruz
Published by Ballantine Books:

F-CUBED

THE GROTTO OF THE FORMIGANS

THE AYES OF TEXAS
TEXAS ON THE ROCKS
TEXAS TRIUMPHANT

MIXED DOUBLES

TEXAS
TRIUMPHANT

Daniel da Cruz

A Del Rey Book

BALLANTINE BOOKS • NEW YORK

A Del Rey Book
Published by Ballantine Books

Library of Congress Catalog Card Number: 87-1176

ISBN 0-345-35878-3

Manufactured in the United States of America

First Hardcover Edition: December 1987
First Mass Market Edition: November 1989

Cover Art by Barclay Shaw

CONTENTS

For
Leila

1. HOLOCAUST
2 AUGUST 2008

GONE WERE THE KREMLIN, RED SQUARE, LENIN'S TOMB. Vanished were the University of Moscow, Gorky Park, Lubyanka Prison, GUM department store, the 5,000-room Rossiya Hotel. Drifting over Central Europe was an enormous cloud of dust—atomized remains of block after soulless block of gray apartment buildings, bridges that had spanned the Moskva River, museums, sports stadia, and monolithic Soviet ministries.

Moscow was no more.

Most of the uniformed men around the conference table had not yet fully grasped the implications of the sudden disappearance of the hub of Mother Russia. In one atomic instant had disappeared not only the city itself, but a rich cultural tradition and the intellectual and political leadership of the land. Those present were themselves the most eminent survivors. Men who had commanded army corps, presided over provincial universities, chaired party apparatus of autonomous republics, headed KGB directories—these were the new masters of the Soviet Union, and they sensed that they must act quickly and with decision to solidify the power history had thrust upon them.

The Deputy Minister of Defense, Marshal Evgeniy Luchenko, had by grudging common consent become Acting Premier. After all, the marshal, who had been on an inspection tour when the atomic explosion leveled Moscow, had the support of the remaining army commanders, and as always in the Soviet Union, power came out the barrel of a gun. A career officer, Luchenko saw the military option as the best means of asserting and consolidating his new power, and the target was not only obvious but vulnerable. "The Republic of Texas," he intoned.

1

"Why Texas?" asked Uzbek Communist Party chief Vladimir Dmitrevich Pirogov. Pirogov knew that Luchenko had been a liaison officer with the ill-fated 17th High Seas Fleet when Admiral Grell led it to a watery death in the Battle of the Black Channel against the Texans.

"Because the Texans are responsible for the annihilation of Moscow."

Acting KGB chairman Pavel Pavlovich Milstein laughed mirthlessly. "Nonsense! Moscow was destroyed by a hydrogen bomb—or bombs. The Texans do not themselves manufacture nuclear weapons, and our agents confirm that American bomb stockpiles show no loss accountable to diversion of warheads to the Texans. Your own radar reports indicate that no incoming missiles were sighted before Moscow was destroyed. And as for a bomb's introduction through, say, the diplomatic pouch—that's preposterous, given the KGB's meticulous inspection of all cargos destined for Moscow."

Luchenko feigned deep thought and gave Milstein a little rope. "Then what is *your* theory, Comrade?"

"Doesn't the explosion speak for itself? The only atomic warheads in the Moscow area were those concealed among the antimissile missiles of our ABM net. They weren't—*couldn't* have been—set off simultaneously . . . by accident. Therefore, it stands to reason that the explosions were deliberate, detonated by suicidal internal enemies."

"Would you care to name names, Comrade?" Luchenko's voice held a hint of menace.

Milstein's smile was bland. "All I can say is that the KGB, at least, doesn't have access to warheads in the custody of the military."

"You are accusing the military of this monumental crime!" Luchenko thundered.

"I make no accusations. The facts accuse."

Luchenko paused to allow Milstein's challenge to take root in the minds of the fourteen men around the conference table. They would remember Milstein's insinuation, his disloyalty, his appalling failure to get the facts that he thought damned Luchenko—a criminal dereliction in a KGB chief. And, when Luchenko proved that Texas was indeed the author of the Moscow holocaust, Milstein would cease to be a contender for power.

Marshal Luchenko built a pyramid of fingers. "The facts are these: Analysis of radio traffic between Odessa and Moscow, monitored by RU Kiev MD on that fatal day of 22 July, indicates *one* cargo *did* pass KGB scrutiny and entered Moscow uninspected. Apparently authorized personally by General Grigoriy Aleksandrevich Piatakov, late chief of Room 101—which I think everyone here is aware was a KGB operation. The cargo consisted of a sealed steel shipping container delivered to Odessa by submarine. The submarine was acting on the orders of that same General Piatakov.

"And where did that container come from? According to radio traffic, from the Turkish steamer *Kara Deniz*—which a Soviet submarine intercepted. The container was listed on the ship's manifest as a Computerized Milling Machine. Its point of origin: SD-1 in Houston, the underground research center of Ripley Forte. Where and how Forte laid hands on a hydrogen bomb is still a mystery, but it is known that shortly after the container's scheduled arrival in Moscow, the city went up in a mushroom cloud." Luchenko smiled seraphically.

The other fifteen men around the table were silent. In the battle of wills, there was no doubt that Luchenko had emerged the winner over Milstein.

Pirogov presented the laurel to Luchenko by saying, "What do you recommend we do, Comrade Marshal?"

"Attack Texas, of course. We cannot allow the capitalist dogs to destroy our capital with impunity, to play at David and Goliath. We shall crush it underfoot as if it were a cockroach."

"Nuclear missiles?" came the question.

"Yes. Swift, sure, conclusive. Texas will never bother us again."

"On the other hand," said Geli Sergeevich Bryntsev, a soft-spoken theoretician whose views everyone respected, "perhaps the United States will. Once we begin dropping nuclear bombs on the American continent, we cannot be sure that the Americans won't retaliate, claiming that we are trying to kill them with radioactive fallout, using our defensive strike on Texas only as a pretext."

"Nevertheless," Luchenko insisted, "Texas must be punished with the fullest rigor at our command."

"Unquestionably," Bryntsev agreed, "but why barbecue the cow when we can capture it, milk it, and enjoy its butter and cheese forever after?"

"How do you mean?"

"Well," said Bryntsev, "Texas is on its way to becoming the richest small country in the world. By next year, in the form of icebergs, every fortnight it will be bringing a billion tons of fresh water to Matagorda Bay. Within a year or two, the harvest of fresh water will be reaped every five days. That water, sold to the parched United States, will pour gold into Texas' coffers. More will come from the electricity sold to the U.S. as a result of ocean thermal energy conservation, with icebergs supplying power for Forte's OTEC units. And, according to our sources, down the road Forte plans to drill geothermal wells, thus exploiting the enormous heat far under the earth's surface to drive generators with superheated steam."

"You're suggesting we do *not* destroy Texas but rather capture it and load its riches on the Soviet war chariot?"

Bryntsev shook his head. "No, I do not recommend that course of action. We've tried it, and it failed. After World War II, we stripped conquered Europe bare—we even got the Americans to help, using the good offices of our agent White in the Treasury Department—and it took a generation for Europe to recover, but at no advantage to ourselves. Rather, I suggest we *conquer* Texas, in the process visiting a necessary and precautionary punishment on Houston, Ripley Forte's home town. It should be severe enough to quell forevermore the Texans' natural delight in rebellion."

"And then?"

"Occupation. Let the Texans work for us. We will, periodically, drain off excess capital to keep them honest and hungry. But Texas, of course, isn't the major prize."

"What is?"

"The United States, naturally. Within two years the

U.S. will be dependent on Texas for the water and power it needs to survive. We will graciously allow it to survive. We are, after all, lovers of our fellow man."

"But at a price..." Luchenko nodded, grinning broadly. "And on our own terms. Without firing a shot."

"Correction," said Bryntsev. "*One* shot: to avenge our national honor, Ripley Forte must die."

2. THE GREAT TEXAS TURKEY SHOOT 12 SEPTEMBER 2008

THE DIM GLOW OF FALSE DAWN TINGED THE EASTERN sky as Soviet Task Force Aleksandr Vasilyevich Suvorov—aircraft carriers, missile cruisers, frigates, destroyers, supply ships and tenders, oilers, and troop ships totaling seventy-three ships—steamed at flank speed toward the coast of the Republic of Texas.

"Thirty minutes to H-hour, sir," murmured Commander Yuriy Akhromeyev, aide to Fleet Admiral Piotr Solyman Maximov.

"Very well." The task force commander scanned the coastline south of Galveston with high-powered binoculars. Empty.

It was just as well. Maximov was a humane man. He didn't enjoy killing people even when the circumstances demanded it. Of course, Houston would have to be obliterated, along with those of its three and a half million inhabitants who had lacked the good sense to flee. This was only just, if woefully insufficient, retribution for the monumental crimes visited upon the Soviet Union by the Forte family of Houston. But Maximov would be happy to avoid any further bloodshed, and the undefended Texas coastline seemed to promise there would be none.

"Updated surveillance reports, sir." Chief of Staff

Captain, first rank, Rodion Yakovich Yakovlev saluted and proffered a clipboard.

"Read them." The admiral, though squat, thick-shouldered, and already bald at forty-seven, was still vain enough to wear his reading glasses only in the privacy of his own cabin. He put the binoculars to his eyes and pretended to examine the vast panorama of Soviet seapower stretching out to the horizon.

"Satellite reconnaissance indicates virtually no activity anywhere within Houston's eighteen-hundred-square-kilometer city limits, sir. Factories and oil refineries throughout the metropolitan area have ceased operations—not a thread of smoke or a burning flare-gas jet is visible anywhere. Highways are deserted, and local traffic is at a standstill. Schools and offices are closed, hospitals emptied. It's a dead city."

"Not quite yet," Fleet Admiral Maximov replied grimly. "But in two hours it will be, without the option of resurrection. We're going to have what Texans call a 'turkey shoot.'"

"I doubt there will be many turkeys left to shoot, sir. In the three weeks since our task force left Murmansk, most of Houston's civilian population has run for its life."

That was true—and odd, now that Maximov thought about it. Abandoning their sprawling metropolis was inconsistent with the Texans' traditional arrogance, bravado, and recklessness, so evident during the Battle of the Black Channel in 1998. Had they lost their nerve, or had they merely become wise, acknowledging that Soviet power was overwhelming, refusing to immolate themselves on the funeral pyre he would soon ignite?

"But I suppose the Texas Defense Forces will feel compelled to die to the last man—Alamo spirit and all that," Maximov commented. "Pity we have to destroy brave men fighting for a hopeless cause."

Chief of Staff Yakovlev laid his clipboard on the pilot house radarscope, took off his hat with the scrambled eggs on the brim, and mopped his forehead. Even at that predawn hour, a hot and clammy mist hovered above the oil-smooth waters of the Gulf of Mexico, and the bridge of the flagship *Beria* was not air-conditioned. "Perhaps not, sir. The TDF seems to have followed the Houstonians' excellent example: it has apparently taken to the hills, too."

"I don't believe it."

Captain Yakovlev held out the clipboard. "See for yourself, sir. These are the latest satellite and long-range aerial reconnaissance reports. We've not had a single sighting of any hostile force around Houston during the past twelve hours. Infrared surveillance photographs indicate that Houston's Air Defense Squadron flew to bases in north Texas during the night. As for ground forces, Intelligence believes they were part of the general exodus from Houston over the past ten days."

Maximov didn't read the reports. No matter what they said, he knew the Texans would fight back. Even if they did, though, there was little to fear. Although they were conceded to be first-rate in terms of discipline, efficiency, and advanced weaponry, the Texas Defense Forces were inconsequential compared with the Soviet task force now approaching the southern coast. To be sure, Ripley Forte's Sunshine Industries was rumored to have perfected some ingenious weapons. But rumors and boastful lies had always been among Texas' principal exports. The only reliable intelligence the GRU and KGB had provided was that each of their infantrymen, who numbered a mere two reinforced regiments comprising 12,600 men, was a highly mobile assault force in himself. Individually mounted on air-cushion vehicles, the infantrymen could cover 425 miles a day over rugged terrain, deploy, and hold their own against units several times their size.

Their Waka tanks were similarly fast and deadly. The low-profile, two-man jet-propelled surface-effect craft, weighing a mere seven tons, skittered across the Texas landscape like hummingbirds, depending on agility, stealth, and speed to evade enemy gunners. Unfortunately for the TDF, it had only eighty Wakas and, as satellite photos showed, they had joined the general flight northward.

As for the Texas Air Force, it was a joke: two squadrons totaling twenty-four single-place Doozer aircraft. They were small and slow—top speed was a pathetic

Mach .87—although nimble, thanks to vectoring jets.

Against the Texas Defense Forces, which would have been hard-pressed to conquer Kansas City, was ranged the might of Task Force Aleksandr Vasilyevich Suvorov, the most powerful fleet to put to sea since World War II. Fleet Admiral Maximov's 140,000-ton flagship, the carrier *Beria*, could easily have annihilated the Texas Defense Forces all by itself. Its seventy-eight MI-37 Baez helicopter gunships, thirty-six heavily-armored two-man MiG-53 Spock fighters, and forty-four Sukhoi-38 Fonda bombers would be part of an armada of nearly four hundred aircraft blasting Houston into rubble.

The *Beria*'s formidable striking power was backed up, moreover, by seventy-two other ships, many of them loaded with naval infantry capable of fighting a protracted campaign ashore. This time, the Russians were taking no chances.

"Ten minutes to launch," said Captain Yakovlev.

"Very well," Fleet Admiral Maximov said. It was going to be the shortest war in history, he reflected, glancing at his watch. H-Hour was at 0545, less than two minutes away. The aerial assault would level Houston in a single wave—the devastation of the heavy bombers completed by the tens of thousands of incendiary bomblets dropped by nearly a hundred Clark heavy-lift helicopters. By 0700 Houston would become the center of a gigantic firestorm dwarfing that of Dresden in 1945. By nightfall nothing would be left of the proud city but twisted skeletons of buildings, heaps of smoldering cinders, and bodies charred beyond recognition. Whatever forces Texas mustered to oppose the Russian tank advance would be mowed down like a field of summer wheat.

"Coming up to H-Hour, sir," said Captain Yakovlev.

"Very well." Fleet Admiral Maximov looked down on the flight deck, where all faces were turned toward him on the bridge, awaiting his command. "Launch strike force!" he ordered.

From nine aircraft carriers with the huge Red Star painted on their flight decks, MiG-53 Spock fighters were shot aloft from twin catapults to provide high cover for the Sukhoi-38 Fonda VTOL bombers, which rose vertically from the same flight decks at five-second intervals. As the last of the bombers cleared the deck, the leaders, far out of sight overhead, eased their thrusters into a horizontal plane and shot forward, pulling the rest of their groups along in their wake like a string of water skiers.

At 0555 radar operators aboard the *Beria* reported that 380 Sukhoi-38 Fondas in successive waves were headed northward toward Houston at two thousand meters. Another 120 MiG-53 Spocks were flying cover at eleven thousand meters.

Just as the last formations of aircraft were crossing the Texas coastline, the first of Fleet Admiral Maximov's amphibious forces were landing upon it, disgorging hundreds of PR-94 main battle tanks, which rumbled down bow ramps and across undefended beaches. By 0927 forty-four columns of twenty-five tanks each were rumbling unopposed toward Houston, sixty miles away.

Aboard the troop ships, a *spetsnaz* regiment and four brigades of naval infantry were loading their armored personnel carriers aboard landing craft, preparing to follow the tank advance, suppress any remaining resistance, and occupy the principal cities and communications centers in the Republic of Texas.

By Sunday night, 14 September, two days hence, the conquest would be complete.

"Red Leader to Wolf Pack—southern boundary of target area coming up in thirty seconds. Arm all ordnance." Red Leader Colonel Fyodor Petrovich Primakov looked up from his instruments to the brightening sky overhead. Formations of Spocks were spread across the heavens, invisible except for their condensation trails ten miles above him. The parallel contrails were as regular as if drawn with a straightedge, which meant that no Texas bogies had been sighted—if they had been, the contrails would have curved as the Spocks changed course. Intelligence was right, for once—no resistance.

Primakov glanced down at the earth, alternate rectangular patches of green and brown, dotted here and there with clusters of houses and farm buildings. Of human activity there was no sign. Up ahead three or four miles away the city began. His own target was beyond, an ugly, decrepit industrial complex of a company called Air Products, Inc. He wondered about the health of a nation where even the air had to be manufactured.

"Target in sight, Colonel," his weapons systems operator said over the intercom. "Please come to course 007."

"Acknowledged," said Colonel Primakov.

It was the last thing he would ever say, for an instant later an invisible knife sliced four feet off the starboard wing, fuel from the ruptured wing tank was ignited by the jet's flaming exhaust, and the Fonda vanished in a huge fireball that cartwheeled across the sky like an exploding star.

In the one or two seconds they had to live, pilots behind Red Leader were frozen with horror before their planes were cut in two and they joined their commander in fiery death. Back in the pack, other pilots jinked wildly to escape, some switching to afterburners and diving toward the ground, others breaking off into acrobatic turns and rolls as if to escape the phantom fighters right behind them. The menace *had* to be behind them: MiG-53s were providing top cover, and no enemy streaked toward them from any other quarter. As for ground-based antiaircraft artillery or missiles, their radarscopes showed no sign of them.

And yet, when they had come out on top of their loops facing to the rear, pilots found the sky there empty, too. And Fondas-become-fireballs kept lighting up the sky; neither speed nor altitude nor evasive action seemed to offer any protection. Only distance from Houston. Echelons far to the rear observed that only when their comrades neared Houston's city limits were they blasted out of the sky. Not all of them, to be sure. A few had firewalled their throttles, even while their wingmates were going up in flames, and pressed in upon the city to drop their bombs. The pilots who managed to complete their mission were the exception—but at a terrible cost: while attempting to return to base, every one was blasted out of the sky.

The leaders of following wings, after quick radio consultation with the chief air operations officer aboard the

Beria, broke off before they reached the danger zone and led their wings back to their carriers, where the air staff would consider what to do in this grave emergency. And emergency it was, for of the 380 Sukhoi-38 Fondas that had taken off, 66 had been shot down, all within the space of five minutes. Enough operational aircraft remained to destroy the city, to be sure, but even a fleet admiral's career could come to an abrupt end over such losses.

Maximov personally interviewed the first pilot who landed his plane aboard the *Beria*. "What the hell happened?" he demanded.

"I wish I knew," said the shaken pilot. "The lead planes were flying normally, when all of a sudden a wing seemed to shear off, the plane torched and went down. One plane two miles ahead of me was bisected right down the middle. The two separated sides were a couple hundred meters apart when they disappeared in a ball of fire. It was as if the plane had been cut with a—with a—well, *razor*."

"You mean laser."

"No, sir—razor. There was no visible beam, and nonvisible light would have triggered the detectors."

"Razors don't fly, Lieutenant. So what the hell *was* it?"

The pilot looked at him, his mind as blank as his eyes.

"Will they be coming back?" asked the scared young radar technician as he tracked the cloud of blips on his screen, heading back across the Texas coastline and out to sea.

Major Gerard Murphy of the Texas Defense Forces, commanding Baker battery of four rail guns, nodded. "Probably. The Russkies don't give up easy. We surprised them, and Russians sometimes come apart at the seams when the unpredictable happens. But they have all day to figure it out, and when they do—yes, they'll be back."

"From the south?"

Murphy, a transplanted Dubliner whose lips were made for laughter, laughed—mirthlessly. "Look, son, these guys aren't television Russians. They're real.

They're professionals. Next time out they could come from *any* direction—any direction *but* south."

And when they did, Houston was doomed. The TDF had only seventeen of the rail guns, and the TDF Chief of Staff Major General Mark D. Raymond had decided against dispersing them. Reasoning that the Russians, seeing Houston apparently undefended, would send their planes on the most direct course to reach the city, he had deployed all seventeen kinetic energy weapons on the city's southern approaches. By sending away most of the Texas Defense Forces, he had disarmed the natural Russian instinct for tactical finesse, and they had barreled straight on in, just as he hoped they would. But next time around, they'd spill out of the skies from the east or west, perhaps even the north. And they would find those approaches undefended.

Major Murphy swore, in Gaelic, a language whose oaths had been honed to needle sharpness by dint of much usage against Ireland's English oppressors over the centuries. If only, he thought . . .

If only Sunshine Industries, which had perfected the Jim Bowie rail gun, had been able to deliver a hundred of them—or even seventy or eighty—Houston might have been completely ringed with iron, and thus spared. Unfortunately, the weapon had been rushed into production only three months earlier.

The rail gun's range was only thirty-one miles, but the weapon fired projectiles at the rate of one every four seconds, and with passive radar had a kill ratio of 91 percent. But it required an enormous expenditure of electrical energy. So General Raymond had ordered Houston's factories closed and the population evacuated from the city. While the exodus was still in progress, new high-tension lines were being laid under cover of darkness to the Jim Bowie batteries south of the city. There, in conical shafts sunk into the ground, the kinetic energy weapons were mounted. The Jim Bowies were electronic slingshots fired automatically, aimed and triggered by radiation of an enemy plane's own active radar as it passed overhead.

* * *

It was toward the southern approaches that the Russian armored spearhead also thrust. Eleven hundred tanks rolled north from the coastal city of Freeport in a great pincers movement aimed at surrounding the city then pounding to dust what was left after the bombers had done their work. The tanks advanced in a wide front over range and farmland, then separated into two extended formations at Angleton. The two divisions of tanks on the right flank, comprising the Operational Maneuver Group Karaganda, pounded through Danbury, five kilometers to the northeast of Angleton, then headed for the Houston suburb of Pasadena. Leading elements of the two tank divisions of OMG Ulanbator, simultaneously passing through West Columbia, would swing in a wide circle around Houston from the west and link up with OMG Karaganda. The four divisions would then converge on the town center, destroying anything and anybody the air assault had missed.

Two kilometers north of Danbury, the open plain that lay before OMG Karaganda was suddenly obscured by a curtain of smoke rising from the ground. OMG Karaganda commander Colonel Valentin Starozhilov, in the lead tank, radioed orders to close up the formation and prepare for action, and plunged ahead through the smoke at full speed. Three hundred meters farther on the smoke cleared, to reveal the totally unexpected presence of what must have been the entire TDF tank corps, three score hovertanks.

The earth heaved beneath the tank on Colonel Starozhilov's left, keeping strict formation at forty-eight kilometers per hour. It flipped over on its back, gouged a thirty-meter ditch with its turret, and blew apart as its ammunition ignited. Starozhilov's ears rang with the crash of gunfire as his tank commander began to return the surprise barrage. Within seconds the Wakas turned and fled, with the Russians in hot pursuit. The Soviet tanks kept up a steady fire with their cannon, but while the earth erupted all around the enemy tanks, half a minute later they all disappeared, unscathed, into another cloud of smoke.

The Russians followed, only to emerge on the other

side of the smoke curtain, but of the Texan tanks themselves—no sign.

The Soviet losses had been light—only five tanks destroyed in the ambuscade. But where had the enemy gone?

Twice again the TDF Wakas were sighted through a veil of smoke. Twice again the enemy inflicted a few casualties before turning tail and disappearing under the cover of smoke. The chase had taken no more than fifteen minutes, all told, but in pursuing the Texan tanks OMG Karaganda had veered off its course and was now heading due west.

"What the hell is going on, Colonel?" exclaimed his exasperated tank commander. "We're hot on the heels of the bastards, and they disappear in a puff of smoke, only to pop up out of the blue."

"I don't know," said Starozhilov. "But whatever it is, I don't like it." The fact that they had reached the crest of a long, sloping hill, beyond which he could discern outlying buildings in Houston's suburbs, did nothing to reassure him. Nor did scouts' reports that their present position was bordered by an antitank ditch running parallel to their line of advance on the west, while to the east his flankers reported the presence of an extensive minefield that the Texans had not troubled to camouflage. He ordered the group to close up, cut its advance to fifteen kph, and keep a sharp lookout on all sides.

The Russian tanks rolled slowly forward at close intervals, almost tread to tread, occupying a front fifteen tanks across and some thirty-five ranks deep. Ahead was nothing but kilometer after kilometer of emptiness, broken only by occasional farmhouses and outbuildings. Colonel Starozhilov called a halt, opened the turret, and carefully examined the countryside around them. Deserted, but its very quiet was somehow ominous.

"Tank 277," he radioed to the behemoth on his right flank. "Scout the area dead ahead. Deploy your mine detectors and report anything suspicious. Look for concealed entrances to underground tank parks." The tank rumbled forward for nearly four hundred meters at walking speed, then suddenly stopped.

"Tank ditch ahead, sir. Camouflaged with painted canvas."

Tank 277's turret opened and a tanker jumped down to investigate. A minute later the radio crackled again. "The ditch is five meters wide and six deep, sir. It looks as though it extends clear across our front."

So *that's* what it was. The Texans had led him into a trap. Colonel Starozhilov heaved a sigh of relief. It could have been a lot worse. As it was, he'd merely swing OMG Karaganda to its flank, proceed a few kilometers, then resume his descent upon the city.

The voice of Tank 227's commander suddenly broke through the static: "Colonel, the camouflage cover is afire!"

Starozhilov put his field glasses to his eyes. The camouflage was indeed aflame, spreading faster than a man could run. Within seconds it had spread from directly in front of Tank 227 to the extremities of the ditch, three hundred meters in each direction. Then, to Starozhilov's horror, the fire was racing back toward them, on both sides of his tank force. The ditch was not merely on their front: like a fiery claw, *it surrounded three sides of the entire OMG.*

"One-hundred-and-eighty-degree turn, all units!" Colonel Starozhilov bellowed into his throat mike. "Full speed to the rear! On the double!"

The tank commanders had practiced the maneuver countless times, and all swung 180 degrees to the left without undue haste or confusion, and lumbered in good formation back toward the crest of the hill they had just descended. The fire behind and on both sides was moving fast, but the tanks were moving faster. Once they passed the hill crest they'd be safe, for the ground there had been solid, or else it wouldn't have borne the weight of more than five hundred heavy tanks.

The foremost rank of tanks was only a hundred meters from safety when the crest itself was engulfed in flames. To try to break through the barrier of flame, which might be a hundred meters wide, for all anybody knew, would be suicide. The fire would ignite the external reserve fuel tanks, the rear ammunition storage racks would blow, and the tank and its nine-man crew would become a spectacular fireball.

As one, the tanks ground to a halt. Colonel Starozhilov, whose heart was beating rather faster than usual, didn't panic. He reasoned that the fuel that fired the flames would soon be consumed. When it was, OMG Karaganda would return to Danbury and then resume the advance on Houston. Meanwhile, they'd wait it out. Advising his commanders to keep on the alert, he opened the turret and climbed to the ground, lighting a cigarette casually to demonstrate to his men that they had nothing to fear.

He walked among the tanks, exchanging a quip here, giving a word of reassurance there, but all the time observing without seeming to the flames that surrounded them. Ten minutes passed, and the flames did not slacken. Starozhilov was embarrassed, and a little afraid, for his impetuous departure from the plan of attack would not go unnoticed. Walking back to his tank to see if the tanks on the flanks had anything to report, he noticed that the ground seemed to have gone soft beneath his feet, as if soaked in the rains of autumn.

It wasn't rain. It was crude oil.

Colonel Starozhilov ran back to his tank, climbed down the hatch, and pressed the mike to his throat. "Attention all personnel! All engines are to be turned off and smoking is prohibited until further notice. To avoid causing sparks, be careful where you step. And don't worry —we'll be out of here within the quarter hour."

Colonel Starozhilov was as good as his word. Ten minutes passed. The ground underfoot became too soggy to walk, and the tankers had emerged from the interior of their machines to take the soft if oil-soaked summer air before they cranked up their engines once more. At the crest of the hill the fire had about burned itself out. In a few minutes it would be safe to move.

Colonel Starozhilov was looking in that direction, impatiently counting the minutes, when a lone horseman appeared on the skyline. Though he was a good three hundred meters away, Colonel Starozhilov saw that the rider was dressed in movie-Texan fashion, wearing a white ten-gallon hat and a spangled jacket that flashed in the morning sun. The horseman stopped and looked down the slope at the scores of tanks, their treads slowly sinking in the oil-soaked earth. Then he pulled what looked like a long-barreled revolver from a scabbard on the saddle and pointed it at the sky. The flare made a slow, majestic arc and flamed down among the tanks. . . .

During that same hour of the morning, another horseman, similarly attired, paid one brief last call to Operational Maneuver Group Ulanbator, some miles to the west of the small town of West Columbia. He, too, fired a flare pistol.

It was the last shot fired in the Russo-Texas War of 2008.

When the radios of the two OMGs suddenly fell silent, one shortly after the other, Admiral Maximov dispatched a squadron of helicopters to determine what exactly had happened. Their report confirmed his fears.

That same day, fearing that if further disasters occurred to Task Force Aleksandr Vasilyevich Suvorov the Americans would feel emboldened to declare war—and win—Premier Luchenko recalled the fleet to Russia.

3. PROSOPAGNOSIA
19 SEPTEMBER 2008

PRESIDENT TOM TRAYNOR WAS GAZING DOURLY OUT THE window of the "Little White House" office overlooking the capital of the Republic of Texas when Ripley Forte was announced. Cherokee Tom turned, his expression still grim. He shook his old friend's hand and motioned him to a chair opposite the old oak desk that had once belonged to Sam Houston. Mounted on the wall behind the desk were the strategic defensive initiative of a Texas longhorn, as wide as the smile with which Forte favored Traynor. Traynor didn't return it.

"Why the long face, Mr. President?" Forte inquired. "I thought I'd find you in that special place in heaven reserved for commanders-in-chief whose troops have just kicked hell out of the enemy."

"I was. After all, I'm only human. But I'm also president, and I finally came down out of the clouds to think about where do we go from here. That's when I called you to come pow-wow."

"I'm afraid I don't follow."

"Well, we beat the Russians, all right, but what do we do for an encore? I was musing last night that last week was the second time in exactly ten years that the Soviet Union tried to wipe out Texas. In 1998 your father Gwillam, God rest his soul, pulled our chestnuts out of the fire by sinking the Soviet's 17th High Seas Fleet before he went to the bottom in the old *Texas*. Then, a week ago, they tried again, and again it was a Forte that constituted our defenses. But what happens when they attack again?"

"What makes you think they will?"

Traynor snorted. "History, wounded pride, ambition, hunger for vengeance, political necessity, Muscovite meanness—take your pick. The Russians have been on the march ever since Muscovy was a principality the size of Pecos County, about the year 1500. Since then they've subjugated practically all the real estate in the world worth owning—at the rate of something like twice the area of Manhattan—*every day, for five hundred years*. You know as well as I that, despite this setback, they mean to have the rest."

"Probably, but not in our lifetime, Mr. President."

"That's exactly my point, Rip: not in *our* lifetime. But the time will come. And where is the Forte who'll ride to the rescue then?"

Forte refrained from the downcast eye and modest disclaimer. He knew perfectly well that the president's flattery was calculated to disarm him, to lay him open for some incautious commitment, which honor would then force him to fulfill. "I hope you've got this line of blarney on tape, Mr. President, because I want a copy. It'll help console me when I call in the computers to tote up how much all these kind words are going to cost me."

A slow smile illuminated the Texan's face. "You'll have it. Still, I'm deadly serious when I reiterate that it's only because of the imagination, resources, and patriotism of the Fortes, father and son—along with a generous helping of Texas luck—that there's a Republic of Texas today. But you're the last of the line, and when you pass on—doubtless kicking and screaming—your labs will be split up among your quarreling kinfolk, and the splendid team and the continuity of defense effort made over the years at SD-1 will last about as long as a fart in a whirlwind."

"I see," said Forte, his jaw tightening. "You're talking nationalization."

"Yeah—me and Joe Stalin. I always *was* a closet commie." He chuckled. Then his jollity subsided. "What I'm talking about is preparing for war—the Texas-Russia War, Round Three—while we still have you and SD-1 and the chance to win it."

"I'm just a private citizen," Forte protested, "and SD-1 is merely the R & D arm of Sunshine Industries, a profit-making—sometimes—corporation. What you're asking for is a long-range national defense effort, not a finger in a leaking dike. That's too big for SD-1. That should be bankrolled with public funds."

"Which the public will never willingly part with—not, at least, until the comrades are wading ashore for the third time." Traynor sighed. "That's the American way."

Forte contemplated the white-haired, ruddy-faced man across the desk. Traynor had been his friend and political ally for a long time, and his father's before him. Forte had no compunction about turning down a request from an officeholder; indeed, it was his natural reaction. But friendship was different. "What do you want me to do?"

Traynor's stern features relaxed. "The Russians have come twice in ten years, and many brave Texans died. The bastards will come calling again, as sure as county road commissioners have unnumbered Swiss bank accounts. When they do, we must not allow a single Texan to be at peril. This means that we must be able, at the first sign of Soviet aggression, to defeat them. And when I say defeat, I mean *annihilate*.

"To do this means that we must possess a weapon that is totally secret, totally intimidating, totally effective, and impossible to defend against. The weapon I have in mind will be the ultimate in stealth, speed, and destructive force. Only when it becomes evident that the Soviets are about to launch an attack against us will we call in their ambassador and reveal to him his country's peril and helplessness, and make them leash the dogs of war."

"A piece of cake," Forte said, straight-faced. "I'll have the boys work it out over the weekend. Come down Tuesday for a demonstration. We'll destroy New York State."

"Okay, I'm asking for miracles. But you're in the miracle business, Rip. You're the guy who brought in—brings in every fortnight—billion-ton icebergs from the Antarctic, when the mere idea used to get horselaughs from the scientific community."

Ripley Forte massaged his weatherlined face and looked into space. "Very well, Mr. President," he said finally, "we'll have a shot at it. No promises. But it would help if you could share with me just what kind of weapon you want."

President Traynor pursed his lips. "I can't say at the moment—top secret, you know—but when you've got it built, call me, and I'll tell you if it's what I want."

"The weapons're not the problem," insisted Dr. Ho Yang Pao, the slight young systems analyst whom Ripley Forte had assigned as project coordinator among the dozen department heads who sat around the big conference table deep underground at SD-1. "We have a number of fast-acting alternatives—nuclear devices foremost among them, then lethal bacteriological and chemical agents and their myriad variations. But we must decide which target, or targets, must be threatened with annihilation if push comes to shove with the Russians. Also, how to deliver the weapon virtually instantaneously."

"No doubt about it," agreed Ripley Forte, in the chair at the head of the table. "The target must be so vital that its loss would automatically destroy the Soviet regime. The optimum target, therefore, will be the regime itself. That is to say, the city of Kiev, where the leadership is headquartered."

"Amen," said Leslie Schmida, SD-1's chief of civil engineering, whose family had been exterminated by Russian fire-bombing during the Soviet assault on Houston in 1998. "Better two million Soviet dead than another Texan."

"Discussion?" Forte queried.

There was none.

"Kiev it is . . . Which brings us to the next item on the agenda. As Dr. Ho pointed out, our arsenals bulge with weapons that can destroy a city like Kiev in short order. How to get them there in a hurry is the problem."

"Satellite-deployed munitions?" someone suggested.

"Vulnerable to ground-based lasers, killer satellites, or kinetic energy weapons like the Jim Bowie," Forte pointed out. "Our satellites would be their *first* target in any new assault against Texas."

"And submarine-based missiles would be equally ineffective," Dr. Ho added. "Before the Russians launched a new attack they'd mobilize their defense forces. The 2,000-mile overland trajectory of our missiles would expose them to Russian antimissile missiles before they got halfway to the Ukraine."

Forte nodded. "So that eliminates aerial and subsurface means of weapons delivery. Any bright ideas?" He looked around the table at a dozen blank faces. "Very well, think about delivery methods between now and our meeting tomorrow, and let's get on to the next item on the agenda—the weapon itself."

"Prosopagnosia," said Per Lindstrom, a laconic polymath who headed biological sciences at SD-1.

Forte lifted an eyebrow. "Come again?"

"Prosopagnosia is a rare condition that afflicts persons suffering damage by trauma or stroke to that tiny portion of the brain that processes information about faces. A prosopagnosic looking in a mirror cannot recognize his own face, let alone those of others."

Lindstrom could always be depended on for stimulating observations. Unfortunately, they seldom had anything to do with the business at hand. "Very interesting, Dr. Lindstrom," said Forte, "but the problem that faces us is to decide upon a weapon that will destroy the enemy."

"Prosopagnosia will. The Karolinska Institute for Neurological Research in Stockholm three weeks ago discovered the enzyme that disrupts the neural patterns governing the face-recognition area of the brain. The enzyme's synthesis presents no insurmountable problems."

A slow smile spread across Forte's weatherbeaten face. "Pretty cute, Per. We synthesize the enzyme, suspend it in an aerosol, and at M-Minute, H-Hour, release canisters of the stuff at strategic points upwind of Kiev and—instant chaos! Guards will prohibit their officers from entering military installations—and shoot them when they try. Those officers already at their posts will suddenly see total strangers operating vital equipment and conclude—as the Russians are all too prone to do anyway—that the strangers are spies, and shoot them down. Confusion will multiply. It will be *The Two Gentlemen from Verona* all over again."

"*A Comedy of Errors*," a muted voice corrected him.

"Whatever," said Forte, unabashed. "They'll be too busy shooting 'spies' and 'saboteurs' to shake any spears in our direction. Per, I think you've got it."

"Maybe," put in Dr. Ho. "But what are we going to do with it? There's still the delivery problem. Those 'canisters upwind of Kiev' aren't going to sprout out of the ground with the spring rains."

A somber silence enveloped the conference room. A destructive agent could be delivered to Kiev by only three means: air, sea, or land. The first two methods wouldn't work. And the land route was still more impracticable—innumerable border checks would prevent the enzyme's introduction by stealth, and no armed force Texas could muster would penetrate those concentric circles of armored divisions surrounding the nation's new capital.

"If not submarine," suggested Leslie Schmida, "how about sub*terranean*?"

"Are you giving me the shaft?" joked Forte. "As in shaft drilled from Houston to Kiev straight down through the earth?"

"No," replied Schmida. "I mean subterranean—sub as in subway."

4. THE HOUSTON—KIEV EXPRESS 20 OCTOBER 2008

RIPLEY FORTE DECIDED THAT CHIEF ENGINEER SCHMIDA, who had constructed more than four thousand miles of small-diameter people-mover tunnels for half a dozen municipalities all over Texas, was capable of handling the job. He had the experience, the machinery, the men, and the spirit.

There was only one hitch: the maximum distance his men had ever drilled in a single day was seven miles. But President Tom Traynor had insisted that the ultimate anti-Soviet weapon, whatever it was, must be in place within a year—that is, by September 2009—before the Russians could gear up for yet another assault on Texas.

"What about it, Leslie?" Forte asked Schmida. "Remember, it isn't a simple city subway project, through known geological formations, with easy access to support facilities. It'll be through unknown terrain, areas of volcanic activity such as those you'll encounter at the Atlantic midline ridge south of Iceland, with every nut and bolt and drop of water brought from Houston even when you have reached Kiev itself; we cannot risk discovery by putting down supply shafts anywhere along the route. And on top of all those handicaps, you'll have to triple your best daily production rate, and do it for three hundred consecutive days."

"Twenty miles a day, for three hundred days," Schmida mused.

"That's it."

"It'll mean a terrific strain on our equipment, even more on the men. They'll have to have some incentive."

"Patriotism?"

"That'll be a positive factor, of course. How about

23

pay—can I promise them all top-scale wages?"

"Triple the going rate. Think that will be enough?"

"Maybe."

"Maybe isn't good enough. Let me think..." Ripley Forte put his feet on the desk and closed his eyes. The tunnel would explore terra incognita, a subsurface stratum that in most places had never been plumbed by pick or drill. There was no telling what they would encounter, especially under the unexplored ocean. Mostly, of course, they'd bore through mile after mile of sedimentary rock. But here and there the residue of the earth's surging crustal plates, the cones of extinct volcanoes, the deposits of rivers flowing into the sea, would harbor unexpected treasures, as they did in the Yukon River valley and in the blue ground at Kimberley. No one could predict what they would find—nickel, manganese, diamonds, oil, gold, rare earths were just the most likely of the mouth-watering possibilities.

"Try this on for size, Les," said Forte. "Whatever signs of valuable minerals your men come across during the digging will be recorded for detailed investigation after the tunnel is completed. Forte Ocean Industries will undertake to exploit those minerals when our Houston-to-Kiev subway is in place. A separate company will be established to market the minerals. One-half of the stock in that company will go to FOI for its capital investment, the rest will be distributed among the workers. What do you think?"

Schmida rubbed his hands together like a bookmaker at the approach of a horse player with an infallible system for picking winners.

5. CONTROL
17 OCTOBER 2008

"MISS ILSE FREEMANN, SIR," ANNOUNCED PEASE THE butler.

"Freemann?" said Vice-President David D. Castle. The name was unfamiliar, and he rarely received strangers, especially during weekends at his country retreat in Middleburg. "Does she have an appointment?"

"No, sir. But she seems confident that you will see her. She claims to be the new diplomatic correspondent of the *New York Times*."

That was a different matter. Vice-presidents who intended to run for president in the next election didn't refuse to receive the diplomatic correspondent of the *New York Times*, appointment or no. "Very well," Castle said languidly. "Have the duty Secret Service Officer confirm her identity and credentials, then show her to my study."

Castle reluctantly laid down the tweezers with which he was laboriously applying the miniature bricks to a cardboard backing, which would form the facade of a model nineteenth-century small-town railroad station, faithful in every detail. He leaned back in the chair at his workbench and fondly surveyed the model railroad that filled nearly the entire basement.

The system he had constructed cost more thousands of dollars than he cared to think about, but it was worth every penny. One of the finest model railroads in America, it not only comprised exemplars of steam and diesel engines, reefers, gondolas, tank cars, box cars, and other rolling stock from the beginnings of American railroads down to the present, but exact scale models of turntables, water towers, level crossings, tunnels, trestle bridges, gravity switching yards, and other features of the railroading scene. He had painstakingly fashioned the deserts, farmland, range, mountains, and urban backgrounds through which his hundreds of yards of track passed. He had lost count of the time he had spent alone down there, but every hour had been a welcome escape from the cares of office. Only there, among the make-believe relics of a bygone era, did David D. Castle feel completely relaxed.

He took the service elevator to the second floor, stripped off his blue coveralls and engineer's peaked cap, had a brisk shower, and took his time about dressing. While the goodwill of the press might be indispensable to the politician, letting reporters cool their heels from time to time helped them remember their place.

A man who considered his taste impeccable, he put on gray flannel trousers, argyle socks and loafers, blazer with the Harvard crest on the breast pocket, and foulard. He combed his thinning brown hair straight back, applied a drop of scent to his silk handkerchief, and arranged it with studied carelessness in his blazer pocket. He glanced in the mirror. Glancing back was a patrician gentleman of fifty-four, rather tall, rather lean, with thin bloodless lips and gray eyes. The backs of his hairless hands were lightly mottled with liver spots.

Walking to the window and parting the lace curtain, he observed with complacent pride his eighty rolling acres enclosed by whitewashed wooden fences and his six prize Arabians grazing in the middle distance. He felt the glow of self-satisfaction of a man who had everything—money, health, a first-rate mind, respect, and the second highest office in the land from which, in due course, he would four years hence ascend by the will of the people to the presidency.

Castle took the elevator—he always called it the lift —from the master suite down to the marble-floored foyer, then strode past the library to his study.

The woman who sat in the chair opposite his desk was regarding his favorite seascape with unconcealed disdain. She didn't rise as Vice-President Castle entered, and he rewarded her impertinence by going directly to his high-backed leather chair, flanked by the American flag and the vice-presidential colors. He sat down, folded his hands on the desk, and examined the *Times'* new diplomatic correspondent.

Ms. Ilse Freemann was of indeterminate age between thirty-five and forty-five, short and squat, with disordered graying hair resembling a magpie's nest after a hard winter. She wore thick round metal-rimmed glasses, behind which slightly bulbous eyes stared at him, unblinkingly. Her bust was a large, undifferentiated, amorphous bulge, as though she had buttoned her tweed jacket over a loosely packed knapsack. Her nail polish was chipped, her lipstick the wrong color and apparently applied in poor light, and she wore Adidas running shoes. She looked not quite clean, and Castle was happy he had omitted shaking hands. Her nose was too long and her brows too bushy, but her piercing dark eyes indicated a sharp intelligence, and her first words showed she was anything but intimidated by the vice-presidential presence.

"Is it true, Mr. Castle," she asked in a soft, silky voice that contrasted strongly with her somewhat masculine appearance, "that you are a brigadier general in the KGB?"

Castle was so shocked by the question that the drop or two of blood that seeped sluggishly through the broken capillaries of his nose drained away, giving his face the gray pallor of a cadaver. His throat went dry, and for a moment he masticated air, trying to make words come. When they did, he realized with chagrin that they more befitted an affronted maiden than the Vice-President of the United States. "How dare you!" he gasped. "I have never heard such an odious suggestion in all my years as a public servant."

"It wasn't a suggestion, my dear David—it was a question, and you didn't answer it," Ms. Freemann purred.

"Then I shall do so, *Ms.* Freemann. My answer is that there is not the slightest foundation of fact in your innuendo, and I must strongly protest the intimation that there is. I am most certainly *not* a brigadier general in the KGB."

He spoke the whole truth and nothing but. He was a *general-major.*

His exalted rank was but just recompense for having successfully kept secret his communist affiliation from his undergraduate days at Harvard, through his career as a high-powered Silicon Valley attorney and five-term congressman from California's Sixth District, right up to the present moment when he was but a heartbeat away from the presidency. He had been a mole buried under such deep cover that only a very few men in the Kremlin—and none at all outside it save his controller—even faintly suspected his connection with the KGB. That circumstance, and his meteoric rise in American public life, made him so valuable that from the beginning of his career as a KGB agent until now he had never been required to pass on a single piece of intelligence. The Kremlin was saving him for the day he would be President of the United States.

"I'd be obliged to know," said Vice-President Castle, recovering his poise and addressing his visitor with lofty indignation, "where you heard such a ridiculous, outrageous calumny."

"A little red bird told me. Name of Gideon Sorrow."

David D. Castle's heart flirted with fibrillation. "Gideon who?"

"Gideon Sorrow, as in the remorse you must feel for his untimely death, when the Pan American shuttle from Washington augered into the main passenger lounge at Kennedy last Wednesday."

Castle's fifty-four years had been such a succession of triumphs and rewards that he had seldom cause to curse his fate. He cursed it now. Ever since the Kremlin and its files had disappeared in a mushroom cloud three months before, Gideon Sorrow had been the sole repository of the secret of his treason. When Sorrow died his fiery death, the shackles that had bound Castle to the Soviet Union had suddenly fallen away. Castle was, for the first time since his sophomore days at Harvard, a free man.

He liked the feeling. It was true that his Kremlin masters had been good to him. They had brainstormed the winning strategy and financed his successful run for Congress and the four reelection campaigns that followed. He didn't owe the Russians everything, but he

owed them a great deal, and human nature has always
made debtors restless and resentful of their benefactors.

So it was with David D. Castle. He had felt but conventional grief, and heartfelt relief, when he learned of
Gideon Sorrow's death. Cooperation with Russia, commitment to communism, subterfuge and stealth, obedience to orders—all these unpleasant things were
behind him. He had for some years regretted his attach-
ment to Russia and foolish infatuation with communism.
The utopian ideals he had believed in were twisted and
perverted by the clique in the Kremlin, and the economic
paradise they promised was repudiated by a century of
crushing shortages. He had had enough. From now on,
he had resolved on that fateful Wednesday when the
plane crash was announced, he would devote his considerable energies and abilities to becoming President of the
United States, and when he succeeded, he would be an
ornament to that office. If it were within his power—it
was certainly within his capabilities—he would go down
in history as one of America's greatest presidents. He
could see the history books now: Washington, Jefferson,
Adams, Jackson, Lincoln, Castle. . . .

And now this maculate bedraggled bitch had come to
cast a pall over his dream of redeeming patriotic service.

Perhaps, though, the situation wasn't so bad as it
seemed at first. Gideon Sorrow wasn't one to confide in
a woman, and the fact that she seemed to know of their
connection didn't mean that she understood its nature.

"Now that you mention it, I do believe I have heard
the name Gideon Sorrow," said David D. Castle, putting
on a thoughtful expression. "Wasn't he in international
finance, or something of the sort?"

"Bet your boots, buster. That he was. Also he was
your controller."

"Controller?"

"As in 'I tell you what to do, and you do it, or else
you're up Shit Creek without a paddle.'" She smiled de-
murely. "I'm your new controller."

For some time Vice-President Castle stared at Ilse
Freemann with empty eyes. Only the soft drumming of
his fingers on the desk blotter gave sign that he had not
lapsed into catatonic paralysis. A dozen thoughts rattled

through a mind suddenly incapable of putting them through the wringer of logic. All were variations on the cornered animal's instinct to fight or flee.

Ilse Freemann crossed her legs. Heavy-veined, coarse-grained, and bare, they were nearly as thick at the ankles as at the calves. Every moment, it seemed, revealed some new grotesquerie about the woman. Castle averted his gaze.

"You may dismiss all those ugly thoughts parading through your mind," Ms. Freemann said sweetly. "Our dossier on you goes back nearly forty years, and there's enough there to get you hanged for high crimes and misdemeanors. If you disregard my instructions, I shall most regretfully have to turn it over to the FBI—most regretfully because we have invested an enormous amount of time, money, and thought in your career. We would hate to lose you just as you succeed to a position in which you can perform incalculably valuable services for the Soviet Union, which for years has spared neither money nor wise counsel to promote your political career.

"You may also forget about expiatory suicide—you don't have the guts for it—or about somehow getting rid of me, or running away to a safe haven where you can begin a new life, or making a public confession of your sins. I have studied your life in boring detail, and I know more about your character than your mother ever did. Your greatest weakness is that you love comfort, and any of the alternatives to continuing to work with us—a cold slab in the morgue, life imprisonment for murder, exile, or trial and execution for treason—would be too uncomfortable to bear. Think about it."

David D. Castle thought about it. He thought for quite some time. Finally he said: "What do you want?"

Ilse Freemann smiled for the first time, showing irregular, tobacco-stained teeth. "That's more like it, David. Actually, we were reluctant to activate you, considering the danger of exposure of your cover. After all, the big prize is the presidency, isn't it? But in this case we have no choice. After the successive tragedies of the annihilation of Moscow and the defeat of our fleet in Texas, the Soviet Union is in dire peril. The factories, universities and institutes, libraries and records, raw materials stock-piles, and above all the trained scientists and technicians —all the elements, in short, that gave the Soviet Union its vast superiority over the Americans—have suddenly vanished in a mushroom cloud. And that's only the damage we can quantify.

"Worse has been the damage to Russian morale of the aborted Texas campaign. By hindsight, based on new intelligence, our military leaders realize now that a determined second strike, by air power and naval infantry, would have subdued the Texans in short order. Our naval commanders lost their nerve, our country lost the conquest of Texas, and our people are rapidly losing their confidence in the communist system. Unless we move fast, the masses are likely to become ugly and rise against us."

"I can't believe it!" said Castle.

"You'd better believe it—it's true."

"No, no—I wasn't commenting on your assertion, Ms. Freemann. I was merely expressing my astonishment that, for the first time in history, the CIA's monthly estimate I received yesterday, reporting substantially what you have just told me, actually represents reality rather than wishful thinking."

Ilse Freemann nodded grimly. "It can't have been hard for even the CIA to arrive at the truth. The Moscow district was to the Soviet Union what the entire East Coast, from Boston to Washington, D.C., is to the United States. It's all gone, and now we've got to get back in the game, and fast, or we're done for."

Despite the Texas fiasco, Ms. Freemann went on, the Soviet Union's armed forces were still in excellent shape. For years they had been widely dispersed—mostly on garrison duty in Eastern and Western Europe, South America and Africa—and their morale was still high. The infrastructure that supported the armed forces, however, was practically wiped out.

Three areas in particular had been bombed back to the technological stone age by the Moscow blast: nu-clear-electrical technology, computers—personal and mainframe—and telephone land lines invulnerable to electronic snooping by NSA and GCHQ.

"And you expect *me* to obtain these technologies for you?" scoffed David D. Castle. "Are you aware, my dear woman, that merely to transport the blueprints for these systems would fill a good-size cargo ship?"

"I am aware of practically everything that bears on the security and dominance of the Soviet Union. Of course we don't expect you to risk your position to do such yeoman work."

"Well, then?"

"As you say, the specifications, blueprints, materials, samples, and test results would fill a ship, and it will take many, many sympathetic scientists and technicians working in the right places to obtain them."

"I see. You want to recruit several thousand American scientists to work for the communist cause. Good luck."

"The thousands of scientists and technicians are *already* recruited, David. But they aren't American—yet."

"I don't follow."

"It's very simple. In the Soviet Union and occupied Europe, we have, as you must have noticed, jailed thousands of 'dissidents'—scientists, poets, engineers, doctors—for anticommunist activities. The American government, never content to mind its own business, for the past forty years has been agitating for the release of such people. When we require some diplomatic advantage, like a contract for five million tons of American wheat at below-market prices, we release a couple of dissidents, to the vast joy of the State Department. Well, we are about to do it again.

"Right now we need a great deal of what the Americans consider only marginally strategic manufactures—switches, transistors, heavy trucks, turbine blades, and so on—and we're going to enter negotiations next week to have several hundred of these items taken off the Department of Commerce's export-embargo list. In return for this concession, we are going to 'release' something like three thousand 'dissidents'—among them many committed members of the Communist Party. Just as we did with the ethnic Germans released by Czechoslovakia in the sixties. The State Department will issue them visas and roll out the red carpet, as usual."

"Then you will have no need of my services."

"We may. We are having a senator who espouses Soviet-American friendship introduce a bill that will shorten the waiting period for naturalization to three months. There will be something like four hundred Jews among the dissidents. We can count, therefore, on well over half of the Senate to push for the bill to accelerate the citizenship process. As vice-president, you are president *pro tem* of the Senate. We shall be depending on you to shepherd the bill through the Senate with all haste, pressuring your friends if necessary, and see that it passes by the necessary majority."

"Whereupon your ex-'dissidents' will get jobs with American industries and start filling that ship with stolen blueprints."

"Naturally."

David D. Castle was enormously relieved. He wouldn't even be called upon to vote, except in the off chance of a tie. If that was all that the Soviet Union required of him, he would do it. After all, security had been much more rigorous lately than in those porous old days of the late twentieth century, when the KGB and GRU ran agents in and out of the United States in relays, known but immune—thanks to the American Civil Liberties Union and its concern for "human rights," even of those doing their best to subvert the nation. He had the feeling that it was going to be more difficult than Ms. Ilse Freemann anticipated to fill up that cargo ship. "I will be happy to do whatever I can to facilitate the admission of dissidents from the communist nations to American citizenship."

"I thought you would be."

"And now," said Castle, rising, "I bid you—"

"Sit down, David," Ms. Freemann commanded. "That dissident thing is just for openers. Now let's talk about what you're going to have to do to make lieutenant general."

6. CHRISTMAS PRESENT
25 DECEMBER 2008

"VICE-PRESIDENT CASTLE IS HERE, MISS RED CLOUD,"
said her secretary to the chairman of Raynes Oceanic
Resources, who was staring out across a foggy San Francisco Bay.

Jennifer Red Cloud swung around in her chair and
hurriedly moved up to the shelter of the vast teak surface
of her desk. "Show him in."

"Hello, David," she said dully when the door re-
opened thirty seconds later. "You didn't give me much
notice."

"Sorry, my dear," said Castle, "but this matter came
up suddenly, and if I can't call upon my most beloved
friend on short notice, what the hell's the use of being
Vice-President of the United States?" He leaned across
the desk to kiss her. But instead of her full red lips, he
found himself kissing her cheek, when she casually
averted her head. Well, he couldn't really blame her.
Though he could rationalize his neglect, he *had* treated
her rather shabbily.

He had last seen Jennifer Red Cloud at her Tokyo
home in July, when he stopped in briefly en route to
deliver a personal message to Premier Kawasaki from
President Horatio Francis Turnbull. They had touched
upon their plans for a November wedding, just after the
election that would make him vice-president. But only a
few days later she called him in Washington to say that
she needed some time to think it over—and in the tur-
moil of the election campaign he had let the matter slide.
He hoped she'd think that he was merely doing the gen-
tlemanly thing, not forcing her hand, though in fact he'd
been too busy with his new duties to think much about
anything else.

Looking at her now, he wondered how he could have

been so callous—and so stupid. She was still, at thirty-eight, the most breathtaking woman he'd ever known, a combination of business brains, feminine beauty, and fiery passion that must have been genetically ordained by her Scots, Norwegian, and Apache forebears. What a marvelous campaign asset, hostess, and wife she would make him. And if she seemed somewhat cool toward him now, her attitude would warm when she saw what he had brought.

"As it is Christmas Day," Castle said, settling into an easy chair opposite her desk and crossing his legs so that the crease would be bent, not fractured, "I naturally went to your home first. I was shocked when Manuel said you were at your office."

"I'm always here," she said. "It's been bad—very bad, what with Joe Mansour and Ripley Forte holding my notes for more millions than I care to think about. By selling off the OTEC and the Ash-Brown computer subsidiaries, cutting more than sixteen hundred staff, and persuading the rest to take deep salary cuts or early retirement, I've managed to pay the interest at the end of every month. So far."

"It must have been tough."

"Right adjective, wrong tense. I'm right on the edge of insolvency."

David D. Castle regarded her with compassion. She had always dressed in sheer, tightly fitting gowns to show off her exquisite figure, and her Filipino makeup man was always nearby to attend to her maquillage and long, lustrous black hair. But today her wool gown hung loose and shapeless, a strand of hair had gone adrift, and her lipstick seemed to have been applied with an unsteady hand. "Marry me, Jennifer, and—"

"You'll take me away from all this? That's very sweet of you, David, but I'm not the woman you left in Tokyo six months ago. Then I was rich, successful, independent. Today—well, it's no use being morbid on Christmas Day, is it? In any case, if I married you now, I'd never know whether it was pity or love."

"Nonsense! I've loved you ever since I was a freshman congressman on the Hill. You *know* that. Of course, if you prefer, you can believe I want to marry you for your money."

Jennifer Red Cloud laughed hollowly. She opened the top drawer of her desk and withdrew a slim file. She slid the file across the desk. "The last page will disabuse you, David. The red is not actually written in my blood, though at the rate ROR's going, it soon will be."

Vice-President Castle eased the file to one side without looking at it. He withdrew a white envelope from an inside pocket, leaned toward her, and laid it on the desk.

"A Christmas card. How thoughtful of you," she said.

"A Christmas *present*—with love and best wishes."

Jennifer Red Cloud lifted the flap and took out a rectangle of light-green paper. She stared at it. It was a check for $640 million drawn on Banque Fermier et Fils of Geneva. "I guess this is where I say 'I don't understand.'"

"You're not supposed to—not the details, anyway."

"I don't suppose this is play money?"

"Oh, no. It's real, all right."

"The sum is interesting—just what I need to pay off Mansour and Forte. How did you know?"

Castle smiled cryptically.

"Yes, of course—you have your sources." She brightened. "Well, David, I don't have to tell you that it's the answer to a maiden's prayer, but I'd better take a rain check on the celebrations until I know a little more."

"Ask away."

"Well, I suppose you somehow got together a consortium of bankers to bail me out, hoping that a revived ROR would lock horns with its competition, Iceberg International, Inc., thus breaking Ripley Forte's present monopoly in the delivery of icebergs. Not only would it make you happy to hurt Forte, but water futures would tumble, and your backers, taking a short position now, would stand to pick up a considerable bundle in two or three years."

Vice-President Castle looked at her admiringly. "What a devious Oriental mind you have, *chérie*."

"Well?"

"You're pretty close."

"On the contrary, I'm nowhere near," she snapped.

"You're lying in your teeth, David. Swiss bankers don't believe in female management. If they wanted Raynes Oceanic Resources, they'd have made a deal with Mansour. And they know that Mansour, a man who believes in fast turnover, would have sold. Furthermore, as vice-president, you wouldn't dare act as an intermediary for foreign bankers. . . . It's government money, isn't it?"

Castle nodded sheepishly. "Yes, it is." He didn't say which government.

"That's more like it. Now let's hear the catch: what do I have to do to earn it?"

Castle built a steeple with his thin, bloodless hands. "Not a very great deal, really. As far as the world is concerned, you have negotiated a loan from Swiss bankers, having persuaded them that *because* you're a woman, and one whom Forte has bested in business, he will not view you as a threat until it's too late. Meanwhile, ROR will indeed begin a crash program to develop alternative methods of iceberg delivery."

"But why should the government want to sponsor alternative delivery methods when Forte's is working perfectly adequately?"

"It doesn't. Your 'secret' project—and the more secret it is, the better, obviously—is just a cover. What the government needs is that cover. Under the guise of research for alternative iceberg recovery methods, you will assemble some of the most formidable brains in the United States. I have the list right here." He patted his pocket. "These seventeen young men and women are gifted explorers of operations research, the theoretical sciences, mathematics, and other fields. Right now they're scattered around the United States, Texas, Japan, and Canada. You'll offer them facilities and salaries they cannot resist, and when they're all here, your responsibilities will be at an end."

Jennifer Red Cloud rose from behind her desk and walked to the window. Castle was shocked once more to see how—how *changed* she was. She was even wearing low-heeled shoes. He had seen her barefoot before—she seldom wore shoes at home, even at the parties for eighty or ninety people she liked to throw—but he'd never seen her in low heels. She gazed out at the fog drifting in across the bay.

"If I'm not responsible," she said finally, "who is— your 'Swiss bankers'?"

"Good heavens, no. *I* am. The President has initiated a very sensitive project that requires the best minds available. Bringing them together in a government facility would only attract KGB agents. But if these scientists drop out, one by one, and relocate at a well-guarded ex-Marine base in El Centro—which you're about to buy, by the way—even if they *are* spotted, they'll be traced back to ROR, and the Russians will be forced to conclude they're being used to brainstorm your new iceberg recovery project."

"When they'll actually be doing what?" she asked, turning.

"Can't tell you. Can't tell anybody. Look, Jennifer, I'm going farther than I should telling you just this much. The President has placed the entire matter—budget, planning, personnel—in my hands on a 'must-know' basis. He's scared as hell it'll leak to congressional circles, and we all know what blabbermouths *they* are. So all contacts will be made through me, personally. Lending verisimilitude to the whole operation is the fact that a lot of people know how deeply I am in love with you; that will give me the excuse for periodic trips to California to see you—and pick up my group's reports."

"I see." It all sounded very well thought out. It must have been, for the government to hand over $640 million without asking for so much as a promissory note. The fact that it had, of course, was an indication that David was telling the truth, for only governments were so cavalier with such immense sums of money. She hated the idea of something going on in Raynes Oceanic Resources that she wasn't thoroughly briefed on, but if that was the price she had to pay to get back her company, if it was all in the national interest, she supposed she'd get used to it. "Very well, David," she said with that sad smile he'd seen when he first entered the room, "it's a deal: I have Raynes Oceanic Resources back, you have your seventeen experts working under ROR cover. I have the nagging female intuition that neither of us knows what he's letting himself in for, but—"

"Believe me," he said fervently, "this project is going to change the history of the world. America will never forget you for your part in it."

7. THE BROWNIAN MOVEMENT 28 DECEMBER 2008

RIPLEY FORTE FIRST MET VALERIE VINCENT, THE former wife of a Texas computer tycoon, at the free-for-all annual Christmas party at his El Cabellejo Ranch. He never did remember which of the three-hundred-odd guests she had come with, but by six-thirty the next morning, as the party was shifting into high gear, it was about the only information worth knowing he hadn't learned.

She was a statuesque woman with a long straight nose, steel-blue eyes, and honey-color hair that spilled to her slim waist. There were more beautiful women at the party than this grass widow in her mid-thirties, perhaps some even with a better figure, but few came close to the sexy throatiness of her voice, the intelligence of her conversation, or the magnitude of her bank balance. From the moment she arrived, regal in an unadorned silver lamé gown cut low in the back, she was the subject of determined pursuit by eligible young males and dessicated old married men alike. Yet, as the evening roared on, more often than chance could explain she found herself in some quiet corner talking with her host, Ripley Forte.

Ripley Forte didn't question providence, but he was at a loss for her obvious interest. Though he was generally conceded to be the world's second richest man, with her rumored $30 million in government securities alone

she certainly didn't need more. Nor could it have been
his looks that attracted her: at fifty-one, he had spindly
legs, more hair on his barrel chest than on his head, a
knife scar from ear lobe to the corner of his mouth that
gave him the sardonic smile of a man calling two pair
with a full house, and the piercing dark eyes of a reli-
gious zealot.

Except for his wealth, which impressed others a lot
more than it did him, Forte considered himself a fairly
ordinary bloke. Though well read, thanks to solitary eve-
nings at remote construction sites, he had too little formal education to qualify for a job sorting mail at the
Houston post office. But his four years as a Marine leading men in three nasty little campaigns, and nearly thirty
years since as a builder of dams and bridges around the
world, had given him the confidence and competence to
crown his achievements by bringing back the first iceberg from the Antarctic, a billion-tonner that, even as his
guests were quenching their own, was relieving parched
Midwest American farmlands of their drought-induced
thirst.

Valerie Vincent had asked him an offhand question
about iceberg transport, and before he became aware
that the others surrounding them were quietly drifting
away, he had plunged into the subject, relieved to engage
his mind for the first time that evening with a subject
more rewarding than the latest sex scandal. Mrs. Vincent flattered him with her rapt attention. Forte warmed.
The words that passed between them, lubricated by
twenty-eight-year-old bourbon, became less formal, then
personal, finally intimate. As the morning sun was struggling to break through the clouds over El Cabellejo
Ranch, they found themselves walking arm in arm toward Forte's private quarters on the second floor, their
quickened breathing owing nothing to the steepness of
the stairs.

The bedroom was dark, save for a trickle of light
leaking from beneath the bathroom door. Forte took her
in his arms. One hand circled her shoulders, the other
slid smoothly down her bare back until his fingers encountered the zipper. He kissed her, a long, lingering,

exploratory kiss. When their lips parted, she shrugged her shoulders, and her gown slithered to the floor. Forte took half a step back. What he saw in the half-light sent the blood surging—in both directions. He grabbed his shirt in both hands and pulled, spraying buttons across the room. His hands were fumbling at his belt buckle when the phone rang.

Her eyes held his. "Don't answer it," Valerie whispered.

Ripley Forte let it ring. He kicked off his loafers, stripped off his trousers, and picked her up. He crossed the room with the feline stride of a jungle animal and laid her gently on the bed. Sitting beside her, his hand caressed her cheek, her chin, the silken smoothness of her neck, and her soft upstanding breasts. His hand moved down to her flat hard belly, then—stopped.

He'd been counting the rings. Three rings meant an important call—unless it was really important, his switchboard wouldn't dare ring at all. If it continued to ring, it was an emergency. He picked up the phone. "Forte."

"This is Tom."

"Look, Tom," Forte said to Cherokee Tom Traynor, the President of the Republic of Texas, "can I call you back at a slightly more Christian hour? I'm still in the sack, and you know my brain doesn't begin to function until I've soaked it in a couple of gallons of hot coffee."

"This won't wait—obviously, or I wouldn't have called you in the middle of—well, knowing the parties you throw, Rip—whoever you're in the middle of. But this is an emergency. There's war about to break out."

Forte sat up and reached for the shirt on the floor. "Not the Russians again, for Christ's sake?"

"No. It's our own people. The details are sketchy, but it seems that a couple of dozen men and their families are squatting on some range land out in West Texas, claiming that since the land is unoccupied and unused, according to a Texas Supreme Court decision of 1871— my people are looking into that decision now—they have the right to homestead and incorporate a village on it."

"Private land?"

"Yep."

"Then why drag me into it?" said Forte testily. "Call the sheriff and throw them out."

"It isn't quite that simple. These are good people. The men are all veterans of either the first Russian invasion or the second, and they're upstanding, God-fearing folk, from what the Texas Rangers have reported. They have no clear legal right to be where they are, but I can't allow the law to be flouted, either. On the other hand, they say if the Rangers try to evict them, they'll fight—and they've got the hardware to do it. I want to avoid bloodshed."

"Sure, I understand that. But you say it's private property. Well, why don't you get the owner of the property to go talk to these people? Maybe he can work something out."

"Maybe you've got something there, Rip," said the president. "But what if the owner doesn't agree?"

"He'll agree, all right. Any patriotic Texan would."

"I'm glad you said that. When can you start?"

There was a moment of silence.

"Jesus!" Ripley Forte moaned.

"That's right, son." Cherokee Tom laughed gently. "You own that land. . . ."

Forte put the telephone back in the cradle. "I've got to go out."

"Right proposition, wrong preposition," she said huskily, running her hand gently down his chest.

He pulled her hand away. "Let's get something straight, Valerie," he said. "I want to make love with you. It'd take me about ten minutes just to *tell* you how much I want to. But about a half hour's flying time to the west, people are going to start shooting at each other unless I can get there in time to cool them off. Do you understand?"

"Of course. But really, Rip, would ten minutes make any difference?"

"Probably not—not to them. But it sure would to me. What I have in mind is going to take considerably longer, and I intend to enjoy every hour of it—to the hilt." He got up and took a fresh shirt from the closet shelf. "I don't know how long this will take—with any luck I can be back by noon. I hope you'll be waiting, but of course I'll understand if you're not."

Valerie Vincent studied him as he dressed. Not until he pulled on a leather jacket and took a much-cleaned but battered brown fedora from the closet did she move. She slid out of bed and picked up her evening gown. She shook the wrinkles out of it, then hung it on a hanger in the closet. She pulled back the big silk comforter and slipped in between the sheets. "I might as well get some sleep now," she said with a laugh, "because one way or another, I doubt that I'll be getting much—sleep, that is—later on."

"Amen," said Forte, closing the door quietly behind him.

The Forte Ocean Engineering Piper tiltprop, with Forte in the left seat, let down gradually from 3,000 feet as he studied the airways chart and calculated that his landing point lay just eight miles ahead. A minute later he saw the neat rows of tents in the vast flat emptiness of West Texas and depressed the tilt control. The aircraft shuddered as it lost speed, and just short of stall the twin engines swung to the vertical on their axes, and the plane settled to the earth as softly as a falling leaf.

A Texas Ranger jeep came rolling up in a cloud of dust, and a heavy man bundled up in a sheepskin coat against the cold wind that whipped across the prairie pulled on the hand brake and climbed out.

"Mr. Forte?" he said, sticking out his hand, "I'm Captain Gordon Catlin, of the Texas Rangers. Hate to drag you out on a day like this, but damned glad you could come."

"I hope I can help," Forte replied, shaking the other's hand. "Everything under control?"

"A little tense, but I think good sense will prevail. These people seem determined, all right, but they aren't crazies who start shooting at the glint of a badge."

"Care to fill me in?"

"No, sir, that I wouldn't. You'd better hear their story

from their own lips. It's all too mixed up with philosophy and other big words for a simple lawman like me. They'll explain it all, and if you buy their bill of goods, I'm on my way back to town and my warm office. If you don't, I'll run 'em off, just like it says in the book. It's up to you."

Forte climbed into the jeep, and they drove to the little tent camp in silence. Captain Catlin stopped before a tent that stood a little apart from the others.

A tall, thin, handsome man of forty-odd in jeans and a sheepskin coat pulled back the tentflap and stepped out. He smiled and shook hands with Forte as he got out of the jeep. "I'm Hallelujah Brown, Mr. Forte, and I owe you an explanation."

"That's what I'm here for," said Forte. Except for his name, Brown seemed quite normal, not at all the wild-eyed fanatic he had expected to find.

"Then please come inside. Will you join us, Captain Catlin?"

"No, thanks. I'll just wait outside. Never could stand canvas coming between me and the Lord's fresh air."

"As you wish." Brown preceded Forte into the tent, which was furnished with a long trestle table and benches on each side, and a lamp hanging from the ridgepole. In the corner was a camp kitchen at which a handsome middle-aged woman in tight-fitting wool shirt and jeans was filling thick mugs with coffee. "May I present Mr. Ripley Forte, our reluctant landlord, my dear?" As she smiled and nodded, he turned to Forte. "This is my wife, Mrs. Letitia Brown, or I should say, *Dr*. Brown, our resident physician, lately Chief of Pediatric Surgery at Rice University."

Ripley Forte said it was a pleasure, and wondered what the hell was going on.

"Please take a mug of coffee and a generous slice of your excellent hot apple pie to Captain Catlin, Letty. I'll look after our guest."

"Of course." She put mugs, a pot of steaming coffee, and an uncut pie and china plates on the table, and silently left the tent with a covered tray for the Texas Ranger.

"Now, then, Mr. Forte," said Brown, rubbing his hands together briskly. "Sit down, help yourself to the best—perhaps the *only*—apple pie and coffee for a hundred miles around, while I tell you the story of the Brownian Movement."

"Brownian Movement?"

"A harmless conceit, although in fact our community got its start from my observation of the Brownian movement in my researches—until recently I was Professor of Physics at the University of Texas, you know—in the kinetic theory of molecules. As you know, when microscopic particles are suspended in a fluid, under magnification they are shown to move randomly. Also, the greater the heat, the more vigorous the random movement. Old stuff, and not a fashionable subject of research these days, I'm afraid. But the phenomenon has always fascinated me, and never so much as when it suddenly dawned on me a couple of years ago that not only did Brownian movement apply to liquids and gases, but to *communities* as well—insect, animal, *human*.

"I was on my daily commute from Austin to Houston when it suddenly hit me. Now that the high-speed expressway is in, the hundred-seventy-odd miles is only an hour-and-twenty-minute run, but the density of traffic makes for a nerve-racking twice-a-day ride. Passing the mangled cars one sees every day on the shoulders, I got to thinking, what a difference it would be if I were all *alone* on the highway: the worry and stress would disappear, and it would become a relaxed instead of a nightmarish commute.

"It was but a short mental leap to a consideration of daily life in Houston. I don't have to recite to you the incidence of robbery, rape, theft, mental illness, venereal disease, child abuse, dope trafficking, wife beating, and other social ills that afflicted our state when Governor Traynor became President Traynor and took Texas out of the Union. Despite a wrenching depression from the drying up of our oil reserves and the dessication of our range and wheat land, by imposing draconian penalties for these social ills he's done a magnificent job of drastically cutting down their incidence. But note, Mr. Forte, *those ills have not disappeared.*"

"Of course not. Social ills never do."

"Nor can they, in cities like Houston, because of the Brownian movement of their populations. This was my flash of insight: people, like molecules, come into collision—read 'conflict' or 'sociopathy'—in *direct proportion to their numbers and density.* Physical space, Mr. Forte, and limitation of numbers are the keys to social health.

"Take the South Bronx in New York, that textbook sociological horror: more than two million individuals compressed in a single small borough, each competing in the urban jungle for life's necessities, jostling, pushing, shoving, elbowing everybody else intent on the same objectives. In cities every man is a stranger, and every stranger a potential enemy. And in cities few people can claim to be happy and fulfilled.

"Contrast that with the situation prevailing in a simpler society, such as that of the Hottentots of the Kalahari Desert. They have almost no personal possessions, are perpetually on the brink of starvation, have no system of laws, and yet, living in groups of around thirty, they are among the happiest people on earth. Why? Because, I think, they respect each other's strengths and condone each other's weaknesses. They must, for to live they must cooperate. In short, it is not man's nature that breeds ill so much as his numbers: when they are too many—conflict; when few—cooperation."

Ripley Forte shook his head. "You make it sound simple, Professor Brown. But hell, even families have their troubles. It only takes two to divorce."

Hallelujah Brown smiled. "You're absolutely right. And we've read too much history to believe in utopias. Conflict is not only inevitable but desirable in any society, however small. The difference is that, in what we Brownians consider the optimum-size community, *where every single individual personally knows every other*, a person cannot escape the consequences of his actions. He must accommodate to the prevailing values of his fellow townsman or face loss of a job, ridicule, or ostracism. That's why villages can and often do function perfectly well without courts or policemen. Consensus rules."

Forte topped off his coffee cup and cut himself another slice of pie. A lot of what Brown said made sense, but it still didn't explain what he was doing on Forte's land. He cleared his throat.

"Ah, yes," Hallelujah Brown said, grinning, "you want to know what all this has to do with you."

"Something like that."

"It's very simple. We deliberately picked you because of your reputation for immense riches allied, most improbably, with an open mind."

"It's my mind that's open, not my range."

"I'll get to that, in a moment. First, let me ask you: are you happy with the civic health of our common hometown, Houston?"

"Hell, no."

"What would you give to see slums eliminated, jobs substituted for welfare payments, the rebirth of the family, a society where the individual bears the consequences of his actions?"

Forte laughed and shook his head. And Brown said he didn't believe in utopias!

"Well, Mr. Forte, what I describe is what we here intend to build. The thirty-one families here are the nucleus of a town called Brown—until we decide on a better name. Every family brings, in addition to enough money to subsist on a Spartan level for at least three years, professional or mechanical skills. Our first concern will be to establish schools, where each child will learn the value of manual labor through the study and practice of farming, animal husbandry, carpentry, masonry, or other useful work. Their curriculum will prepare them for university studies elsewhere, should they desire to pursue a professional career.

"There will be no laws except the limitation of population to eleven hundred people, enough to permit cooperative interaction and cultural exchange but too few to breed serious conflict. If every person in the community performs a useful, vital service, no one will dare to risk his ill will for fear of losing that service. By narrowing choices, we create an interdependence that will profit all. As for those whose values or way of life are found to disturb the equilibrium of the community, they will suffer but one punishment: an invitation to depart, in peace."

"It's a point of view," Forte confessed, "and I wish you all the luck in the world. But you still haven't told me why you want to build your Big Rock Candy Mountain on my land."

"You have a great deal of it, and for a hundred miles around it is currently going to waste. A decision of the Supreme Court of the State of Texas of 9 June 1871 gives us squatter's rights to range land after thirty days of unopposed occupancy. It happens that we have been here for thirty-three days. But mind you, we're not standing here on narrow legality. We will irrigate this land, farm it, and make it bloom. We will pay you any reasonable rent, or buy the land we need outright—whichever you prefer. But this is but one part of a greater overall plan, you see. As concerned Texans, we feel that great sprawling cities such as Houston, Dallas, and Fort Worth are an anachronism, a blight to the eye and soul, cesspools of crime and misery, and damned inefficient, too— you only have to think of how wasteful in time, gasoline, and frazzled nerves it is to commute two hours a day to work.

"So we want you to rent or sell to us our thirty square miles of land. But we want something else: that you let it be known that we are actually squatters who are temporarily protected from eviction by some obscure provision of the law. In two or three years we'll have neat farms laid out, village buildings constructed, a school in operation, wells dug, and the business in which Brown will specialize—the manufacture of orthopedic devices that my wife and our staff of scientists have designed—organized and in production.

"We hope and expect that our success, especially if publicized by your *Houston Herald* and your other media, will excite the interest and envy of other groups of people united by a common objective. They will come and look, and go away to find ways to emulate us. Some may wish to start small industry, or computer-programming centers, or stock-fattening operations, or even fat farms. We believe that our plan will help drain the cities of their restless excess populations, create a multiplicity of small communities, each united by a common purpose, and restore a happy, healthy way of life to our people, who God knows deserve it after two Russian invasions.

"Each community will need to get started, though, and they will be able to justify their demand for land by our example. You, Ripley Forte, will personally be able to decide on the viability of each project and lay down conditions for its establishment. Each settlement will quickly develop its unique character. One may become wildly liberal, another politically conservative, a third a center for modern dance instruction, a fourth for handicrafts, a fifth for wine lovers who grow and sell their own product. People whose attitudes change or mature can vote with their feet, by moving to a community more congenial to their tastes. Some will fail, some will succeed. All will give Texans a wider range of choice and the chance to be a real person in a real community, not a faceless prole."

"Good coffee," Forte said noncommittally.

Hallelujah Brown waited.

"It's none of my business," said Forte, finally, "but there's a personal question I'd like to ask."

"Ask away."

"How'd you come by the name Hallelujah?"

Brown laughed. "That was my mother's doing. My folks had a farm about fifty miles from here, struggling to scrape a living out of sorrel-and-sagebrush country. Before I was born they had six girls, one after another. So when I came along—"

"Say no more, Professor Brown. . . . But let me get this straight. You're willing to buy thirty sections—19,200 acres—from me, but you want it noised about that you're squatters and we're in litigation?"

"Right. That way our project will arouse the interest it will need to succeed. The old story of David versus Goliath. People will say, 'If *they* can buck Ripley Forte and make a go of it, so can *we*.' And I believe they can."

"Well, Professor Brown," Forte said, "I've bet on a lot of unlikely propositions, but this . . ."

"You bet your money, your reputation, and, they say, your life on bringing back the *Alamo* from the Antarctic. We're willing to bet our money, our reputations, and our lives on Brown, Texas."

Forte didn't know whether Hallelujah Brown was any good as a physicist, but he'd have made a hell of a bond salesman. "You're asking a lot on faith. But faith don't buy farms. Not from Ripley Forte, anyway. How much do you people think this land is worth?"

"We've put aside $610,000 for land purchase. For land like this, we thought that should cover it."

"Write the check."

Hallelujah Brown took out a checkbook on the Fifth Third National Bank of Houston. His hand shook a little as he wrote.

Ripley Forte inspected the check, nodded, and put it in the pocket of his leather jacket. Ordinarily, he'd have put up an argument over such a bald attempt to con him out of his land. But Forte's thoughts were less occupied with the Brownian Movement than they were with those Valerie Vincent was waiting to demonstrate. "Stake out the thirty sections you want, and I'll have my men come out tomorrow to do the paperwork. . . . And if Dr. Brown designs orthopedics like she bakes pie, I may ask to buy some stock in your company."

On the Piper back to Houston, Forte pulled out the check and looked at it again. He shook his head, turned it over, and wrote on the back: "Pay to the order of Brown, Texas, Community School. /s/ Ripley Forte."

He handed it over his shoulder to Blades, his secretary, and was about to request landing instructions from Houston Control when the radio sputtered, and he heard the voice of Yussef Mansour on the SSB.

"Ripley, this is Joe."

"Where the hell are you, Joe?"

"On the *Linno*, getting some sun near a small island off the coast of Venezuela. It's taken my fancy, and I'm thinking of buying it."

"The sun, or Venezuela?"

"Whichever I can cover with $640 million, actually."

"An interesting sum. What did you do—bust open your piggy bank?"

"I hope you're sitting down, Rip."

"I am."

"Well, Jennifer Red Cloud just sent me a check for the amount of our loans, with accrued interest. As of this morning she is sole owner of Raynes Oceanic Resources."

"The hell you say!"

"On my honor as a Cub Scout," said the little Lebanese financier, the caretaker of Forte's billions.

"But who the devil would bail her out—and why?"

"Oh, the word is that it's the Swiss, in order to mount an effort to develop new technology to contest our monopoly on iceberg delivery. I don't believe it. It's just too pat. Anyway, I'll have my people look into it and let you know."

"Do that. Forte out."

The party was audible from a quarter of a mile away as Ripley Forte switched off the engines of the Piper tiltjet on the landing pad behind El Cabellejo Ranch. More muted were the sighs of Valerie Vincent as he emerged from the shower ten minutes later and slipped into the bed beside her.

She was worth his wait in gold. Forte, who had spent too many nights alone in primitive construction camps on the margins of civilization and beyond, had less experience with women than many men half his age. But that afternoon, and through the night into the next morning, he more than made up for several of those years of deprivation. She was the stuff of dreams, and Forte, like a starving man at a royal banquet, gorged himself on delicious fantasy. Never in his life, he told himself, had he experienced such an agony of ecstasy. Then why did he turn out the bathroom light, and pretend her hair was black and that the intoxicating fragrance that drowned his senses emanated from the wild, pulsating body of Jennifer Red Cloud?

8. IMPROMPTU
2 FEBRUARY 2009

JENNIFER RED CLOUD CUSTOMARILY SUNBATHED IN THE
nude at her Jamaican residence on Montego Bay, but for
this occasion she was swathed in a voluminous ankle-
length terry-cloth robe, her long black hair plaited and
coiled in a tight chignon. Her knees drawn up before her,
she occupied a beach chair, protected from the early-
morning sun by a large striped umbrella, reading ROR's
latest monthly operating report. The ex-marines who
manned guard towers at intervals along the twin barbed-
wire fences surrounding the estate were backed up today
by Dobermans running free, for she had received instructions that no one—not even the household staff—
was to witness the meeting.

Shortly after ten-thirty, a figure in a shiny black wet
suit emerged from the water and stalked clumsily up the
beach toward her. He struggled free of his oxygen tanks
and stripped off his face mask. "A very good morning to
you, my dear Jennifer!" David D. Castle said jauntily.

"So you made it after all. I was just about to give up."

"Sorry, but it took some time to persuade my bodyguards that I'd be perfectly safe on my own. As it is,
they're camped on the beach a quarter of a mile from
here, ready to plunge to the rescue unless I show up
after a reasonable interval."

"Then you can't stay for lunch?"

"I wish I could. But I have time only to confirm the
identity of our go-between, and then back to the loving
embrace of my jailers."

Having supervised many highly sensitive defense
projects for ROR over the years, Jennifer Red Cloud was
used to the government's security concerns. All the
same, David's precautions were extraordinarily herme-
tic. He had insisted, for the sake of security, that even

she—nominally in charge—was to be kept completely ignorant of the operation. All she had to know was that it concerned the continuing struggle between the super-powers. There was, of course, one consolation: with se-curity so tight, at least this was *one* American secret operation whose details wouldn't be spread out on Kremlin desks within a week. In their meeting five weeks before in her San Francisco office, David had outlined steps to ensure that the integrity of Operation Impromptu, as he called it, was absolute. She was to be here, alone on her private beach, at nine-forty-five on this second day of February. Shortly thereafter he would arrive by sea. That was all she had been told.

"What now?" she said. "Little green men dropping from the sky in peppermint parachutes?"

"Nothing so dramatic. One little man, anything but green, will be coming out of the bay in a wet suit just as I have done, any minute now. I know him, of course; that's why I am here—to vet him for you. But he doesn't have an inkling of who I am. This breaks the chain of identification, you see. He is a very competent scientist and has been cleared by the government on the basis of years of top-secret assignments. But his main function is to act as my agent, delivering my orders to the group, seeing that they carry out the assigned research, and de-livering the reports to a dead drop."

"Good Lord, David! All this undercover and subter-fuge. Are you sure," she said lightly, "you're not work-ing for the KGB?"

"Of course I am," he replied. "But let's not waste time. Dr. Oswaldo Edwards—that's not his real name, by the way—will be here any minute, and I want to make sure we understand just how this is going to work."

"Shoot."

"First, how about a glass of that lemonade, or what-ever it is you're drinking? I'm dying of thirst."

She poured him a large glass, which he drank in one draught. He handed it back and asked her to wipe it clean of fingerprints. Well, now, this was a new David D. Castle. She knew him to be a wily and resourceful politi-cian, but never suspected a penchant for intrigue. Maybe there was more to him, after all, than the bloodless patrician grooming himself for the presidency.

"Here's what we're going to do," said Castle, wiping his lips. "When Edwards walks up the beach, I'll put on my gear. With my hood and mask, he won't recognize me, or my voice, for I'm not going to speak. But my presence here will tell him that I'm the man he reports to. When he takes off *his* mask, I'll be able to confirm his identity. I'll nod to you and be off to the briny deep. He'll then arrange with you the administrative and financial details of our little Team B at the research facility in El Centro. Then he'll leave the way he came. Is all this clear?"

"Quite clear, but I have a few questions I'd like—"

"Later," said David D. Castle, pulling on his mask. "Here comes Edwards. . . ."

9. EL CENTRO
20 FEBRUARY 2009

Livia dos Santos arrived in El Centro, California, on 17 February, bearing a load of guilt, and it got heavier every day she spent in the isolation of the barbed-wire-enclosed precincts of the former Marine air base in the arid fastness of the lower Imperial Valley. The author of her discontent was Dr. Oswaldo Edwards, but she was too much a realist to blame anybody but herself for having succumbed to the siren song of instant security.

Dr. Edwards had intercepted her on her daily four-mile walk from her office at the University of Texas to her apartment in the Austin suburbs. A pleasant square-faced man in his middle forties, he fell in by her side and introduced himself as an emissary of a government department whose identity he was not at liberty to divulge. "That old devil security, you know." He'd laughed.

"I quite understand," she replied, "but if it's business, it can wait until lab hours tomorrow."

Edwards gently disagreed. "Authorization came from

Washington just four hours ago, and I chartered a plane in Chicago immediately in order to catch you today. Time is a vital factor, and I need your answer now."

"What's the question?" she said, resuming her three-and-a-half-mile-an-hour pace, reassured. Whatever he said, she could simply respond with a quick no and be rid of him.

"We require your services for three months—four at the maximum. That is to say, during the spring term. I am aware that you are to participate in a graduate seminar in gene engineering this semester, and that your adviser expects you to assist four other doctoral candidates in their researches. Against that, I offer you the sum of $125,000 for the three months' work and the chance to do something which will be vital to the national interest."

Livia dos Santos' pace slowed. "What do I know that could possibly be worth that much money?"

"Perhaps nothing. Perhaps, several months down the road, we'll discover that your vast erudition in plant genetics has nothing to offer Project Frontburner. On the other hand, it may, and we can afford to overlook no reasonable possibility."

"Project Frontburner?"

"A classified project on which, as I have pointed out, this nation's welfare depends. We hope that considera-tion, plus the $125,000 I am authorized to offer you—most of the other eminent young scientific minds we've approached for our Frontburner B-team have come aboard for an even $100,000, by the way—will persuade you to work with us."

Livia dos Santos reflected. She needed a vacation, and maybe a few months of thinking about something else would clear her mind for fresh perspectives on ribo-somal RNA and the translation of messenger RNA into protein chains when she returned. On the other hand, her laboratory cultures were almost her flesh and blood, and she hated to leave them in the inept hands of that three-thumbed idiot, Nathan Prell. Still, she had her *own* child to think of, and unfortunately Anthony was autis-tic. He would require lifetime medical care, and $125,000 would go far toward providing it. She nodded to Dr. Oswaldo Edwards. "When do I start?"

Had it not been for the feelings of guilt for having deferred her studies, Livia dos Santos would have been quite content at El Centro. The company of sixteen very bright young scientists in a wide variety of disciplines was stimulating; the catered food, brought onto the base three times daily, was excellent; the dry weather was delightful after Austin's humidity. Furthermore, Livia dos Santos, an attractive and warm-blooded young woman of twenty-two, enjoyed the nocturnal attentions alternately of Benjamin Whitly, a brilliant agronomist from Tempe, Arizona, and physicist Raoul von Williams. And managed to keep them both separate and happy.

True, the security precautions Oswaldo Edwards imposed were onerous and thought provoking: no outgoing mail or telephone calls, all incoming mail forwarded to them through a mail drop in Akron, Ohio, and no trips off the base. They might as well have been on the far side of the moon. But when they learned what they were expected to do, they quit grousing and got down to it, for the gravity of their mission had not been exaggerated. They were indeed working on a subject of vital national interest: Soviet war plans.

"Since you have all been subjects of the most intense security clearance," Edwards began when all seventeen were assembled for the first time in the project's comfortable lounge, "I am going to be completely open with you about your mission and what the government hopes will be the result of your researches. You all know that much of the Soviet intelligentsia, war machine, political apparatus, and manufacturing resources was wiped out in the blink of an eye by the explosion of a hydrogen bomb, or bombs, in Moscow last year. At first glance, the military balance has swung decisively in America's favor as a result of that catastrophe, especially since the Soviet Union demonstrated its relative impotence in an unsuccessful assault against the Republic of Texas. But in fact, if we examine the problem more closely, we'll see that appearances may be very deceiving.

"For one thing, the destruction of much of the Soviet

Union's war potential has induced among us the apathy common to Americans after a victorious war: we disband our armies, destroy our superb war machine, cut up our carriers for scrap, sell off valuable equipment as surplus. But there is another menace far more insidious and dangerous: the Soviet Union's infrastructure has been destroyed. What does this mean? Weakness? My superiors think not, and I believe you will agree.

"The Soviet system has, until now, dominated the Russian people by an extremely well-organized monolithic power, brutally exercised. It has stifled dissent, killed initiative, and suppressed invention. It has stolen most of its 'innovations' and built the most formidable war machine in the history of the world by dint of forced labor, low wages, paucity of consumer goods, and a single-minded objective: to conquer the world, even if it takes two hundred years. Until last year it had been very successful, occupying every one of the two-hundred-odd nations of the world save the Benipic countries, and Canada, the United States, Japan, Australia, and South Africa. These five remaining bastions of democracy the Russians cleverly weakened for eventual conquest by depending on American political naivete to follow its traditional course: allowing soft-hearted America to impoverish itself by feeding, clothing, and arming the Benipic countries—Bangladesh, Egypt, Nigeria, Indonesia, Pakistan, India, and China—on the foolish assumption that they would 'fight for liberty.'

"But, you will say, everything has changed. The Soviet Union is now hanging on the ropes, waiting for the knockout punch. On the contrary. Remember what Moscow was. It was the heart and soul of the communist world. It was the establishment, the conformers, the *apparatchiki*, the conservatives. The activists, the original thinkers and artists, were exiled to the provinces, where they couldn't rock the boat.

"*Those exiles are the people who rule Russia today.* They have come to power by accident. And who are they? They're original thinkers, experimenters, people who are tired of traditional ways of doing things. But their objectives are the same: destroy the United States, so that the Soviet Union may rule the world.

"This fermenting subsociety has taken over. They will abandon the military sledgehammer method of conquest. Why? Because the last two tries—against the Republic of Texas in 1998 and again last fall—didn't work, and because their conventional war machine has been severely weakened by the Moscow blast. So they will experiment with new methods, new materials, new strategies, while we, the Americans, are asleep in the trenches, clutching the weapons of the wars of yesteryear, dreaming the dream of peace everlasting. When the Soviet Union launches its new-style offensives, it will come as complete a surprise to us as Pearl Harbor. We won't be prepared. And they'll win."

John Ionescu, the molecular biologist from Berkeley, interjected: "What you're getting at, I suppose, is that you expect us to evolve counterstrategies."

"Counter to what?" said Edwards.

"Well,—ah—"

"You see, Mr. Ionescu, that's our problem. We don't *know* what sort of deviltry the Russians might come up with. We could depend on the old regime to plod along traditional lines of research and development—particle weapons, lasers, V/STOLs, hypersonic aircraft, smart missiles. But the new rulers of the Soviet Union, having no respect for the ideas of a regime that made them outcasts, will devise new strategies, and I think we must expect them to be highly original, stealthy—to avoid nuclear retaliation by the United States—and enormously effective."

"But if we don't know what those strategies are, how the hell can we counter them?" asked mathematician Lee Tung Park.

Dr. Edwards smiled, and said nothing. It sometimes amazed him how long it took the superbright to arrive at obvious conclusions. He surveyed the three rows of the bright young scholars he had brought together at El Centro, three women and fourteen men, each among the most promising in their field, each capable of the most arcane and involved speculations, and yet each not able to see the red flag of elementary reason waving in their faces.

"Of course, of course," said Ionescu, finally, with

shamefaced chagrin. "We are to put ourselves in the place of the new-wave Russians, ponder the weaknesses of the United States, and design stratagems to wage unconventional and successful war against it."

"Whereupon," said Livia dos Santos, "you will turn our researches over to the Defense Department think tanks to work out counterstrategies, so that the United States, for once, will be prepared beforehand."

Edwards chuckled. "You will observe that there are no military people among us. The omission is deliberate. We want you to devise, as Mr. Ionescu suggested, stratagems that will require the minimum use of Russian manpower and resources, stratagems that will not set alarm bells ringing in the United States, stratagems that will bring this country to its knees. If the Russians can think of such stratagems—and believe me, given time, they will—the B-team's seventeen savants in this room can do so, too. The more imaginative your solutions are, the better.

"In fact, you were chosen for your youth and fresh approach to the problem at hand. You are the counterparts of the young Russians who will be, even now, addressing the same problem. Meanwhile our A-team scientists will be brainstorming the same problems from more traditional perspectives. Between the two teams, we believe, no significant solution will be ignored.

"Now, do not think in terms of armies advancing across hostile territory. Think what *you* would do, if each of you had absolute power, to bring the enemy to heel, without recourse to armed force. Elaborate your ideas in detail. And when you have taken into account every facet of the operations the Soviets will someday devise, and written the plan as the Soviets would write it, *then* we shall turn it over to higher authority so that countermeasures can be prepared. Never again will we be caught napping.

"Oh, and by the way, so that you can concentrate your formidable talents on the work at hand, I've given orders to remove all television and radio sets and to interdict newspapers and magazines. Our work is too important for such mundane distractions, as I'm sure you'll all agree. Also, to facilitate that work, I have assigned your group five computer technicians who will retrieve any data you may require from the World Data Bank and run whatever programs you desire. Good luck with your assignment. Remember, the fate of the world for the next generation is in your hands."

10. TUNNEL VISION
20 MAY 2009

RIPLEY FORTE SLEPT MOST OF THE WAY TO ICELAND STA-
tion, the farthest point reached on the Houston–Kiev line, and a hundred meters below the ocean floor south of the fog-shrouded island in the North Atlantic.

The windowless maglev train rocketed through the narrow round tunnel with scarcely any movement beyond the monotonous, sleep-inducing vibration of its electric motors. Only as the train finally began to slow eight hours and fifty minutes after they had pulled out of the underground terminal in Houston could Forte tell that they were approaching their destination, a little over four thousand miles from the Texas terminus.

Leslie Schmida, a smallish man with a scholarly air, met Forte at the Iceland Station, within earshot of the shrieking laser drill punching its way through the sedimentary rock just ahead. Schmida would have looked more comfortable in the flute section of a symphony orchestra than in the hard hat he wore.

"How's it going?" Forte asked, shaking the other's hand.

Schmida shook his head. His expression was dour.

By rights, the chief engineer should have been content, even happy. Tunnel excavation, lining, and laying of rail and electrical line was averaging twenty-one miles a day, slightly better than their rosiest projections.

"Troubles?"

Schmida grunted. "Not yet, but there's going to be."

"What do you mean?"

"I'll let you see for yourself." He led the way down the concrete platform, past mounds of supplies stockpiled on either side. At the far end they boarded the low-slung gondola that transported rail to the welding site. Schmida nodded to the engineman, and the train moved slowly toward the workface two miles ahead.

Forte donned bulbous ear defender/earphones and thick-lensed glasses, then switched on the throat mike that would allow him to communicate with Schmida above the din of the rock being shattered by the laser array. The gondola slowed and stopped, and Forte could discern the powerful machine, more than a hundred yards long, that chewed a path through the soft shale underlying the seabed.

The mechanical mole moved at the pace of an arthritic elder, somewhat less than one mile an hour. Though programmed by an engineer who occupied a cab at the rear and with a bank of instruments monitored the mole's progress, the machine itself was entirely automatic. At five-second intervals it blasted the rock face with the evenly spaced beams of thirty lasers, generating instantaneous heat of such intensity that the expanding rock fractured. Moving forward on its treads, the mole then deployed its rotary cutting face, 380 centimeters in diameter, which removed the spoil and dumped it on an endless conveyer belt, and transported it to the station behind them for disposal.

In the wake of the mole came the construction crew, applying an impervious facing to the rough walls of the tunnel with quick-drying liquid ceramic. They were followed by the rail gang, who welded sections of rail into continuous, seamless steel ribbons. Then came the water line, essential for disposal of the rock. Finally came the electricians, who laid the cable that provided the train's propulsive power. It took hundreds of sweating, cursing, dirt-streaked men, working in relays, to keep up with the mole. The heat and noise were overpowering. The seeming confusion was as carefully orchestrated as a ballet, as each skilled worker hurriedly performed his task, then stood ready to aid the specialist who followed.

Simple in conception, the building of the Houston–Kiev subway presented formidable logistical problems.

Problem one was supply of materials—thousands of tons of rail, ceramic mix, fuel for the mechanical mole, chemicals to scrub the air in the tunnel, oxygen for the men and machines to breathe, and millions of gallons of water. It was all brought in through SD-2, the secret nerve center and supply depot four miles from SD-1, both of which were served by the same elevator complex.

Problem two was disposal of the rock taken from the tunnel. It was hauled back to the closest station, fed into rock crushers, pulverized to the fineness of dust, and mixed with water to form a slurry. Each night the slurry was pumped to the surface into the nearest navigable river, where all traces would be carried downstream by morning. Once the tunnel reached the Atlantic, the slurry was pumped directly into the sea through high-pressure locks.

Problem three was the men's morale, which as Chief Engineer Schmida made clear, was a lot lower than the tunnel itself. "It's hot, dirty, and dangerous work," he said. "Furthermore, for security reasons, not one of the men has seen the light of day since October 20—that's seven months, Rip. That's a long, *long* time."

"Not as long as ten months, Les," Forte pointed out. "Everybody who signed up—at triple the standard pay, remember—knew that he was letting himself in for at least 300 days of hard labor. I didn't twist anybody's arm."

"Sure, I know that. But we've had six deaths and more than forty serious injuries, and half the crew is down with cabin fever. They're getting careless, and the accident rate is going up while production is slipping. You may remember that two weeks after we started this tunnel, we were cutting up to twenty-seven miles a day."

"I remember."

"Well, at present projections, we'll drop through the twenty-mile-a-day rate next week. By the time we hit the European mainland beneath Norway, our production will be down to fifteen miles a day. It may take us 350 days or more to finish the tunnel."

Forte shook his head. "We can't let that happen, Les. Nor can we give our men leave topside: security would disappear like a thief in the night. And security is the reason we're building this tunnel, don't forget."

"So?"

Forte ran a gnarled hand over his wrinkled brow. "I guess a couple of platoons of dancing girls would be the best answer. But I'm afraid that if I did that, the men might forget just what it is they're paid to tunnel."

"Well, they sure as hell need a better incentive than their day's pay. And I might as well tell you, Rip, that the rumor is circulating down here that your offer to share the proceeds, even-steven, of all mineral deposits encountered was a sham. 'Rip-off,' they're calling it. They say that we're running through valuable mineral strata all the time but that the engineers are getting back fake results on the rock samples submitted hourly for assay."

"Maybe you've got something there, Les."

"Huh?"

"Fake assays. . . ."

A couple of ex–copper miners from Butte, Montana, noticed it first. They spotted the telltale peacock iridescence of copper ore in the crushed rock carried back by the mole's conveyor belt. Sure enough, the assays of that day's production revealed that the mole had penetrated the margins of a lode of copper-silver-lead ore, and exploratory digging by the engineers indicated that the main vein was more than two feet in thickness, an extremely valuable deposit. The engineers marked the area for in-depth exploration once the tunnel was finished, but for those who didn't want to wait or take shares in the find, Ripley Forte offered $50,000 for the interest of each man willing to sell.

Morale rebounded overnight. The workers, many of them aware that the rich copper mines of Scandinavia were a thousand years old, assumed that their recent find was but the prelude to the discovery of an enormous mother lode. As the tunnel approached the coast of Norway, production soared.

Had the euphoric sandhogs consulted a geologist, they might have learned that the composition of the copper ore was radically different from that found in Scandinavia. As a matter of fact, the assay was identical to that of ores from the mines of Pioche, Nevada. But that interesting fact would probably not have impressed them, anyway. It was only copper, but to the sandhogs their "find" blinded them with the irresistible glitter of pure gold.

11. VANISHING ACT
15 JUNE 2009

"Oh, it's you, David," said Jennifer Red Cloud.

"It is indeed, calling to say how much I've missed you," Vice-President Castle replied unctuously.

"I admire your capacity to conceal your longing," Mrs. Red Cloud said dryly, "considering it's been something like four months since I heard from you. What's the occasion this time?"

"Nothing so earth-shaking, I'm sorry to say. But I thought you'd like to know that the classified project we were conducting at El Centro has been brought to a successful conclusion. Just yesterday, as a matter of fact. You are now free to use the base for regular Raynes Oceanic Resources activities, if you wish. Or you're free to sell it. Of course, the fact that government research has been carried on there must remain our secret."

"Well, I guess we are entitled to one. What a shame it isn't the kind that people gossip about...."

Livia dos Santos packed her two bags with a wistful sigh. Now that it was all over, she regretted that such a stimulating group was breaking up. They had ransacked the data banks of North America, argued lustily over outlandish hypotheses, drawn up meticulous scenarios that were promptly shot down by their colleagues, spent many a beery midnight hour proving the unprovable, and walked hundreds of miles along the perimeter fence by twos and threes framing strategies that the Soviets would, if they were smart enough, one day evolve—by which time the Americans would have airtight defenses against them already in place.

Some aspects of their stay at El Centro, it was true, had raised questions in her mind. This Dr. Oswaldo Edwards, for example. He was supposed to be supervising their work, yet he had appeared only three or four times during the three months, to collect the results of their researches. This absence of bureaucratic regulation was unlike any government operation she'd ever heard of. On the other hand, security restrictions were as tight as if they'd been working on the Manhattan Project, rather than merely brainstorming potential Soviet strategies.

However, in her handbag was the promised check for $125,000. Reading the figures, she felt it small recompense for the long separation from Anthony, left in the custody of her Mexican housekeeper. She promised herself she'd never leave him again.

"All set?" said von Williams, sticking his head into the room.

"As ready as I'll ever be."

"Let me take your bags," he offered. "You'd think they could have afforded a little service, considering the money they're paying us."

"Security, you know," Livia dos Santos said. "That's the answer for everything around here—why we do our own laundry, make our own beds, clean our own rooms."

"We're probably the highest paid dishwashers and laundrymen in history. I figured it out—$150,000 for 101 days' work comes to $1,485 a day—damned near as much as a second-rate lawyer makes."

"You were paid $150,000?"

"Sure. Weren't you?"

She laughed nervously. "Yes, of course. It's just that I—oh, that must be our bus."

Livia dos Santos and von Williams were the last to arrive, and when their bags were stowed they climbed into the bus, a large streamlined vehicle with dark-tinted glass. "Where's Dr. Edwards?" she asked the driver, a stocky red-haired man who sat in his little compartment cut off from the passengers by a black plastic curtain. "He said he'd be here to see us off."

"He had to go ahead to San Diego to make last-minute changes in the travel arrangements. It seems that a couple of your carriers overbooked for the Memorial Day weekend."

"Good Lord!" said von Williams. "Is it Memorial Day already?"

"Next Monday it will be." He climbed into his seat, and the door whooshed shut. Cool air from the air-conditioning system was welcome after the searing heat of the desert. In the back of the bus the bar was opened, with Waldo Finnegan, the meteorologist, acting as bartender. The bus rolled down the sticky asphalt road toward the inner perimeter gate and stopped while the bus driver himself unlocked it, drove through, and stopped to lock it after him. A quarter of a mile on, armed guards waved the vehicle through. It turned west and picked up speed. In the west, the sun had just been swallowed by the mountains, beyond which lay San Diego.

Inside the revelry continued as the bus rolled down the four-lane highway toward the darkening mountains in the distance. But five miles beyond the main gate the sounds suddenly diminished. One minute there had been a *clink* of ice in glasses, good-natured banter, a voice raised in song; the next minute a deathly silence. If the bus driver observed the abrupt change in mood, he gave no sign.

When he reached the foothills twenty minutes later, he turned on the bus's ventilation system full blast. Ten miles farther on he pulled onto the shoulder, stopped, and set the brakes. He levered himself out of his seat and walked back through the bus, looking into every face. Then he returned to the driver's seat, removed his gas mask, and drove on.

At his official home at the Naval Observatory in Washington, Vice-President David D. Castle received the diplomatic correspondent of the *New York Times* in a private interview on the eleventh of June.

"Why didn't you tell me you were going to have those seventeen—ah—ah—"

"Killed, murdered, assassinated, rubbed out?" Ilse Freemann laughed. "Because, David, my dear, you might have raised objections that I had no time to listen to. But you knew what would happen. You knew that we couldn't let them go back to their homes and families and blab their heads off about the sensitive work they had done 'for the government.' You knew, but you just didn't want to think about it."

Vice-President Castle pulled his chin and looked glum.

"As of Thursday, the twenty-eighth of last month, my dear David, you became accessory before and after the fact to the murder of seventeen of America's more promising young scientists. These days conviction on first-degree murder charges is, a hanging crime. Just remember that, if at any time you have second thoughts about which country you're working for, sweetheart."

12. AGAINST THE GRAIN
25 JUNE 2009

RIPLEY FORTE SPREAD THE MAP OF THE REPUBLIC OF Texas out on the drafting table in the Abilene office of Forte Ocean Engineering. At his side was Mark Medina, the courtly, white-haired Mexican-Texican who had been his first mentor in the construction business, and now acted as engineering chief of staff for all Forte enterprises. Grouped around them were the division heads of FOI, Triple Eye (Iceberg International, Inc.), and GRIT (Gwillam and Ripley International Traders), the foremost commodity traders in North America.

"The main oil product lines were, of course, already in place when FOI rescued Phil Guthrie's Texas-Southern pipeline in June 2006," said Medina, pointing at the red schematic tree whose trunk was planted in Houston and ascended to Kansas City, with branches extending to Cincinnati and Chicago in the Midwest and to Albuquerque, Denver, and Billings on the eastern slopes of the Rockies. "Phil's been working like a Turk ever since,

building subsidiaries off the trunk lines to every agricultural and range area within the T-S Corp network, which
covers approximately two million square miles of the
United States and Texas. To conserve the iceberg water,
we've opted for drip irrigation, about 50 percent more
efficient than any other means. On a fifty–fifty basis
with tens of thousands of farmers, we've also built thousands of small plastic-lined, plastic-covered catchments
to minimize winter-rain runoff; the dammed waters will
be distributed by means of the pipeline throughout our
operating areas during the dry season."

"So the pipeline's now fully in operation?" asked Dr.
Roger Nucho, GRIT's president.

"Not quite," said Medina. "We're melting down
something on the order of three billion tons of iceberg
every month at Matagorda Bay. That's not nearly enough
to reverse the drought the Republic's suffered these past
four years. Our first task has been to recharge the soil,
start rebuilding the aquifers, and finish the pipeline network. By next year this time we hope to be melting
eleven billion tons a month, and we'll be able to restore
adequate farming conditions as far north as mid-
Nebraska. Eventually, with thirty-four billion tons—
that'll take three more years—we'll be providing water
right into Saskatchewan and Manitoba."

Nucho's eyes glinted behind his granny glasses. "It's
going to be one hell of a harvest, once all that water
starts flowing."

"Right," agreed Forte. "And we're depending on you
to find markets for it. What are the prospects?"

"Couldn't be better. The world's population is rising
1.83 percent per year. With just over seven billion people
in the world today, that's an addition of 128 million a
year, more than the population of Japan. A lot of the
food they'll need will come from the Plains states, and
more from Triple Eye's Nullarbor Plain holdings in Australia when they begin to come into production in 2011.
There is, to be sure, the problem that more than two-
thirds of those 128 million are in equatorial regions, and
rice eaters. That will mean the conversion of a considerable part of our acreage to rice production."

"And this year?"

"An improvement, but nothing to shoot off rockets about," said Dr. Nucho. "Remember, we started from dust-bowl conditions. The percentage increase in yield will be phenomenal, but the actual tonnage will be way below the ten-year average. We'll get an idea of the possibilities when the Panhandle wheat harvest figures come in in a few days. If it's as good as I think it's going to be, then—" He smiled and gave a thumbs-up sign.

As Nucho pointed out, prosperity seemed to be just around the corner, but how long was it going to take to reach the corner? The triple depression of the oil, cattle, and grain industries in Texas—brought about by the simultaneous disasters of an international drought and a drying up of oil reserves—had exacted an ugly human toil. Businesses and schools closed, wages plummeted, unemployment-compensation lines grew ever longer, and crime and vagrancy, along with drug and alcohol abuse, became the only growth industries. Downtown Houston, never an aesthete's joy, was rapidly becoming a skid-row slum. Suburbanites habitually carried handguns, even to church. Vigilantes began to hang rapists, murderers, and robbers—and a few mistaken for them—when law enforcement broke down along with other civic services. Only the sweeping emergency political powers given Governor Tom Traynor, when he became president after Texas declared its secession from the United States, halted the Republic's slide toward catastrophe. Even now, after he had imposed draconian economy measures, instituted compulsory fifty-hour work weeks for relief recipients, beefed up the courts and police forces, and made the work ethic and lowered economic expectations basic elements of state policy, it was still touch and go. Traynor was hoping the people would see a good wheat crop that year as a symbol of national recovery and thus they would edge back from the popular revolt that had seemed imminent for some months.

Ripley Forte had used his considerable fortune to bankroll any and every enterprise that gave promise of increasing production. He didn't give a penny to publicized charities. But his Texas-wide banks gave low-interest loans to small industry, family farms, and students whose records demonstrated a serious interest in scholarship. His many corporations hired men and women who agreed to do an honest day's work, and fired them when they didn't. He paid annual bonuses based on each worker's productivity. He didn't countenance unions: if his workers voted to organize, which they were free to do, he sold his companies to the workers on easy terms. When the new entity failed, as it did more often than not because the owners spent more time jockeying for position than working, he bought it back again at a fire-sale price, fired the work-floor politicians, and reinstituted hard-nosed management. Not everybody in Texas loved him, but those who worked for him seemed to prosper more than those who didn't.

"Well," Forte summed up after all the division chiefs had had their say, "it looks like we're still walking a tight-rope. If we keep our noses to the grindstone, if Texans see that their fortunes will soon take a turn for the better, if Antarctica doesn't suddenly stop calving icebergs, *and* if Russia leaves us the hell alone, *maybe* we're all going to end up dying with our boots on instead of at the end of a rope on some friendly Texas Telephone and Telegraph pole. Breathe shallow for the next three months, and if the harvest is what Roger expects it to be, we'll be able to cancel our unlisted telephone numbers and return to the living."

"Amen," said all.

"Trouble," said Joe Mansour the next day, calling from his yacht *Linno* off the island of Maui to Forte in his Houston office.

"Handle it yourself," Forte advised. "I've got a plateful."

"Everybody's going to have a plateful, it looks like . . . of our wheat. In the past five weeks I've received orders for more than 1.6 million tons of wheat for delivery during the next six months, and orders are piling in every day."

"That's trouble?"

"Considering the origin of the orders, that kind of market movement is totally unexpected and unexplainable, and *that's* trouble."

"Translation?"

"The orders have all come from Bangladesh, the Philippines, Malaysia, and Indonesia."

"The hell you say!" All four countries were rice consumers; when they were starving, which was most of the time, they wouldn't touch wheat, even for free.

"I thought that would fetch you." Mansour chuckled. "Any idea what it means?"

Forte had an idea, and it wasn't reassuring. The pipeline system he'd been inspecting just the day before would begin significant water deliveries within months. As a result, the season's harvest would be by far the best in years. Accordingly, wheat prices, now at record highs, would tumble. Wheat futures would tumble along with prevailing prices.

"Joe," said Forte, trying to keep his voice steady, "what does the wheat futures picture look like?"

"That was the other point I was going to mention. Despite Nullarbor wheat soon coming into production, and a bumper crop this season in traditional growing areas of Australia, prices for October delivery, while still relatively low, are going *up*, not down. I can't understand it."

Forte understood it, all right. Somebody was gambling that, come October, the price of wheat would rise. They were gambling on a catastrophe that would ruin the fall harvest—blight, tornados, drought, unseasonal rains, fire, or locusts. But these calamities were all acts of God, and speculators in wheat futures seldom put their faith in the Lord. Yet it was entirely conceivable that they'd put their faith in a couple of truckloads of dynamite that, strategically placed, would destroy the pumping stations on which the pipelines depended, creating a manmade drought. If that happened, the economic recovery of the Republic of Texas would be stillborn, there'd be food riots, a quick plunge from gray recession to black depression, and the very existence of the country would be at risk.

Malaysia and the Philippines had long since become satellites of the Imperial Soviet Union. Citizens of free countries were free to travel there, providing they brought plenty of dollars to exchange at the ruinous legal rates, but they were followed wherever they went.

Though they lived hand to mouth on American aid, Bangladesh and Indonesia were theoretically independent. Forte didn't know a single word of Indonesian, but the official languages of Bangladesh were Bengali and English, and Forte could get along in one of them.

That night Forte boarded a jet at Dallas–Fort Worth for Honolulu and Tokyo. At Haneda, he was transferring to a flight for Dhaka, the capital of Bangladesh, when the radio message from President Horatio Francis Turnbull caught up with him. He caught the next flight back to Washington, D.C.

13. SHISHLIN
25 JUNE 2009

VALENTIN SHISHLIN WASN'T VERY BRIGHT, NOR WAS HE very honest, but he was extremely lucky.

He cheated on his examinations whenever he could, advanced with his class, and graduated without having learned anything useful except that deceit, diligently applied, was the road to preferment in the Soviet Union. After his compulsory two years in the army, he applied for flight training, for he had discovered that the relative freedom of movement accorded pilots enabled them to get away with a little discreet smuggling, thus capitalizing on the shortages that always afflicted one part of the country or the other. The proceeds of the traffic allowed pilots to live well above their nominal salaries.

Shishlin wasn't a very good pilot, but again, his guardian angel was looking out for him. Failing proficiency tests for fighter pilots, he was relegated to flying support and liaison aircraft, in which service he built up quite a nice little trade in American cigarettes, vodka, caviar, nylon stockings, hard currency, and other articles of small bulk and high profits. By the time he attained the rank of captain, he was making more and living better than most colonels. His friends envied him, and more than one jealous subordinate had reported his delinquencies, but lightning had never struck. This surprised no one: corruption was customary in all branches of Soviet society, and it was taken for granted that Shishlin had bought immunity by sharing his spoils with his superiors.

Shishlin was too preoccupied with his own comfort to worry about abstractions such as political theory and the withering away of the state. So long as he had a steady supply of vodka to help the young women around his base in Novosibirsk forget that his hair was thinning and his waist a bit flabby, he was content. When he thought about the future at all, he saw himself as Lt. Col. (ret.), living happily on his pension plus whatever he managed to put aside from his speculations. He might have done so had it not been for a sudden and unexpected transfer, assigned to pilot the KGB courier plane, whose usual circuit between Novosibirsk, Tashkent, Zyryanovsk, Irkutsk, and Krasnoyarsk vastly expanded his sphere of operations.

Though not a member of the KGB itself, his position deflected questions and criticism. His standard of living went up a notch, and his promotion to major in 2007, while still in his early thirties, gave him hope that he would become at least a full colonel. When the vodka flowed freely, he dreamed of the day when he would be *General* Valentin Shishlin.

The dream ended abruptly in the first week of June 2009, and a nightmare took its place. He had been doing better-than-usual business in gold coins and in fact had just received a consignment of old Ottoman and Iranian coins from his contact in Balkhash to unload on his semiannual trip to Kiev. En route back to his base in Omsk, he kept the coins in cloth strips wrapped around his ankles, concealed from view by his flying boots. He was carrying them when his copilot Ivan Dubinin, as they were landing on the evening of 4 July at Alma Ata, remarked having heard a rumor that the Politburo was cracking down in one of its periodic attempts to eradicate corruption, drunkenness, dealings in foreign currency, and other crimes of social parasitism.

"In fact," Dubinin said as he depressed the gear lever, and the Yak-237 two-engine turboprop shuddered and

pitched nose down on its approach, "they say they're
going to impose penalties of five to ten years for even
minor offenses."

"Is that right?" Shishlin's heart was beating hard.

"So they say. And as for 'economic crimes'..." Dubinin made a chopping motion with his hand across his
throat.

Economic crimes included such offenses as possession of foreign currency and trafficking in gold.

Shishlin had survived such sweeps before, but they
had taken a toll on his nerves. Just then the timing
couldn't have been worse. If the police or KGB chose to
shake him down before he had a chance to hide his loot
in the hollow beam in his quarters, they would find not
only the 400-odd grams of gold wrapped around his ankle
but the wad of 14,300 yen he had concealed in the bottom of his flight bag.

"They've added a nice capitalistic touch this time,"
Dubinin went on casually. "The word is that whoever
turns in one of these rotten dogs gets to keep five percent of whatever the *gebeshniki* turn up." He looked at
Shishlin and smiled blandly.

The landing was bumpy, and Shishlin nearly put the
Yak-237 in the mud on the rollout. Unaccustomed to
thinking fast, he tried to recollect whether Dubinin,
who had been his copilot only two weeks, had somehow seen the lumpy cloth that adorned his ankles. Or
had Dubinin seen him transfer the wad of yen from his
inside jacket pocket to his flight bag on their last stop,
at Frunze, where Shishlin had picked up the money
from the line boss while they were refueling? Everybody knew Shishlin was running contraband. Who
wasn't? But this five-percent bounty for turning in an
"economic criminal"—that was new and very disquiet-
ing. It destroyed the atmosphere of live-and-let-live
that allowed private enterprise to support the fantasy
of the socialist state.

Shishlin turned the Yak-237 onto the taxiway, eased
back the twin throttles, and considered the problem. If
routine were followed, the courier would open the five-
tumbler safe welded to the frame in the rear of the eight-
passenger plane, remove the files requested by the KGB

committee holding its monthly meeting in Alma Ata, and take them to the conference room at the military base adjoining the airport. As darkness had already fallen, he and Dubinin would remain overnight, and be ready at daybreak to fly the general to his next meeting at Zyryanovsk.

Now, if Dubinin knew he was carrying contraband and were going to turn him in, it would be insanity to accompany him back to the operations shack, where a word from Dubinin would place him under instant arrest. The best plan was to send Dubinin ahead and do the ground checks himself. As soon as Dubinin was gone he'd somehow ditch the gold and the smuggled yen in the darkness, then make his appearance.

With the props still windmilling, for Shishlin would have to taxi the aircraft to the hangar for the night, Dubinin and the general's aide climbed out in front of the operations shack and went inside. Shishlin released the brakes and let the plane roll forward toward the hangar two hundred meters away. In front of the open doors, he swung the craft around, cut the lights, throttled the engines back to idle, and picked up his binoculars.

He could make out Dubinin standing in front of the operations shack, talking with two men with brassards and sidearms. Military police. And Dubinin was gesturing toward the plane. The three men started toward the military police jeep parked alongside the operations building.

Valentin Shishlin made his decision. They would be upon him within the minute, not enough time to ditch the gold and the banknotes. He didn't have the luxury of examining the situation at leisure. If he hesitated, he would face the firing squad. And if he made a run for it? Well, the Chinese border was but fifty kilometers away. By the time they scrambled the fighters, he'd be over the Tien Shan mountains and into Sinkiang. As for antiaircraft fire, the three airfield batteries would be shut down for the night, since it was hardly likely an enemy would attack.

He buckled his shoulder harness and firewalled the throttles. The plane lurched across the muddy field, bucking like an untamed horse. The runway ran diagonally across his front, and he'd lose valuable time trying to get there. Instead, as he approached the narrower taxiway, he swung the plane around, flicked on the lights, and in twenty seconds was airborne, hugging the ground to gain airspeed.

From the tower, KGB Brigadier General Evgeniy Tomskiy watched the plane stagger into the air. He turned to the station commander. "Sound the alarm."

The colonel hit the horn button. The high-pitched wail echoed from hills surrounding the base. Within a minute the four MiG-61 duty pilots were speeding in their jeeps toward the hangar where mechanics were already pre-flighting their aircraft. Four minutes later they were airborne.

"You briefed the pilots personally, did you not?" General Tomskiy asked the base commander.

"Yes, sir."

"They understood the orders?"

"Perfectly, sir."

Missiles appearing from out of nowhere and flashing by his wings so terrified Major Valentin Shishlin that he almost rammed his aircraft into the towering blackness of the Tien Shan mountains dead ahead. He dodged as much as he dared, and after what seemed like a hundred missile tracks had shot by harmlessly, there was sudden surcease. His radio altimeter showed the ground dropping away sharply, which meant that he had cleared the mountains and left the Soviet Union behind. He switched on his mayday beacon and landing lights, tuned his transmitter to the international distress frequency, and called the tower at Aksu, the closest Chinese airport.

After some time, Aksu—or somebody—replied, in basic English, and in the distance runway lights flashed on. Ten minutes later he was on the ground, the sweat congealing in his flying suit, his pulse still hammering, and his mind working at forced draft to compose a plausible story to cover his defection. Shortly after he saw the runway lights, he put the Yak-237 on autopilot and divested himself of his contraband by shoving it out the cockpit window. He wouldn't need it now that he was on foreign soil: American propaganda broadcasts advertised a bounty of $500,000 cash for any pilot who defected from Russia or its satellites with his aircraft.

In the end he was rewarded with $600,000, for not only was his tearful story of flight from communist oppression swallowed by the gullible Americans, but the safe that was in the back of the plane yielded papers in which the Americans were most interested. Shishlin was flown to the United States and spent two weeks at CIA headquarters in Langley, Virginia, undergoing a thorough debriefing. He could throw no light on the documents from the Yak-237's safe, but he did provide a most comprehensive account of his background, leaving out only his illegal activities.

To the bulging archives of the CIA, Valentin Shishlin added details of his childhood, schooling, military training, and reminiscences of the hundreds of individuals with whom he had come into contact in his years as an air force pilot. Among the names he mentioned was that of a frequent flier, one General-Major Evgeniy Tomskiy of the KGB. The Americans took note of the name, but if it meant anything to them, they didn't show it.

"And that's *all* we've got, Rip," said President Turnbull. "A lot of questions, no answers."

"And this man, Shishlin—couldn't he throw any light on the wheat shipments?"

"No."

"Well, how about the forced-draft construction of those factories whose plans were in the safe in Shishlin's plane? What are they manufacturing?"

The president shrugged. "You see, nothing but questions. But all the indications are that something big's afoot. I've talked it over with my scientific adviser, Dr. Sid Bussek, and he's of the opinion that it all relates to some new Soviet secret weapon."

"A weapon made from *wheat*, for Christ's sake?"

Turnbull laughed self-consciously. "Yes, I know. It sounds preposterous, but Sid's been right before. It's a hypothesis that needs testing."

"That would seem to be the next step, all right."

The president cocked an eyebrow at Forte.

Forte raised his hands. "Not me, Mr. President. That's a job for the CIA."

"Unfortunately, the KGB's penetrated the CIA. We don't know the good guys from the bad guys anymore. Can't risk the Soviets finding out that our suspicions have been aroused. You, on the other hand, will keep your mouth shut. Also, you have the private resources to do the job. If I go through the budget process to finance the operation, all the wrong people will get wind of it. Finally, you were on your way to Bangladesh when my message caught up with you, by your own say-so to find out the story behind the wheat shipments."

"But I—"

"So all I'm asking is that you pursue that line of investigation and see where it leads. Now—while there's still time to act. Through government channels, it'll take ten days to get the inquiry off the ground. You, on the other hand, you can leave tonight."

"It doesn't—"

"What it comes down to is a question of national security. I wouldn't be asking if I thought anybody else could do the job."

Forte grimaced but was silent.

The president smiled benevolently. Forte's pride wouldn't allow him to refuse.

14. CHITTAGONG
26 JUNE 2009

"ZIAUR SATTO, AT YOUR SERVICE." THE SWARTHY LIT-tle man wore immaculate white ducks.

Camouflage, Forte decided, was not going to be difficult: it was going to be impossible. He weighed eighty pounds more and was a head taller than any man in sight and had fair skin. Ziaur Satto might have better fit in with the surroundings had it not been for his starched whites, carnation buttonhole, and monocle. He was a caricature of the British *sahib* who had ruled this part of Asia more than a half century earlier. He was as out of place as Forte himself in the sea of Bangladeshis—short, thin, sun-scorched, and mostly clad in undershirt and wraparound *lungi*—who clamored to carry his canvas carryall.

"Glad to meet you, Ziaur." Forte surrendered his bag to a porter, who balanced it on his head and trotted ahead of them to the waiting taxi. An old Volvo, it was one of the few four-wheeled vehicles at the Chittagong airport. Because of a chronic fuel shortage, Bangladesh made do with three-wheeled motor scooters, which snarled about them like a pack of angry jackals as they roared down the highway toward the city.

"Mr. Mansour instructed me to put myself at your entire disposal, Mr. Forte," said Satto. "Without undue modesty can I lay claim to be knowledgeable about affairs of commerce more than whatever other in the metropolis of Chittagong where have I specialized in export import bills of lading invoices and letters of credit lo! these many years as a result of which I have earned the complete and abiding faith trust and confidence of our esteemed Mr. Yussef Mansour whose word is my command."

Forte took a deep breath. "He said you know where the bodies are buried."

"Yes indeed I do although was I given to understand your respected self wished to initiate inquiries as to the status of the corn trade and not into subject of cemeteries about which needless to say am I also eminently qualified to discharge the function of informant and confidant." He paused and looked at Forte conspiratorially. "Whose bodies?"

"That's a figure of speech," said Forte. "It means you know the local situation."

"How very true is what you say my dear Mr. Forte for in fact my business calls for what in vulgar parlance is termed an ear to the earth which apprises me not only of commercial happenings but events in the political realm frequently reacting one with the other to produce the utmost droll consequences an example of which happened yesterday when at the orders of aforesaid esteemed Mr. Yussef Mansour I attended the press conference of our premier—"

Forte tuned out and turned his attention to the crowds, which parted like the Red Sea before Moses as the Volvo hurtled down the highway. The population of Bangladesh was estimated—it had been thirty years since a census had been taken—at 163 million, and it seemed that they had all come to impede Forte's progress from airport to city. Along both sides of the road hordes of naked little children with big bellies and hollow eyes played in slow motion before flimsy huts of corrugated iron and cardboard. There wasn't a well-fed human being in sight along the road, and while Forte realized that airport roads were a common refuge for the poor, his suspicion about the import of wheat now seemed thinner than the poor devils he was looking at: surely people that hungry would eat *anything*.

"That's very interesting," Forte broke in finally, as the monologue threatened to go on forever, "but I—"

"Ah here we are at last at the Hotel Bengal which as you must know was established in the year when Colonel Powers and the Second Bengal Lancers put down the insurrection in Mymensingh and thus became when convalescing from his wounds the first guest at this august establishment."

Forte gave up. He allowed himself to be steered into the somewhat seedy hotel, where ceiling fans sluggishly churned the fetid air. Satto with a self-important flourish signed the register in Forte's name, objected to the room assigned, and picked out one more to his liking, sweetening the rejection by sliding a 100-taka note across the desk to the clerk.

In room 443 Forte slung his bag on the bed and reached for the carafe of water on the bedside table.

"It's not so hot as rooms go, but at least it isn't bugged," said Satto. "I had my men check it out."

Forte stared at him. "What happened to our fine little subcontinental conversational style?"

"Oh, that. Well, Mr. Forte, our cabbie is a well-known KGB man. I picked him for that very reason. You must have stopped listening before I casually dropped the purpose of your visit to Bangladesh: to see the Minister of Human Resources to contract for 6,200 Bangladeshis as seasonal labor for Mr. Mansour's Nullarbor wheatlands. Our driver's English is fairly rudimentary, so I spoke in the local patois to make sure he didn't miss anything."

"Fine. Now you've got to make sure *I* don't miss anything. I sure as hell didn't learn anything in Dhaka, and frankly, Chittagong doesn't seem any more promising."

"Exactly what is it you want to find out, Mr. Forte?"

Forte leaned back in the patched upholstered chair, shucked his shoes, put his feet on the varnished pine coffee table. "Don't ask *me*. All I know for certain is two things—one: Bangladeshis eat rice, and two: two hundred thousand tons of Australian wheat have been bought by an organization called Ali Khan Trading Company, which exists only as a nameplate on 115 Khadoorie Street in Dhaka, with two clerks who know absolutely nothing."

"Yes. At Mr. Mansour's request, I have been keeping those shipments under observation. Of seven vessels scheduled to bring the wheat into Chittagong, two have already unloaded. Another—the S.S. *Princess Potter*— is heading into port. At the moment, it is seven or eight miles off Cox's Bazar in the Bay of Bengal. It will be tying up sometime early tomorrow morning."

"What about the wheat already landed?"

"It's distributed among five warehouses on the waterfront."

"Can we have a look tonight?"

"Why not?"

That evening Forte and Satto made the rounds of bars frequented by foreigners, staggered back to Forte's room—where Satto made a quick and professional search for bugs—and left in place the two he discovered. He smiled and handed Forte the battery-operated tape recorder he had picked up from a bartender who did odd jobs for him. For nine hours the tape would play night sounds—the flushing of a toilet, the click of the bedside light, intermittent snoring, the creak of bedsprings. He held up two fingers and said blearily: "It has been quite an evening Mr. Forte and I do hope you have enjoyed yourself and will be able to receive me when I pass by your presence at the only slightly ungodly hour of ten o'clock ante meridian on the morning and I wish you pleasant dreams and a very good night."

It was ten minutes past twelve, and Forte had topped off the evening with two bottles of warm beer, confident that they would awaken him before two hours passed. He stripped off his sweat-soaked clothes and was asleep within minutes.

He awakened at one forty-five, went to the bathroom, and dressed in dark trousers, a navy-blue silk turtleneck, and running shoes. He turned on the tape recorder on the dresser and silently left the room. As briefed by Satto earlier, he ascended the stairs to the top floor, where he found Satto. Satto nodded and led him out the door onto the roof. They threaded their way among the mats on which the service staff of the hotel slept beneath the stars, across low walls to the roofs of adjoining buildings, and finally descended the musty stairs of an apartment house on the far side of the block. On the ground floor, an old man in a dhoti waited with two bicycles, and Satto and Forte rode off through the darkened streets toward the waterfront.

Despite the darkness, Satto several times turned corners and stopped, or doubled back, to make sure they weren't being followed. Then, assured that they were unobserved, he pedaled directly toward the long, low warehouse where the first shipment of wheat had been stored two weeks earlier.

Two guards were sitting on one side of the building, chatting over a small fire they'd made to brew tea. Satto led the way to the other side, improvised a platform from abandoned packing crates, and on the third try found a window unlocked.

The two men eased through the window. Bags labeled DURUM WHEAT—PRODUCED IN AUSTRALIA BY AUSSIES were stacked to the rafters of the low building as far as the beam of Satto's light would penetrate. The ledge on which they stood led to a narrow catwalk running the length of the building. They walked carefully down the catwalk, guided by the masked beam of the flashlight, stopping from time to time to inspect the bags that filled the long chamber.

"Well?" Satto whispered, when they had made a tour of the premises and were back at the open window.

Forte shook his head. The wheat was there, all right, but why? This was the first shipment. It had been there two weeks. Whoever the Ali Khan Trading Company represented had invested a huge sum in the contents of those burlap bags. Sound business practice dictated moving the wheat to market—wherever the market was —as soon as possible, to make a profit for further investment. It just didn't make sense to let the wheat accumulate warehousing charges while being eaten by rats.

Rats! He hadn't seen or heard the squeak of a single rat. If it was impossible to prevent rats running free in the best-protected warehouses in America, certainly he'd have seen some sign of them here. It stood to reason: where there was wheat, there were rats.

But what if there *wasn't* any wheat in the warehouse?

Forte crouched on the beam on which he stood and swung himself to the bags just below. The moment his feet touched he knew he had been right. He motioned to Satto to toss him the flashlight. In its beam he flicked open the switchblade he carried and slit one of the bags. It deflated like a punctured balloon.

In fact, it *was* a punctured balloon. . . .

The activity in the fifth warehouse, where bags of wheat were being carried in from the S.S. *Princess Potter*, docked only an hour before, did nothing to enlighten them. From a window in the side of the warehouse, they observed a procession of coolies, each bent almost double with the weight of a sack of wheat, stacking their burdens in orderly rows.

More than a hundred meters back along the dock was the fourth warehouse with wheat from Australia, and here they found the answer. From the darkened depths of the warehouse, forklift trucks bearing pallets of bulging jute bags labeled POLISHED RICE—PRODUCT OF BANGLADESH were rumbling to the front of the warehouse, where the bags were shouldered by coolies and loaded onto the S.S. *Malcolm Miller* tied up to the opposite quay. Forte was tempted to steal back into the interior of the warehouse, but decided it wasn't worth the risk. Besides, he already had the answer he came for.

"How do you figure it?" Ziaur Satto asked out of politeness as they were bicycling back to the hotel through the ill-lit streets, although he thought the answer was pretty obvious.

"Why they're doing it—why they're going to the immense trouble of transshipping the wheat, I can't guess, but *how* they're working it is easy: they're unloading the wheat from the ships, filling one warehouse at a time. As they begin filling up the *second* warehouse, they begin *emptying* the first, after having transferred the wheat to bags labeled rice. Into the bags that held the wheat are then inserted prefabricated balloons—and this means that we're onto something big, for special heavy-duty rubber balloons to be manufactured for this specific purpose—and the balloons inflated. Then the empty but now inflated durum wheat bags are stacked in the warehouse. The last step: the wheat is shipped out."

"Shipped out—where?" asked Ziaur Satto.

"How the hell do *I* know?"

"Okay, then—why?"

"When I know where," Forte temporized, "maybe I'll know why."

15. SEVASTOPOL
4 JULY 2009

"THAT'S RIGHT, MR. PRESIDENT," SAID RIPLEY FORTE, "I need to borrow a missile frigate."

A bushy silver eyebrow rose interrogatively over President Horatio Francis Turnbull's left eye. "Is *that* all? For a moment there I thought you were going to ask for a whole damned task force."

"Well, now that you mention it, maybe a task force *would* be appropriate."

"I should have known better than to try to sink you

with sarcasm," Turnbull muttered. "Let me get this straight. You observed a switch of 'rice' for wheat taking place in Chittagong. Your Forte Ocean Engineering hydrographic satellites tracked the ship on which the wheat-disguised-as-rice was loaded, the S.S. *Malcolm Miller* of French registry, to Sevastopol in the Crimea. And now you want me to lend you one of the navy's missile frigates to—"

"Task force," Forte corrected.

"—missile frigates to do exactly what—bombard Sevastopol and start a new Crimean War? Over a shipload of *wheat*?"

Forte shifted in the straight-backed wooden chair in front of the president's desk in the Oval Office. Turnbull had ordered the White House cabinetmaker to design the most uncomfortable chairs possible, so that his visitors would not overstay their welcome. "I don't anticipate any shooting, Mr. President. But you'll appreciate that while *I* cannot sail a ship just outside the Soviet Union's twelve-mile limit in the Black Sea, the U.S. Navy does all the time, just to demonstrate it has a legal right to do so. My idea was, when the task force—a task force would be less suspicious, you see, than a single ship—gets close enough, I'll disembark in scuba gear and have a little look-see. When I get the dope I want, I'll rendezvous with the task force and they can drop me off in Istanbul."

President Turnbull waved his hand dismissively. "If you think you've convinced me of the need for such a provocative operation, you're mistaken, Rip. So the *Malcolm Miller* took aboard a load of wheat in Bangladesh. So it took a roundabout route to Sevastopol, presumably to throw off any surveillance. So what?"

"So something is distinctly fishy, Mr. President, that's what. Look," he said, glad for the chance to get out of the chair and walk to the big map of the world on the wall. "Wheat from Australia bought by elaborate subterfuge by the Soviet Union, shipped to Bangladesh, transshipped to Sevastopol via South Yemen, Oran, and Genoa. Wheat bought at premium prices by the Soviet Union, which this year has the best harvest in prospect in fourteen years, in addition to stockpiled purchases from the West sufficient to last sixteen to eighteen months. They don't need the wheat, yet they take extraordinary precautions to prevent our knowing that they bought it. We've simply *got* to know what's going on, sir."

"I disagree. At the moment, the world wheat situation is not critical—what with the Midwest crop soon to be harvested. And if Russia is not threatening us in any way, I cannot afford to let you commandeer one of our ships—let alone a whole task force. Sorry, Rip, but that's final."

The lights of the carrier *Parris Island* were ablaze, as were those of the guided-missile cruiser and eight ASW frigates that accompanied her. At unnerving intervals Russian destroyers loomed out of the darkness of the Black Sea and cut across the carrier's bow, in flagrant contravention of the rules of the road and at more risk than they dreamed.

"Let's have a little mo-board exercise, Lieutenant," said Captain Dan Doon to the Junior Officer of the Deck on the bridge of the *Parris Island*. "When radar plot picks up that Red tin can turning to make another high-speed run across our bows, I want you to compute a collision course, and instruct the chief engineer to have the engine room ready to pour on the power to clip the bastard's fan-tail."

"Aye aye, sir," replied the JOOD, his hands not quite steady as he laid out the problem on his maneuver board. Themistocles' remark that "a collision at sea can ruin your whole day" floated across his mind. His hands began to sweat.

"You're not really going to ram that can, are you?" said Ripley Forte, standing beside the tall young captain with the wild-Cossack moustache.

"I'm going to try. Have to teach those people a little respect for their betters." He smiled. "Don't think me hard-hearted, Mr. Forte. We'll drop over life rafts for survivors. . . . Don't you think you should be getting in some sack drill?"

"Can't sleep. If I get back in one piece, I'll make up for it on the run back to Istanbul."

It was a big "if," but Forte was confident. For one thing, he wasn't going alone but with four native-speaking Russians, two of whom were defectors, one of them a former naval infantry officer stationed for two years at Sevastopol. For another, their mission would be brief and involve a minimum of movement. Analysis of satellite reconnaissance films had shown that the wheat from the S.S. *Malcolm Miller* went from the ship directly to waterfront silos. But, as in Chittagong, as one silo was filled, another was emptied and its contents trucked thirty miles up the peninsula to what seemed to be a factory two miles inland. That, again, was unremarkable. It could have been a flour mill—except that while a steady stream of trucks dropped their loads of Russian wheat and returned to Sevastopol empty, nothing came out of the "flour mill." Nothing . . .

At 2230 Ripley Forte suited up in the ejection compartment below the waterline aft. Captain Doon checked his oxygen supply and other equipment himself, for President Turnbull had given him strict instructions to do everything possible to avoid detection and giving the Russians the opportunity to embarrass his administration. "The trip in should take no more than forty minutes on the sea sled," said the *Parris Island*'s skipper. "The sled's detection gear will pick up magnetic anomalies, alerting you to mines. Recon reports indicate that the beach you're landing on is rocky, with scrub brush right down to water's edge, affording good concealment for your gear. You'll each carry a satnav box, which gives your position to three meters. Any questions?"

"Yes," said Forte, pulling on his black rubber hood. "I'm a little concerned about the rendezvous."

"No problem. When you get the dope you're after, suit up and head out from the beach on a bearing of approximately 210 degrees true. By the time you reach international waters twelve miles out, the sea sleds will home in on the underwater marker beacon. Once contact is made—we'll be cruising in the vicinity—the beacon will trip a signal, and we'll make a sweep in to pick you up. Won't take more than twenty or thirty minutes—less if you hit the ETA at 0400 as planned."

Forte nodded. He climbed through the open hatch of the sea sled and lay down on his stomach, facing forward, his hands on the diving plane and throttle controls. Already in his position next to him was Chief Fire Controlman Harry Elmer Smit, and behind them the other three men, crowded together side by side in the torpedo-like undersea vehicle.

"Masks on, oxygen on," Captain Doon ordered.

The men checked their masks and oxygen supply.

"Cycle hatch control."

Forte hit the switch that lowered the leaves of the hatch over them, then raised them again. "All set."

"Good luck—and see you all back aboard at 0400," said Captain Doon, crossing his fingers.

Forte closed the hatch again. Inside he could see nothing but the faint glow of the navigation dials and the sea sled instruments. He felt the sled being raised by hoist and inserted into the ejection port. "Stand by," came the signal in his headset. He tensed.

"Eject!"

Forte felt himself slammed backward as they were ejected from the stern of the carrier, cruising at two-thirds ahead, and tumbled widely as the sled fought the turbulence of the wake. He switched to automatic pilot, and the sleek craft descended from two meters to nine meters, curving in toward shore as it followed the programmed course.

Forty-five minutes later the craft slowed and nudged the bottom at three meters. Forte touched the switch that opened the two leaves of the hatch. Sea water flooded in. The five men disengaged their belts and one by one floated to the surface. Ahead, in the light of the quarter moon, the rocky beach seemed deserted. It was CPO Smit's job to see that it was.

He swam parallel with the beach, systematically scanning it with an infrared detector and low-light goggles. Ten minutes later he was back. "All clear," he whispered.

The five men swam in among the rocks, quickly shed their gear and cached it among the bushes, and moved out toward the factory whose lights were barely visible to the east. They were dressed in black, their faces were blackened, and they wore black rubber-soled sneakers. There was a footpath from the beach inland, but they didn't follow it. They moved as silently as shadows in a long, looping curve that brought them to a high wire fence.

Forte checked a meter to see if there was an electrical field. He gave a thumbs-up signal. One of the Russians flung a thick cotton mat over the top, barbed strands. One by one they climbed over swiftly and made themselves small on the ground until the last man was inside the compound.

The Russians with the party had studied the satellite pictures of the plant and offered the opinion that the factory's work schedule was probably no more than two shifts. Except for guards, if any, they'd have the plant to themselves until 0700. The stillness that pervaded the factory site confirmed their estimate.

The plant was protected by only three or four sentries, lethargically walking post outside the plant. In the darkness, Forte and his men easily evaded them, picked the lock on a side door, and entered.

By the dim glow of the flashlights, they followed the wheat-processing operation from the beginning. One end of the low building was little more than a huge hopper in which wheat was stockpiled. By means of a screw-feed mechanism, the process seemed to be automatic and continuous. The grain was first soaked in vats containing a noxious-smelling chemical, then passed through crushing rollers and subjected to another chemical bath. The wheat mash was then centrifuged, kiln dried, and pressed into blocks of what seemed to be cattle feed. The liquid in which the grain was soaked after crushing passed through a dozen stages of distillation and separation, the final product being collected in a ten-liter glass receptacle, which was only two-thirds full.

At each stage of the process, Forte and his men collected minute samples in stoppered glass vials. Of the clear liquid that seemed to be the end result of the refining process, Forte drew off two samples, and gave one to Chief Smit in case his own was broken. A small office yielded papers and instruction manuals, which were photographed before being replaced.

From the time the five-man team landed until they got back again to the beach, suiting up for return to the underwater rendezvous, less than three hours had elapsed. They set off no alarms, saw no sign of hostile forces. This fact did not surprise them, for the processing plant they entered, according to satellite reconnaissance, was but one of more than two hundred like it located in wheat-growing areas of the Soviet Union. All seemed to be automated.

As they slipped into the water to reenter the sea sled, Forte glanced back at the placid countryside through which they passed with such ease. With sound intelligence and planning, he reflected, almost any operation would be a success.

16. BETA-3
12 JULY 2009

"TAKE A LOOK AT THIS, RIP," SAID DR. ROGER NUCHO, pressing the button on SD-1's magnetic resonance synthesizer, which projected its image onto the big screen.

The molecule meant nothing to Ripley Forte. It looked like a conical bedspring, with a couple of branching hydroxyl radicals. The formula shown below was as long as a loser's alibi, and composed of the elements oxygen, hydrogen, nitrogen, carbon, phosphorus, and, unexpectedly, cobalt. Chemistry had ever been a mystery to Forte, and the structure of the molecule did nothing to temper his ignorance.

"That was the only anomaly in the liquid sample we took from Sevastopol?"

"No. Actually it *is* the sample you got from Sevastopol. Pure stuff. Chemically, its name begins with *beta-3* and as you see, goes on and on. We call it simply beta-3."

"A deadly poison, of course."

Nucho smiled. "Only in the sense that a lover's kiss, a

$20,000 raise, or Dallas beating the Redskins by eighty-three to zero is poison."

"Come again?"

"*Beta-3* is euphoria, happiness, bliss. But I'd better start back a way. A graduate researcher at the University of Texas, a young woman by the name of Livia dos Santos, isolated beta-3 from samples of cereals grown in Russia's podzolitic soil. Dos Santos—until her recent disappearance—was on her way to becoming a major authority on the biochemistry of cereals. At the time of her disappearance, she was studying derivatives that can be extracted from the grains on which man mainly subsists—adhesives, pharmaceuticals, fibrous materials for strengthening cement, and so on, as well as unsuspected vulnerabilities of various grain strains to disease. We at Gwillam and Ripley International Traders were of course vitally interested in her work, and in fact funded her researches at UT."

"Back up, Roger. Way back. What's 'podzolitic'?"

"Podzol—from the Russian. It refers to soil characteristic of coniferous forest areas, which is grayish white in its upper, leached layers."

Forte nodded for Nucho to continue.

"Podzolitic soil produces wheat that contains a minute fraction of beta-3, the stuff up there on the screen. Dos Santos tested beta-3 from Russian wheat samples in rhesus monkeys. The results were so dramatic that, with the secret consent of President Tom Traynor, it was tested on convicts awaiting execution." He paused.

Forte reached into his pocket and extracted a ten-dollar bill. He handed it to Nucho solemnly. "So far, this is shaping up as good as any movie I've seen in the past few months. Okay, I've paid the price of admission—pray continue."

"A good investment," said Nucho, pocketing the bill, "because it gets better. Every man who took the beta-3 went to the electric chair with a pulse rate of seventy-five and a smile on his lips. In short, beta-3 produces instant and lasting euphoria. Anybody taking it doesn't care whether school keeps, whether he's out in the rain, whether he's just lost his job, or whether his wife has switched from hooking rugs to hooking thugs. Those plants in southern Russia are processing beta-3 in significant quantities. And for the next chapter in this commie cliff-hanger, allow me to introduce Dr. George Ashkar, who has flown in from Washington, where he heads a think tank with such an awesome security clearance that its name is spoken only in whispers."

Forte gripped the hand of a tall man with a wild moustache and a spade beard. "Whisper to me, George."

"The way we figure it," said Dr. Ashkar, who had a whisper like a hoarse bassoon, "we've stumbled onto a secret weapon that could annihilate the free world. It couldn't do the United States or the Republic of Texas any good—the wheat they produce doesn't contain beta-3. But it would be worth more than a whole nuclear arsenal to the Soviets."

It didn't take much imagination to guess why. If convicted murderers and rapists serenely marched to the gas chambers after taking a dose of beta-3, then the whole North American continent would with similar tranquility welcome an invading Russian army, once the American army had been disarmed with beta-3. But that unpleasant prospect could now be dismissed: since the Americans had warning—just in time—they would be on guard against any adulteration of their food by beta-3 the Russians might have planned.

"Yes, but how about their *water*?" said Dr. Ashkar.

"Water?"

Ashkar unrolled a map of the United States and Texas. "This is a facsimile of a map found in the safe of the Yak-237 aircraft whose pilot defected to China in late June. The pilot, Shishlin, is in Washington being debriefed at this very moment. While he knows nothing of the map or the other goodies found in his aircraft's safe, he does report that he routinely flew Brigadier General Evgeniy Tomskiy of the KGB, whom the CIA has identified as one of the Soviet Union's sharpest brains in subversive warfare."

Ripley Forte examined the map. It was marked with dozens of tiny spots that Ashkar told him represented key watershed areas where the great rivers of the United States were born. Beta-3 air-dropped in those areas would soon contaminate every drop of water supplying more than 95 percent of North Americans. "Bad, very bad," Forte said after a moment's reflection. "But not fatal. We could conceivably distill all drinking water. It would cost us dearly in energy, but it can be done."

"True," replied Ashkar. "But what of the food plants —the wheat, corn, rice, tomatoes, potatoes, celery, beets—that absorb the water? We have to eat as well as drink to survive, and it will take a long time—if we can at all—to devise a way to flush out the trace contamination." He raised his hand as Forte opened his mouth to intervene. "Believe me, Mr. Forte, we've thought this through, and our conclusion is that the Soviets have us stymied at every turn.

"You see, it's not only the water. It's not only the food. It's the very *air* we breathe." He unrolled another Russian map. It was of the Pacific coast of the United States. "You see these dots in the Pacific in a band five hundred miles deep off the coast?"

Forte nodded.

"They are dump points for beta-3. Their submarine fleet will simultaneously dump quantities of beta-3 at each of these seventy-odd points. It will be quickly absorbed by the sea and—"

"You don't need to go on," Forte growled. "Evaporation from the sea will form clouds carried inland by prevailing westerlies. When rain is precipitated, they'll add to the beta-3 contamination."

"Yes, indeed," Dr. Ashkar affirmed. "But there's something even more sneaky about beta-3; it has a strong chemical affinity for salt. Since you're in the oceans business, Mr. Forte, you know that minute salt crystals are kicked into the atmosphere by wave motion at the rate of 300 million tons a year. In fact, if it weren't for these salt particles, there would be a worldwide drought for they, like dust particles, form the nuclei of the raindrops precipitated from the clouds. Many of the salt particles float free, however, permeating every cubic centimeter of air we breathe. When you consider that the average individual inhales 5,000 quarts of air every day, you can readily imagine how slim are our chances of avoiding contamination by beta-3 from Pacific waters."

Forte was too stunned to speak. Despite their recent

nuclear disaster, here the Soviet Union was again knocking on America's door. They had elaborated the beta-3 extraction technology, imported foreign wheat as an edible substitute for *their* wheat, which could then be used to produce beta-3, built factories. . . .

"Hey!"

"Sir?" said Dr. Ashkar.

"You've laid this load of grief on me, but you haven't really built your case."

"I don't understand."

"So far, it's all theory. This Livia dos Santos has disappeared, you say. It doesn't mean she's working for the Russians."

"No, it doesn't. But sixteen other young scientists seem to have disappeared, as well. . . . And *you* collected the proof of Russian intentions and capabilities yourself, Mr. Forte, on your foray into Sevastopol. By whatever means, the Russians have obtained Livia dos Santos' manuscript, or theories, and are busy implementing them. The way we—our Washington group—see it, the Russians will be able to launch a knockout punch against North America this very summer if we don't do something. Their harvest is just beginning: the beta-3 you abstracted represents first fruits."

17. APACHE
15 JULY 2009

"Mr. Daniel Cragg," announced Marietta Molenaar, Forte's statuesque personal assistant.

"Shoot him in," said Ripley Forte from behind his desk in his fifty-eighth-floor office of the *Houston Herald*. He forced himself to do at least half an hour of paperwork a day and had only just begun plowing through the stack when Miss Molenaar ushered in the man with the ten-thirty appointment. With a sigh of relief, he consigned the unread letters, memoranda, and reports to the

OUT basket and told his aide to handle them herself.

"Now then, Mr. Cragg," Forte said as she closed the door behind her, "what have you got for me?"

"Not so much as I'd have if you'd given me a little more time—but something. The police, FBI, and CIA gumshoes checked out all the obvious leads—family, friends, and business associates—and came up blank, so I passed on all that. I concentrated instead on people and institutions owed money by Livia dos Santos and the other sixteen scientists who vanished at the same time. They were all reputable people who paid their debts, and I figured that, even though lost to the sight of man, they'd—"

"Good thinking, Mr. Cragg," Forte said to the muscular, straight-backed former deputy chief of the Criminal Investigation Division of the U.S. Army, who had been recommended to him as a specialist in redeeming lost causes. "Any luck?"

"Some. I ran down a Miss Patricia Fairweather, formerly Mrs. Raymond Leeb, singing for her supper in a Cincinnati nightclub. Raymond Leeb, you'll remember, was one of the *desaparecidos*, a top student of operations research, Ph.D. candidate from the Utica/Rome campus of the State University of New York. Leeb was—is?—a pretty smart fellow, but not so smart as the bookies. He's into them for better than twenty-four thousand dollars. And he's delinquent in his alimony payments, too, as you can see." He laid a postcard on Forte's desk.

"Dear Pat," it read. "Sorry about missing last month's check. Unfortunately, I'm going to miss the next three, as well, due to a hush-hush assignment. But when I surface, you'll get it all with interest. Plane's about to depart—got to run. Best, Ray."

"Postmarked 16 February, Utica Municipal Airport," Forte noted.

"Exactly. I checked all passenger manifests for that day and came up blank. But twenty-four small planes—business jets, sports craft, and so on—also took off from Utica Municipal on 16 February. Checked *them* out, too. It appears that Leeb left Utica aboard a Cessna Consortium that went to St. Louis. At St. Louis I flashed his picture and found a ramp rat who had seen Leeb walking to another Cessna—with a woman." He smiled and passed over a photograph.

Forte examined the picture. "Livia dos Santos... And where was that second Cessna headed?"

"Its pilot filed a flight plan to Denver, then amended it in flight with destination El Centro, California..."

Ripley Forte caught up with the *Apache* about fifty miles off San Clemente Island. The yacht was built along the lines of her owner, Jennifer Red Cloud—beautiful, graceful, proud, and classy. He motioned with his thumb to the pilot to take him down. Five minutes later he was bracing himself against the chopper's prop wash on the yacht's heliport.

The reception committee, four brawny sailors togged out in white bell-bottom trousers and white skivvy shirts, blocked his path to the ladder leading down to the main deck. As the chopper's blades slowed to a stop, they parted to let pass the ship's captain, a distinguished man in white uniform, a jaunty peaked cap, and a neatly trimmed white beard. He nodded pleasantly to Forte. "Hail," he said, "and farewell."

"I'm here on business with Mrs. Red Cloud."

"You must have an appointment. Mrs. Red Cloud grants none."

Ripley Forte essayed a smile that belied his rising choler. The friend and confidant of presidents, he wasn't used to being told no. "My business is urgent. Tell her it's an affair of state."

"The only state Mrs. Red Cloud cares about is the state of her nerves. You're getting on them by being aboard this ship. I suggest, accordingly, that you push off—now."

Forte calculated the odds. Five to one. He had faced bigger ones in his time, but he was fifty-two, now, and he didn't feel up to fighting an entire yacht's complement single-handed. Anyway, he didn't have to. He nodded. "Very well, I'm going. But when I get aboard my chopper, I'm going to put in a call to a fellow named Horatio Francis Turnbull, whose business I'm here to transact. He may be unhappy that I'm unable to carry out his instructions. He may decide to have this ship, its crew, and its owner taken into custody at your next U.S. port of call and taken apart plank by plank looking for contraband gold, parrots, jaguar skins, cocaine, and Russian spies. It could take months, but maybe Mrs. Red Cloud's got nothing better to do."

The captain regarded him with a cold eye, then shrugged. His job was to drive the boat, not to second-guess tycoons and presidents. "Stand by."

He returned five minutes later to report that Mrs. Red Cloud would be enchanted to have Mr. Forte's company at lunch.

She was stunning, as usual. He'd expected it, for the Jennifer Red Clouds of this world, like fine cognac, only mellow with the years. The simple white silk caftan concealed her soft convexities as she stood, as regal as a maharani, in the center of her salon to receive him. But when she moved toward him, hand outstretched, it molded itself against a body whose hips seemed slimmer and bust incredibly fuller than when he had last caressed them so lovingly.

That had been at her Tokyo home. He even remembered the day, 21 July, a day which would live in ecstasy for them both. He had gone there to rape her, as she had raped him by swindling him out of his share in Forte Oceanic Resources fourteen years earlier. But what began as rape swiftly turned into a collision of body and soul whose passionate intensity they realized was the emotional fulfillment for which both had always unconsciously yearned. The next morning she had declared her love for him, *love*—after years of perverse sabotage of every project he undertook. That her declaration was sincere he could not doubt, but Ripley Forte had come to take possession of her body—temporarily—and her company, Raynes Oceanic Resources—permanently—and he was too proud to admit that one night of rapture could change his rules for corporate warfare. He walked out on her. It was the hardest thing he ever did, but he was a man, and a man moreover who never allowed himself to succumb to such feminine fantasies as "love."

Yet, looking at her now, holding her warm hand in his

own, for the thousandth time second thoughts assailed
him. She was to every other woman he'd ever met, even
exotic, erotic females like Valerie Vincent, what a raging
sea is to a mill pond. Her Apache-Scots-Norwegian
blood churned with guile and candor, cruelty and tender-
ness, her violet eyes never giving a hint which of her
volcanic moods would surface next. She was flint to his
steel, and he had now to keep his distance, or risk the
spark that would set their lives again afire.

He released the hand he wanted to hold fast forever.

"Hello, Rip," said Jennifer Red Cloud. "Whatever it
is, it must be important to drag you away from your
ocean scows and society cows. Sit down and tell Mother
all about it."

"I'm sorry I'm so pressing," Forte began, "but—"

"Don't apologize—you're *always* pressing, as I remember so well from our last meeting."

"Yes, well—" Forte hurried on, "I'm here on a matter
of national security, and I need your help."

"I thought you'd already taken from me everything
you wanted."

Forte ran his calloused hand over his near-bald head.
This was going to be worse than he thought. No matter
what he said, she was going to bend it into a spear to
skewer him with. "Look, Red, I know how you feel,
but—"

"I should hope so, *especially* where the butt is concerned."

"Hey—can we get off this subject?"

"And onto the four-poster, do you mean?"

Manuel saved him. The old Filipino retainer brought
in a tray with a silver coffee service and put it on the low
table between them. He kept his eyes averted from Ripley Forte, the wild man who, when they last met at Mrs.
Red Cloud's Tokyo home, had threatened to kill him
when he had answered her cry for help, before Forte had
disappeared upstairs with madam across his shoulder.

Jennifer Red Cloud poured coffee into one of those
paper-thin china cups Texans hate worse than quiche,
and handed it to Forte. He put it gently on the table,
fearful it would disintegrate on contact with his hand.

"Why did you come here, Ripley?" said Mrs. Red Cloud, now all business, in one of her mercurial changes of mood.

"Like I said, it's a matter of—"

"National security. You said that. Get to the point. I am a busy woman."

Forte described the disappearance of the seventeen first-rate researchers and graduate students, how the FBI and CIA assumed they had defected en masse to the Russians, how he had learned that the Russians planned a sneak offensive against North America that would without question destroy them all.

Mrs. Red Cloud nodded. "I fail to understand your concern. You'll lose your billions, to be sure, but after the Russians deploy their laughing gas, you'll die happy. Would you rather die miserable?"

"I don't intend to die either way just now."

"You mentioned needing my help, I believe."

"That's right. I am convinced that those seventeen men and women didn't defect to Russia. None had any problems defection would help. The logistics of spiriting seventeen people out of the country would be formidable; none was sighted at any point of departure. Yet it is apparent that their researches are in the possession of the Russians, who are using them to wage a particularly sneaky kind of war against us."

"Yes, yes, you said that," said Mrs. Red Cloud impatiently. "Tell me where I come in, before I tell you where you can go out."

"The seventeen have been traced to El Centro. To your recently acquired ROR facility, in fact."

"Oh, I *see*. I am collaborating with the Russians now."

"I didn't say that."

"Near enough. Now stop talking to me as if I were a fool and listen. I was approached by a government official with impeccable references, asking to use my El Centro facility for secret work. I agreed. When the disappearance of the seventeen scientists was made public, I assumed, naturally, that they were the ones at El Centro, and the government had good reason not to divulge their whereabouts."

"When did you see them last?"

"I never *did* see them, actually. Had no reason to."

"So, far as you know, they're still at El Centro?"

"No longer. Around the middle of last month, my government contact informed me that their researches had been successfully completed and the team disbanded."

"When?"

"The day before, I believe."

"Can you be more precise?"

Jennifer Red Cloud spoke into the intercom, and a moment later her secretary produced a leather-bound diary. Red Cloud flipped through the pages. "The researchers left on June 15. Now maybe you'll tell me why you think all this is significant."

Forte reached for his coffee cup, thought better of it, and leaned back in his chair. "I was in El Centro this morning. Made some inquiries. I found, for example, that the food was catered."

"So?"

"I spoke with the chef at the Barbara Worth Hotel, from which the catered food was dispatched three times daily. I asked whether the food was sent out in individual portions, or whether it was served out family style, thinking to get a check on the number of people served. It figured out to about twenty to twenty-five portions, which is what you'd expect seventeen young people to eat."

"How shrewd of you!" said Red Cloud, her voice throbbing with synthetic wonder.

"Then I asked if the people requested any special food. Oh, yes, he said, they ordered hamburgers and dogs and fries, pizza, and lots of soft drinks and sugary desserts. Again, what you'd expect of a bunch of young folk. Finally I asked him when he made the last delivery of food. He said it was on 28 May. So I was wondering, what did they eat between that date and 15 June?"

Jennifer Red Cloud sat transfixed. Anger suffused her face. The seventeen young scientists had left the El Centro facility more than two weeks earlier than David D.

Castle claimed. Why did David lie? Obviously because it gave him two weeks in which—to—do whatever he wanted to do with the seventeen, who had not been seen since. All sorts of unpleasant thoughts assailed Jennifer Red Cloud. But among them was one certainty: David had lied to her about their departure date, and if he'd lied to her about that, he could just as easily have lied about everything else.

"You've been taken, haven't you?" Forte asked quietly.

She nodded. "Not for the first time," she said grimly. "But, I promise you, for the last."

"Who was it?"

She shook her head. "You'll know soon enough. All I can say is—"

Her words were cut short by the striking of six bells on the *Apache*'s bridge.

Before the sound of the last bell died away, the salon door opened and a woman in a white nurse's uniform stepped across the combing. In her arms was a baby, swathed in a blue blanket. When she saw that Mrs. Red Cloud had a visitor, she blurted an apology and started back through the doorway.

"That's all right, Carmen," Mrs. Red Cloud said. "Mr. Forte is a friend."

The nurse smiled shyly and brought the baby to where Mrs. Red Cloud sat. She took the baby tenderly in her arms and smiled down at the restless child. Carmen hurried from the salon.

Mrs. Red Cloud unzipped the front of her caftan, revealing a swelling breast to which the infant immediately attached itself, punching with both tiny hands.

Forte sat speechless, his jaw sagging foolishly.

"I guess you'd have found out sooner or later that I had a child, Rip."

"But I—I—"

"And your natural curiosity would have brought you blundering into my life again. Well, now that you're here, take a good look, because this is the last you're going to see, for a very long time, of your son—Ripley Forte, Jr."

18. BLACK MAGIC
15 JULY 2009

"DAVID?"

"My dear, how wonderful of you to call."

"I hope you don't change your mind after we switch to scramble code 1137."

"Switching." The vice-president punched in the code. "But frankly," he said in a ponderous attempt at gallantry, "I'd be flattered if everybody knew that the most desirable woman in the world wanted to talk with me."

"You bet I do," Jennifer Red Cloud said crisply. "And I'll get right to the point. An hour ago . . . This line *is* secure, by the way?"

"Checked out by the Secret Service this very morning, my dear Jennifer. Nobody here but you and me."

"Good. As I was saying, this afternoon Ripley Forte dropped in—I'm calling from the *Apache*, by the way, off Catalina Island—and raised a very interesting question about garden paths."

"Garden paths?"

"Yes. The questions he asked made me wonder whether you haven't been leading me down one."

"I'm afraid I don't follow."

"He tried to pump me about what was going on at El Centro. I got the impression he thought I was set up."

"Did Forte tell you that?" Castle said sharply.

"Not exactly. But the hints he dropped would have squashed a fair-sized elephant. He was wondering aloud whether the people in El Centro were the seventeen missing scientists."

"What did you tell him?" Castle asked tensely.

"Not a damned thing. It's none of his business, after all—or is it?"

"Certainly not!"

"That's what I told him—that it was none of his business what Raynes Oceanic Resources does. Well, he got a little huffy and said that he had some good leads he intended to run down, and I told him to run as much as he pleased, so long as it was in the other direction. He started to go, but then it occurred to me I'd better talk with you before he stuck his big hoof into your secret government project."

"Brava, my dear Jennifer!"

"So I made an appointment with him for the day after tomorrow—Wednesday. We're to meet at—well, the exact spot where I met your Dr. E—at eleven in the morning."

"Fine. Tell him nothing."

"You should know Ripley Forte better than that by now, David, after the way he tied you into knots on the iceberg *Alamo* project. He's very persuasive, and unless I have quite a convincing story to tell, he may go blundering into the matter and compromise your security."

"True, true... Look, Jennifer, this matter requires some thought. It's ten-twenty Washington time. Give me a few hours—say, until midnight your time—and I'll figure out the best approach to use with Forte and call you on the *Apache* before you fly off. Agreed?"

"Very well, David. I don't know what you have in mind, but it'd better be good."

"Have I ever failed you?"

"Good-bye, David," she said, hanging up before her answer to that question brought a chill to the proceedings.

It was 1 A.M. when the taxi rolled through the gates of the U.S. Naval Observatory and stopped before the mansion, the official residence of the Vice-President of the United States. Ilse Freemann, who had been summoned by Vice-President Castle for "an exclusive backgrounder," strode up the steps and was conducted to the study where the vice-president awaited her.

"You must be out of your mind," she grated when they were alone. "Vice-presidents don't give exclusive backgrounders at this time of morning. How do you think I'm going to explain this?"

"You're the brains," said Castle contemptuously.

"You're the control. You'll think of something. And while you're thinking, listen to this." He switched on a tape recording of his conversation with Jennifer Red Cloud.

Ilse Freemann listened with a frown, enveloped in cigarette smoke, as the tape played through. When it was finished, she sat staring ahead, nibbling thoughtfully on her knuckle. "Well, it could be worse," she said finally.

"I don't see how," replied Castle. "She didn't tell him about my connection with the El Centro operation, but she will, when Forte starts working on her under that romantic Caribbean moon. It will only take one word, and I—*we*—will go down in flames."

"Yes."

"Well?"

The *New York Times* diplomatic correspondent shrugged. "It could have been worse," she repeated. "At least we have thirty-six hours to take remedial measures."

"Such as?"

She smiled sadly. "Somehow, I don't think you *really* want to know."

It was three-thirty in the morning when Ripley Forte's corporate jet landed at Newark International Airport. The pilot taxied the aircraft to its designated tie-down and shut down its engines. He and the rest of the crew exited by the forward hatch, leaving Forte, who had turned in before the plane reached the Nevada border, to sleep on his king-sized bed aft. The grind of international intrigue, running one of the world's biggest corporations, trying to lead what passed for a love life, and now the new and unexpected battle with Jennifer Red Cloud to share their son were taking their toll. He was tired, and he needed his nine hours a night, preferably alone.

He awoke to a rainy, dismal, New Jersey Tuesday, and taking the chopper to a rainy, dismal Manhattan only made matters worse. He had scheduled a full day: board meetings, a business lunch, an appearance at the opening of Texas' refurbished New York Consulate, and hearings with the State of New York Commerce Commission, which had offered to dredge the East River and provide berthing facilities if Triple Eye would agree to bring a minimum of six one-billion-ton bergs to New York annually.

Between the Consulate inauguration and the Commerce Commission hearings, Forte took a taxi to Sleight-o'-Hand, on Sixth Avenue, the foremost magician's prop suppliers in North America. By prearrangement, he met with the proprietor of the shop and Danno the Magnificent, a leading practitioner of illusions. He stayed an hour, and left with a large package and a thoughtful scowl adorning his pleasantly ugly features.

The chopper hovered five feet above the roiled waters of Montego Bay. A figure in fins and goggles poised for a moment on the starboard skid, then plunged into the emerald sea. The chopper whipped around a half turn and roared away toward Kingston. The sea became smooth, disturbed only at twenty-second intervals as the swimmer broke the surface, took a breath, and plunged again into the coral depths. Each time he came up, he was closer to the beach.

At shortly after ten-thirty, the figure reached the shallows and waded ashore. Ripley Forte stripped off his fins and mask and tossed them on the sands near the beach chairs, already shaded by a striped beach umbrella. He picked up a big beach towel from the stack beside the chairs and dried himself. From the cottage two hundred meters up the sloping beach, shielded from the sea by a thicket of palms, a small brown man in a white jacket came toward him, bearing a tray with things that glittered in the sun.

Forte took a glass from the tray, passed a few words with Luis, Mrs. Red Cloud's personal manservant, as he arranged glasses, pitcher, and ice bucket on the low table between the chairs, and drank it down. Luis bowed, not so deferentially as to break the sharp creases in his whites, and trudged back up the beach toward the house. Forte was alone, except for the sea and the semicircle of palms that afforded Jennifer Red Cloud the privacy that allowed her to bathe undisturbed in the nude.

Ten minutes later, as Forte soaked in the hot morning sun, a woman in a one-piece white satin bathing suit came out of the trees and walked toward him with a springy, hip-swinging stride. Her long black hair was swept back by the breeze, and her lithe legs contrasted nicely with her swelling breasts, like twin spinnakers in a thirty-knot wind.

Forte rose at her approach, and they exchanged a few words before the woman took off at a run for the sea, followed by Forte. She hit the water in a shallow dive, and surfaced fifty feet offshore. Every time Forte nearly caught up with her, she plunged toward bottom and emerged, laughing, at some unexpected spot. At last, tiring of the game, she swam toward the beach with regular, powerful strokes and was toweling herself dry when Forte came up behind her, wrapped her in the towel and his embraces, and deposited her gently in one of the deck chairs. He picked up another towel, straddled her chair, and wrapped it about her head. When he stepped back, her legs were outstretched, her arms folded behind her head, luxuriating in the sun. Forte sat beside her looking out at the blue waters and far horizon.

They sat like this for some time, immobile, as the morning sun rose toward its zenith.

Shortly after eleven the surface of the shallows, some two hundred feet from where they sat, gave birth to a figure all in black. The figure broke the surface, stood on the shallow bottom with head and shoulders exposed, and without haste pulled back the mask, raised a carbine to its shoulder, and squeezed off four shots in rapid succession into the body of the woman next to Ripley Forte. Four gushers of red poured out on the white suit as Forte, startled by the shots, hit the sand with arms and legs outspread to offer the smallest target, instinctively following the lessons of his Marine training.

The figure dropped the rifle and disappeared beneath the sea. From the line of trees armed men came running down to the water's edge where they searched for a trace of the vanished assassin. Almost at once the waters began to churn not far from where the rifleman had stood, and three frogmen broke the surface, dragging the figure, struggling in vain, toward the shore. From the deeper waters other frogmen came into view at intervals, and now swam ashore.

"Let's have a look," said Forte.

While two frogmen held the rifleman's arms, the other stripped off the mask and rubber hood.

The rifleman was a tall, handsome black woman of about thirty-five.

She smiled, her dark eyes luminous with satisfaction. "Tough luck, man," she said.

"Good luck, you mean. You missed me completely."

She laughed. "Hell, I wasn't supposed to shoot *you.*"

Forte nodded to the dozen men who had come running from the trees. "She's all yours. See what you can beat out of her."

The black woman snorted. "Try a gang bang. That way we'll *all* have some fun. And believe me, fun's all you're going to get out of this baby."

Forte turned away as the men escorted their prisoner up the beach to the house. He lifted the red-stained dummy from the deck chair and threw it to one side. Then he hit the spring lever, the chair flip-flopped, and a sweaty female appeared. She released the transparent belts that had held her in place and wiped the sweat from her forehead with the black wig she had worn over her short-cropped blond hair.

"What a girl does to make a living these days."

"Mustn't grumble, Miss Pace, and I doubt that you will want to when you see the size of the bonus that's waiting for you in the little white envelope. Now, if you'll just go up to the house, shower and dress, my men will see you get back to the mainland in good order."

"No warnings about not talking?" said the young woman.

"What would you say, and to whom? Besides, if you said it to the wrong people, they might turn out to be baddies. The world's full of them."

At lunch Jennifer Red Cloud was glum. "Some judges of character *we* are. How long do you think he's been working for the Russians?"

"Who knows? David thinks you're dead, and you're going to stay that way for the moment, while we give him some rope to hang himself. Anyway, none of that's important right now."

"Oh! And if it isn't important that the Vice-President of the United States of America is a communist mole, pray tell what *is*?"

"When you're going to be reasonable and let me have —*see*, I mean—my son."

Jennifer Red Cloud smiled her Gioconda smile. "Have a glass of this lovely 1998 Musar Cabernet Sauvignon," she said, pouring red wine into his glass. "It's a vintage year. It'll help you forget what is beyond your reach."

19. FIRESTORM
21 JULY 2009

"IF IT WERE ANYBODY BUT YOU SAYING THAT, RIP," SAID the President of the United States, "I'd have him hauled away by brawny men in white coats."

"Nevertheless, sir, it's a fact—your vice-president is taking orders from the Kremlin."

Horatio Francis Turnbull shook his head. Unbelievable as it seemed that the man next in line for the presidency of the United States was a covert agent of the Soviet Union, he had to admit that precedents abounded. In England, the Queen's adviser on art had been a commie, as at various times were the head of and number-two man in MI-5, a brace of MI-6 senior officers, a gaggle of Foreign Office types, communications specialists, and ranking military officers. In the United States, the top-secret Manhattan Project had been riddled with commies homegrown and imported. The United Nations charter had been entrusted for delivery to San Francisco in 1945 to Alger Hiss. And the assistant secretary of the treasury, Harry Dexter White, was Red. If those traitors had positions of trust among the mighty, why not David D. Castle?

Forte's evidence was convincing. Utterly damning was the fact that only Castle had been advised of Jennifer Red Cloud's imminent trip to Jamaica; not even her own staff had been told of her intentions until the moment of departure. Even more conclusive was the bail-out of Raynes Oceanic Resources by "the government." Only the president himself could have authorized such a transfer of funds, and tonight was the first time he had heard of it. It followed from these two bits of evidence that David D. Castle was up to his neck in the disappearance of the seventeen scientists. That they had all defected simultaneously without leaving a trace was preposterous. The only alternative explanation was that they had been forcibly removed to the Soviet Union, or even murdered. Both murder and kidnapping were hanging offenses. So any way one looked at it, David D. Castle was going to hang by the neck until dead.

Or was he? He had been tried and convicted in the minds of a jury of three: Ripley Forte, Jennifer Red Cloud, and Horatio Francis Turnbull. The Fifth Amendment required a presentment of a grand jury, while the Sixth guaranteed the right to a speedy and public trial. While such a trial would satisfy the natural thirst of duped Americans for revenge, it would ruin Turnbull, who had picked Castle for his running mate. It would make America an object of the world's ridicule. Its political damage would exceed the catastrophes of the Tea Pot Dome scandal, Watergate, and the Viet Nam War combined. The president just might escape impeachment, but he could never thereafter captain a ship of state whose sails were filled with gales of laughter.

There was another way, of course. David D. Castle could poison himself one day by ingesting tea accidentally spiked with botulism toxin. Or he might suffer a fatal fall from a high place, or be shot by an assassin, or be crushed under a runaway tractor on his Virginia farm. The possibilities were legion, and the men Turnbull could rely on to carry out such a patriotic project only slightly less numerous.

"But would that be wise?" he mused, half aloud.

"What's that, Mr. President?" said Ripley Forte, whom President Turnbull had completely forgotten about while concentrating on the many attractive possibilities for bringing David D. Castle's career to a prompt and vigorous close.

"I was wondering whether we should confront him with evidence of his treason," said the president glibly. "Give him a chance to take the gentleman's way out."

Forte snorted. "Fall on his sword? More likely he'd need a hearty push."

President Turnbull was aghast. "I hope you aren't suggesting anything illegal, Rip. While I quite sympathize with your indignation—and share it—I cannot permit such a line of thought. No, we'll have to do something else."

Forte waited.

"Yes," the president went on, "we'll have to handle it in another way, without either jeopardizing the effectiveness of the remainder of my term by a public disclosure of Castle's treason or committing upon him the mayhem he so richly deserves."

"There's another way?"

"Certainly. We'll proceed as if nothing had happened —providing you can persuade Mrs. Red Cloud to stay out of sight for the time being. Thus our vice-president and his employers will be convinced their operative has killed Mrs. Red Cloud and that his secret is safe. And then we will be able to plant whatever disinformation we wish with Castle, knowing it will be immediately relayed to the Russians. An agent, once uncovered, can be a very useful weapon in our battle with the forces of darkness."

Spoken like a true politician, thought Forte. "One thing: what happens if—may the evil be far distant from you—you should die while in office? We'd have a Russian mole surfacing in the Oval Office. What then?"

"Then I'd expect you, my dear Ripley, to take appropriate measures."

"Speaking of which, what do you intend to do about the Russians?"

"Do?"

"Sure. They're about to convert the population of the United States into a nation of lotus eaters. You *are* going to act, I hope?"

President Turnbull shook his head. "Anything I did to prevent the Russians from unleashing an offensive that, so far as I know officially, exists only in the mind of a

single citizen of a foreign country—you—would constitute an act of war. The world would become embroiled in
immediate hostilities, leading to a nuclear exchange
punctuated at last only by our mutual extinction."

Forte regarded the president sourly. "Double-talk for
doing nothing, is that it?"

"That's right." Turnbull nodded, rising behind his
desk. "Nothing. On the other hand, Rip, you being a
citizen of the Republic of Texas and all—I have no control over what you might do as an outraged individual
acting in your own interest. From what I've heard, you
Texans don't get mad—you get even."

That bit about the "outraged individual" was right on
the mark, Forte decided as he left by the West Wing
tunnel that took him directly to the White House helipad,
its lights extinguished to conceal the identity of the midnight visitor. He didn't know whether he was more outraged by Castle's treason, or the Soviet scheme to make
zombies of Americans, or the president's decision to let
Forte do the job the American people elected him president to discharge. Forte was a businessman, not a states-
man. His function was to make money, not war. But if
making war was the only way he could continue to pursue his business of selling water and electricity and
growing wheat, then so be it.

On the flight from Dulles International Airport back
to Houston that night, Forte considered the interrelated
problems of preventing the poisoning of the water and
atmosphere by beta-3 and teaching the Russians that getting Gwillam Forte's boy Ripley riled was bad politics. It
would have been in the realm of the possible had he
commanded half a million battle-hardened Marines, in
the purlieu of the probable with 1,000 intercontinental
bombers or an arsenal of missiles. On the other hand, he
had what might prove far more useful: a vast organization peopled by men and women with brains and imagination.

"The problem is this," said Ripley Forte the next day
to his top computer scientist in the SD-1 research labora-

tories under Houston. "I want to bust into the Strategic
Defense Initiative control system."

Dr. Victor Reston, a wiry, well-preserved man who
once had been Golden Gloves boxing champion of Texas,
returned a thoughtful look. "Well, Rip, I foresee no great
difficulty. That little chore should be simple enough after
we've laid some preliminary scientific groundwork—like
determining the extent of the universe, reversing the aging
process, figuring out why teenagers hate their parents, and
discovering how a man smart enough to accumulate an
estimated twelve billion dollars can be dumb enough to
think he can bust into SDI."

"Spoken like a man who wants to add to his collection
of pink slips."

"Sure," said Reston, "you can fire me for telling you
the facts, and then you hire some yes-man who'll take all
your loose change and give you the same answer five
years down the road."

"Now, now," said Forte, contrite, "don't take me literally about the pink slip. It's only that I know you play
a Brown-Ash Mark IX computer like Ormandy used to
play the Philadelphia Symphony Orchestra. All I ask is
that you purge your mind of preconceptions and think
about whether there *is* a way in."

"Yes and no. Yes, I've thought about it; and no, there
isn't."

Forte draped his hairy forearm about the shoulders of
the smaller man and led him from his laboratory, where
he felt compelled to think like a scientist, to the comfortable lounge, where he could put his feet up and dream
like a civilian. Forte poured the good doctor a cup of
coffee and sat in the leather club chair opposite him.

"Let's approach this thing systematically," Forte
began. "First of all, the SDI satellite system is controlled
by electronic impulses from the ground. We could break
into it—"

"—if we had maybe twenty or thirty billion man-
years," Reston interposed. "They have an elaborate
code to authenticate orders, and the code changes each
day randomly according to an algorithm that is more secret than the formula of the silver hair dye that President
Turnbull uses. Next idiocy?"

"So it's impossible for us to get control of the system?"

"Absolutely—from a technological standpoint."

Forte frowned. "Are you trying to tell me something?"

"Maybe. How far are you prepared to go to break into the system?"

"As far as I have to."

"Who'll run the operation?"

"The most competent man we can find."

"Okay." Reston smiled. "You talked me into it. . . ."

Six days later Captain Merle Plash of the U.S. Army, designated custodian of the "football," the briefcase containing the go-cards with which the President of the United States would authenticate his strike commands in the event of a Soviet missile attack, sat in an anteroom of the Oval Office reading the *Armed Forces Journal*. It was his responsibility to accompany President Turnbull at all times, never to be more than a few steps from the president's side, and never to relinquish possession of the black briefcase chained to his wrist to anyone except his authorized relief, who had to identify himself with a special card issued by the Joint Chiefs of Staff in the presence of the president's military aide.

Lieutenant Colonel Henry Haperman, who had reported two days earlier for duty with the National Security Council, stuck his head through the doorway, did a double-take when he saw Captain Plash, and said, "What the hell are *you* doing here?"

Captain Plash rose to attention, a puzzled frown wrinkling his forehead. "I'm on duty, sir. It's my watch."

"But where's Hudson?"

Lieutenant (jg) Hudson was Plash's relief, but he wasn't due to report for more than twenty minutes.

"He comes on at sixteen hundred, sir."

"I know that," replied Haperman impatiently. "But I thought he'd relieve you at once, when he heard the news."

"News?" Captain Plash felt a sudden roaring in his ears. "*What* news?"

Haperman hesitated. "I thought you knew. Your wife

was just arrested by the Secret Service. When she drove through the gate to pick you up, they made one of those unscheduled inspections and found a quantity of amphetamines under the front seat."

"*What?* Where is she?"

"Still at the gate, so far as I know, trying to explain that it's all a mistake. That's why I'm surprised that Hudson's not reported, knowing that you could get down there and straighten everything out in five minutes."

Plash agonized. To leave his post carrying the football was unthinkable. Not to intercede for his wife was equally unthinkable—considering what the shock of arrest might do to the baby Sheila was carrying. *Where the hell was Hudson?*

"Maybe I'd better go look for him, or maybe you should just wait until your watch ends. After all, it's only twenty min—"

Plash cleared his throat. "Colonel, you can do me a great favor, if you would, sir. You're cleared for Muckraker material, and the president just went into conference with the Speaker of the House. He won't be out for at least half an hour."

"If you're going to ask me to hold the football, forget it." Lieutenant Colonel Haperman shook his head. "That would be a breach of regulations, and you know it, Captain."

"Just five minutes, sir," Plash pleaded. "Nobody will know, and—I've got to go to my wife." His forehead was damp, his eyes agonized.

Lieutenant Colonel Haperman came to a sudden decision. "Five minutes, Plash, and not a second longer. If anybody comes while you're gone, it'll be my ass. . . ."

Twelve minutes later Captain Plash was back, flushed and sweaty but with a triumphant smile on his face. Switching the handcuff and chain from Colonel Haperman's wrist to his own, he explained: "I stepped into the guard shack and pissed into a bottle for them, then got them to take Sheila downtown to run a test on her. It's all a mistake, and I think the Secret Service realizes it. Obviously, some malicious son of a bitch planted that stuff in our car, and they'll have proof of it when they test us with the polygraph, which I've already volunteered us to take."

"I'm relieved you got it straightened out," Haperman said. "Meanwhile, let me have a word with the Secret Service officers to see if we can't keep this incident off your record."

"That's damned decent of you, sir. I won't forget this."

Haperman smiled. "Look, Captain, we've both done something that could ruin our careers and get us demoted to Pfc and a tour of the stockade. I think the best thing would be for us both to forget the last fifteen minutes ever happened. What do you say?"

Plash extended his hand. "You've got my word," he said thankfully.

On 28 July 2009, at dusk, as the Russian wheat harvest was getting into full swing, the iodine lasers of American Strategic Defense Initiative satellites transiting the Soviet Union, in what was later found to be a major malfunction, sent a 150-millisecond burst of energy that could theoretically destroy even the thickest-skinned spinning target.

Actually, since no missiles were launched, the American alert that would have responded with its own massive missile launch against Russia were the SDI system to fail caused a number of heart attacks and much mystification, but no other casualties. The iodine laser beams, which failed to connect with ascending missiles, expended their energy on the first solid matter they encountered, which happened to be the huge grain-growing areas of central and southern Russia and the fertile flatlands west of the Ural Mountains.

Even as the President of the United States was sending an urgent message of apology for the SDI malfunction and promising appropriate punishment for the culprits responsible, along with generous indemnities to the Soviet Union, scattered fires broke out in an area of more than one and a half million square miles, and soon the isolated fires joined to produce a firestorm whose

200-mile-an-hour winds spread the fire still further, defeating all efforts to bring it under control.

For the next twelve hours of darkness, while the firestorm raged out of control across the Soviet Union's heartland, the President of the United States was airborne in his Boeing 797 aerial command post, ready to give the order that would cause a four-star general's finger, poised over a computer keyboard, to fall, unleashing America's response to the expected Russian retaliatory ICBM strike.

To the surprise and enormous relief of American politicians and defense staff, satellite reconnaissance showed that the Russians who would have been preparing missiles for launch were instead trying desperately to bring the fires under control. Whole cities emptied as millions of Russians, with shovels and rakes, bulldozers and burlap bags, fought a losing battle against the flames.

The fire, unprecedented in the history of the world, was not the only source of heat. The hotline between President Turnbull's air command post and the Kremlin crackled and burned with accusation and recrimination from the Russians on one hand and abject apology from the Americans on the other. But even before the fires began to burn themselves out, President Turnbull had convinced Premier Evgeniy Luchenko that the Americans had nothing to do with the fire and that, indeed, the United States would empty its grain storehouses and silos to make good the Russian loss as a gesture of international amity, and at no cost to the Soviet Union.

As for the unknown criminal who had somehow broken through SDI security, President Turnbull strongly hinted that it must be someone known to bear obdurate hatred for the Soviet Union and possessing the means to pervert the peaceful Strategic Defense Initiative system into a weapon that could devastate the heartland of Russia.

Premier Luchenko suggested that only one enemy of Russia could marshal the immense resources such sabotage would require: that renegade Texan, Ripley Forte.

President Turnbull pointedly declined to disagree.

20. SLOW BURN
25 JULY 2009

"STILL BURNING?" PRESIDENT TURNBULL ASKED WORriedly.

"Still burning, sir," replied his National Security aide, Marine Major General Habib T. Noonie.

President Turnbull massaged his face, trying to rub the tension away. His eyes were bloodshot and puffy from fatigue, the lines that usually gave him the appearance of graceful maturity now were those of a tired old man. "Goddammit," he protested, "those wheat fields *can't* still be on fire. Our Department of Agriculture experts said they'd burn out in a matter of hours. But it's been four *days* now, and they're *still* burning. I don't understand it."

"You're not alone, Mr. President. *No* one understands it."

"What do the Russians say?"

"Merely that the great Russian people are valiantly battling the flames set by that arch-capitalist villain Ripley Forte."

"Well, for once, they're half right. But it still doesn't account for the fires still burning."

"According to Premier Luchenko, before they could get one fire extinguished it had spread to adjacent fields and is now burning out of control."

Turnbull made a gesture of disbelief and emitted a ripe raspberry to go along with it. "They've mustered every able-bodied man and woman in the wheat-growing areas to fight those fires. They've hooked up harrows and discs to their tractors and gang-plowed firebreaks to cut off the spread of the conflagration. Our wheat-belt farmers would have done the job in a day; the most it

117

could have taken the Russians is double that. But *four* days?"

Nevertheless, whatever the cause, the Russians weren't faking the fire. American reconnaissance satellites reported that not only had the pall of smoke over the Soviet Union not dissipated, but it had actually thickened during the four days since the American lasers had been manipulated by Ripley Forte's scientists into setting Russia's wheatlands afire. Another anomaly: the Russians had registered a bitter but pro-forma protest and demanded the extradition of Ripley Forte to stand trial in Kiev for crimes against humanity. Considering the gravity of the situation, the Russian response to this nationwide catastrophe had been astonishingly mild. The least Turnbull expected was a Russian demand for some sort of symbolic retaliation, perhaps the nuking of an expendable American city, like Detroit.

Of course, that initial reaction might have been deliberately restrained in order to put the Americans off their guard, so that they would be unprepared for a sudden deluge of Russian nuclear warheads. But President Turnbull had anticipated that ploy, and American nuclear and conventional forces remained on full alert. The reserves and national guard were in the first stages of mobilization, and citizens of both the United States and Texas were stocking up on food and water and hastily digging shelters. Supermarket shelves had been swept clean, and the price of shovels, plastic sheeting, premixed concrete, and handguns had quadrupled since the beginning of the crisis.

Still, the Soviet Union protested that it harbored no aggressive intent against the United States—and Intelligence reports from within Russia, backed by satellite reconnaissance, confirmed that the Russian armed forces had indeed been diverted from defense to firefighting duties and nowhere were preparing for a nuclear confrontation. The Americans were at a loss to explain the remarkable absence of Russian counteraction to an obvious Western provocation. It was totally out of character. Turnbull and his advisers waited with apprehension for the other shoe to drop.

On Day Six of what the news media were describing

as the Great Russian Burn-Off, a hint that the crisis might be some kind of smokescreen came as General Noonie strode into President Turnbull's office unannounced, clutching a handful of glossy photographs and trailing yards of the latest satellite photos and computer readouts. He spread the strips across the president's desk. "Take a look at that, Mr. President," he said, pointing at the shadowy area on the right side of the map.

President Turnbull regarded the image blankly. "What am I supposed to be looking at?"

"Those black smudges."

"When you've seen one black smudge, you've seen them all."

"Except that you didn't see them *there* in the earlier shots," General Noonie said triumphantly. "The clouds of smoke were concentrated in European Russia—over the Ukraine and the so-called Virgin Lands opened up by Nikita Khrushchev when he was premier back in the fifties. Those were the primary wheat-growing areas fired by our lasers when Forte got cute with the satellite sensors. But *these* clouds of smoke are far to the west, over Siberia, in Asian Russia."

President Turnbull made a gesture of dismissal. "I thought you graduated from the Naval Academy in the sciences," he scoffed.

"That I did, sir," General Noonie said proudly.

"Then they must have taught you that the prevailing westerlies of the northern hemisphere would have blown that smoke from the Ukraine westward a couple of thousand miles to Siberia during the six days the wheatlands have been afire."

"I see what you mean, sir. But you know the old saying, 'Where there's smoke, there's fire.' That's especially true here. A lot of the smoke *is* indeed from the wheat fields. But not all, by any means. In fact, the smoke that you see here photographed is mainly being produced in Siberia itself."

"How do you know that?"

General Noonie pointed to red-circled entries on the computer readout. "These are infrared readings. The smoke, even over the Ukraine, where the wheat fields are completely burned out, is warm. As it drifts west, it should grow cooler. But that smoke over Siberia isn't cool—it's *hot*. And the earth beneath that cloud of smoke is hotter still."

President Turnbull stroked his chin in puzzlement. "But how can that be? Unless my geography teacher was all wet, the lower latitudes of Siberia are grass rangeland or covered with sparse brush and trees."

"Your teacher didn't lie."

"Then how did it catch fire? We've already reviewed the computer programs Forte used to trick our SDI lasers, and they show conclusively that he targeted only wheatlands—not the steppes of Central Asia. To my recollection, not a single fire was ignited east of the Urals."

"Right."

"Then why the hell are the steppes afire?"

"They're not, Mr. President. The fire is not general, but confined to something like 870 specific and relatively tiny areas." On the desk he spread a large photograph on which were marked the locations of the current heat sources.

The president looked at it. "What is this supposed to tell me?"

"Nothing, sir—not until you see this overlay." He produced a piece of clear plastic that fit precisely over the map of Russia. On the overlay were dots that masked every one of the fire symbols.

"What's this?" said Turnbull.

"A map of reserves of lignite—sometimes called brown coal—billions of tons of the stuff, in Siberia. Many of these mines have been listed on natural resource maps since way back in czarist times, but they've never been exploited because they were uneconomical. Well, they're being exploited now—with a vengeance."

"I don't understand."

"As of this morning, when these satellite photographs were taken, they're producing at full capacity."

"*Lignite?*"

"No—smoke."

During the next two weeks, smoke boiling up from the nearly one thousand Siberian lignite mines blackened the sky over Asian Russia. It ascended to more than forty thousand feet and oozed eastward, like a gigantic amoeba, along a two-thousand-mile front, borne by the prevailing westerlies toward the American continent. When it reached Alaska, it was seized by polar winds whistling down the vast Mackenzie Basin and spread like a pall from northern Canada southward as far as the Mason-Dixon line.

The United States that year was suffering one of its periodic heat waves. At first the advancing black mass, now gray from dilution with polar air, brought surcease from the blistering sun in a cloudless sky. But within days the heat rose slowly but steadily.

"And it's only going to get worse," Major General Noonie reported glumly.

"How do you figure that?" said the president. "That blanket of soot over the northern half of the United States won't win any friends except maybe the dry cleaners and laundrymen, but at least it will keep off the sun's rays."

Noonie shook his head. "Doesn't work that way, sir. Look—the sun's rays are composed of visible light, with a wavelength of about one two-millionth of a meter, and IR—infrared radiation—ranging from one- to five-millionths of a meter. About half the total solar radiation that hits the earth is usually absorbed. That's what keeps the earth's surface warm. Come night, the earth radiates a lot of that heat back into the sky at wavelengths between five- and a hundred-millionths of a meter. That's why nights are usually cooler.

"But if clouds are interposed between the earth and the sky, the situation changes. Clouds absorb solar radiation—and clouds black with carbon particles absorb it extremely well—and reradiate that energy in all directions. In effect, land covered by clouds radiates its daytime warmth to the clouds overhead, which reradiate a lot of it right back to the earth. The balance between nighttime heat loss and daytime heat gain is upset, and the earth progressively heats up. That's the greenhouse effect scientists fear might trigger a new ice age. Now, an ice age occurs because—"

"Hold it, Habib T.," cautioned President Turnbull.

"One catastrophe is all I can handle right now. Are you telling me that this damned heat wave is going to get *worse* because of the black cloud?"

"No question about it. But the heat is not the whole story. When it rains, it will combine with the combustion products of the burning coal, producing dilute nitric and carbonic acids and other pollutants."

"Acid rain?"

"Like *aqua regia* coming out of a firehose. Clothing will rot on our backs and off the clotheslines, exposed skin will blister, well and spring water will become undrinkable, and stone buildings will dissolve in front of our eyes—eyes that will constantly stream with tears from the acrid pollution."

President Horatio Francis Turnbull meditated on the implications of what his aide had told him. The Americans were helpless. They could hardly declare war on Russia for rendering the air unspeakably foul, because Ripley Forte, a Texican-American dual national, was ultimately responsible for the environmental disaster, not the Russians. The Russians could now rest on their oars and let America drown in acid rain, let its crops be scorched in acid rain, let its proud buildings be dissolved in acid rain and dribble down its acid rivers to the sea.

"That bastard Forte," Turnbull thundered, wheeling on his hapless Marine aide. "He's the one that persuaded me to allow that Lieutenant Colonel Haperman into the White House. I'll have his hide if it's the last thing I do on earth!"

"Excuse me, sir," protested General Noonie, "but if I may say so, you're being unjust."

"You may not. The man has brought this country to the brink of extinction, and I'm going to bring him to trial on charges of high treason."

"Forte didn't do it," Noonie persisted. "He couldn't have. The whole scheme must somehow have been engineered in Russia, probably by the seventeen missing American scientists."

"How do you figure that?" said Turnbull, suddenly wary. When Major General Habib T. Noonie contradicted the president so firmly, it was usually for good reason.

It was simple, Noonie explained. Forte had indeed engineered the laser shots that ignited Russia's summer wheat crop. But within forty-eight hours, the first signs of smoke from the burning lignite mines had appeared over Siberia. The Russians could have set fire to a thousand mines that contained a tremendous national resource only after long and careful consideration. They *never* made such far-reaching decisions on the spur of the moment, as the United States often did. That meant that it was all part of a long-standing Russian plan, in which Ripley Forte had unknowingly been persuaded to play a leading role.

President Turnbull demurred. "That line of thinking rests on the programs and data Forte made available to us. They showed he maneuvered the iodine lasers into zapping the wheat fields, and only the wheat fields, during the thirty-seven seconds he had control of the SDI system. But he could have cooked the readouts. He might just as easily have zapped those 870 lignite mines to boot."

"Beg to differ, sir. The shallowest of those mines lies tens of meters beneath the surface. The energy powering those orbiting lasers is not a fraction of that needed to penetrate the dirt overburden. Those fires were set. And only the Russians themselves could have set them. . . ."

By the fifteenth of July, the situation in North America was becoming desperate. The Canadians were worst hit, but the black cloud that covered the regions of the United States in which more than three-quarters of the population lived also cast the long shadow of economic hardship, respiratory ailments, depression—Americans now began to learn why so many Swedes commit suicide during their long winter nights—discord over diminishing reserves of food and clean water and, among those who panicked easily, outright hysteria.

It was the Russians who suggested a remedy for America's ills. From a very unofficial but authoritative Russian government source, a message was brought to President Turnbull suggesting that if the Americans stopped stonewalling and handed over Ripley Forte immediately, it would be a great morale booster in the Soviet Union. His trial, conviction, and hanging might, indeed, inspire the laboring masses to the superhuman effort needed to extinguish the fires the running dog of Westheimer Avenue had set.

On receipt of the message, President Turnbull summoned Ripley Forte to Washington. He showed him the communication.

"What are you going to do, Mr. President?" Forte asked.

"What *can* I do?" replied Turnbull helplessly. "We all know the Russians are liars. They'll hang you, and somehow not be able to extinguish those fires, and have the laugh on us while admiring your alopecic scalp nailed to the outhouse door."

"Well, then?"

"But maybe not. There's a chance in a thousand—make that a million—that they're on the level this time. And, you see, I can't afford not to do everything possible to make them douse those fires. The very survival of the United States depends on it."

"You invited a friend to come from his home in Texas to tell him you're going to hand him over to the Russians to be executed?"

Turnbull sighed. "A politician has no friends—only constituents, and you don't even vote in the United States."

Forte couldn't think of anything to say to that.

Turnbull brightened. "There may be one other way."

"Shoot."

"Exactly. If you're shot while resisting arrest so that we can send you to Russia for trial, surely the Russians will take that as an earnest of American good faith. Unless, of course, they insist on delivery of the body, in which case perhaps we can accommodate them there, too."

21. ACCESSION AND ABSCISSION
28 JULY 2009

ONLY THE PRESIDENT'S COLLAR WAS CLEAN, FOR ONLY the president had not been outside that day.

Their shirt collars rimmed with black, their hair flecked with soot, their eyes bloodshot, the men had come to the White House conference room for an emergency meeting of the War Council: the president as chairman, the director of Central Intelligence, the director of National Security, the president's national security adviser, the secretaries of state and defense, the chairman of the Joint Chiefs of Staff, the leaders of the majority and minority of the Senate and House, the House speaker, and the vice-president. President Turnbull, comfortable with superstition, would have gladly eliminated one of the thirteen men, but none was really dispensable in this crisis.

"I have the unpleasant duty to report," President Turnbull began, bringing the meeting to order, "that the Soviet Union has made no attempt to bring the lignite mine fires under control. If anything, they are getting worse."

The Speaker of the House, as famed for his certitude as for his ignorance, said complacently, "No need for alarm, Mr. President. The crisis will be over in a couple of days. Those jet winds blow right around the earth, and they'll blow the smoke right back in Ivan's face. *Then* they'll change their tune."

"I wish I could be as sanguine," replied the president. "But our meteorologists tell me that the combination of polar winds, moist air, and particulate matter coming together over the North Atlantic will cause most of the soot to precipitate out in rain, with very little coming to rest on the European continent."

"Then they'll burn themselves out."

"True—but when? Coal fires in Illinois have been burning out of control for seventy years. Another well-known hydrocarbon fire, the so-called fiery furnace of Nebuchadnezzar of Shadrach, Meshak, and Abednego fame, has been burning steadily in Kirkuk, Iraq, since biblical times." He smiled bleakly at the speaker, whose snow-white hair was now salt and pepper. "Are you suggesting we wait?"

The Speaker fell silent.

"The chair is open to constructive comment and suggestion."

"Nuke 'em," said the chairman of the Joint Chiefs. "—Or rather," he added when he observed the shocked reaction around the table, "*threaten* them with a dose of ICBMs unless they shut down the fires."

"Thus gaining immortality—if anyone is left to remember—for us as the men who started the Last World War? I think not."

"Anyway," added the secretary of state, a man with the face and backbone of a boiled turnip, "we must exhaust diplomatic initiatives before we even *think* of direct action. We must protest this gross violation of human rights in the strongest—"

"Write up your protest, Mr. Secretary, and I'll sign it. Anybody else?"

The CIA chief, whose heavy-lidded eyes had been almost closed during this colloquy, woke up to ask: "Why don't we talk about the one thing the Russians have indicated would bank their fires: handing over Ripley Forte."

"What makes you think you can trust the Russians?" Turnbull said.

"We can't, of course. But it's the only course short of war that offers some hope."

"You'd sell out an honorable and upstanding citizen, a wounded Marine veteran, a man who has fought the Russians and won, the *son* of a man who has fought the Russians and won, for the sake of 'some hope'?"

"In the national interest—yes."

"I ask for a show of hands," Turnbull said. "The question is, should we turn over Ripley Forte to the tender mercies of the Russians in return for their promise to put out the Siberian fires?"

His eyes went to the secretary of state, on his right, whose hand shot into the air. One by one every hand was raised. Smiling a wintry smile, Turnbull raised his, too. "Rare unanimity, gentleman. But of course, it's the life of another man we're talking about and, after all, he's only a Texan, isn't he?"

In the office outside the conference room, a light that he had been awaiting lit on the presidential staff secretary's intercom. He picked up a folder with a top-secret red slash across its cover and entered the conference room. "This report just arrived, sir," he said to the president, and left the way he had come.

President Turnbull opened the folder, glanced at its contents, and read aloud:

REPORT
From: Chief, Special Executive Operations Unit
To: The President
Subject: Ripley Forte

In accordance with Presidential Directive OS/311/26, subject-named civilian was put under surveillance at his El Cabellejo Ranch in Houston, Republic of Texas, at 1026 local 26 July 2008, with the view to accession and abscission.

The SEOU consisted of 31 operatives plus locally recruited informants of established reliability.

Subject-named civilian left his ranch for his downtown office at 1135 by helicopter. Due to Republic of Texas control of airspace, it was considered impracticable to take any action at that time.

Interception of optical cable transmissions permitted surveillance of telephone and telex traffic into and from SNC's office. At 1307 a telex message arrived from SNC's partner and financial adviser, Yussef Mansour, advising him in code—which SEOU was able to break without difficulty—that he had heard through his contacts in the USSR that the Soviets were willing to extinguish the fires in the 870 lignite mines in return for America's handing over SNC.

A flurry of outgoing calls followed. At 1423 SNC left his office under heavy guard. He was escorted in a four-car convoy to Hobby Airport in Houston where he boarded a waiting Piper 311 executive jet. The pilot and steward were the only other persons observed to be aboard. Five minutes later, on a flight plan listing New York City as refueling stop and Lagos, Nigeria, as ultimate destination, the Piper 311 took off on a heading of 049° true.

SNC's selection of Nigeria as ultimate destination is, it is believed, due to the fact that Nigeria has in force no treaty of extradition with either the United States or the Soviet Union.

The SEOU tactical aircraft standing by at the Naval Air Station, Pensacola, immediately took off to intercept in the vicinity of Tupelo, Mississippi. However, ten minutes after takeoff SNC's aircraft lost altitude and suddenly disappeared from air traffic control's radarscopes. No more was heard of the Piper 311 until we received a report that at 1655 it had landed at Orlando, refueled, and taken off at 1714, again with destination Lagos.

ATC reported that apparently the pilot of the 311 suspected he was under surveillance, altered course, and descended to treetop level to evade detection.

Four fighter aircraft from the carrier U.S.S. *Iwo Jima* locked onto the Piper 311 just north of Cuba. The 311 was, at that time, on a Great Circle course for South Africa. [It is believed that, at some point in his flight, Forte suspected that his communications might have been compromised and therefore changed his destination.] Since the 311 tiltjet has carrier-landing capability, the aircraft's pilot was instructed by both radio and signal lights to alter course, follow the Navy aircraft, and land aboard the *Iwo Jima*.

No notice was taken of the signals by the Piper 311, which proceeded on course at 7,000 meters.

The last attempt to make contact came at 2020, as darkness was falling. The plane altered course slightly to the south, apparently seeking cover of cumulus clouds in that area.

Contact was made, in code, by the pursuing aircraft with the commanding officer of the *Iwo Jima*, for the purpose of receiving instructions. The CO radioed Forte aboard the Piper 311 on its assigned frequency. There was no response. The lead plane tried to contact the Piper 311 on the emergency frequency. The call was unanswered. The CO, *Iwo Jima*, thereupon radioed orders to shoot the plane down.

Meanwhile, the target plane had descended almost to mast level in a local squall, apparently hoping to evade surveillance. Nevertheless, we followed on radar. When the Piper 311 was in range, one missile was launched. It struck the Piper's port wing, and the plane cartwheeled into the water. No fire was observed, and no survivors were seen.

Search-and-rescue helicopters from the *Iwo Jima* arrived on scene within half an hour, and a thorough search was made of the area. Numerous bits of flotsam and the shark-ravaged remains of two men were retrieved.

The remains were flown back to the Dade County Forensic Laboratory in Miami and subjected to examination. Positive I.D. was not possible from photographs of SNC due to the lack of identifiable remains. A thumb and forefinger of one of the bodies was, however, intact. Prints raised were faxed to the FBI in Washington, where they were compared with those on the Marine enlistment records of Ripley Forte. The FBI reported positive identification.

The remains of SNC, as well as those of the steward, also identified by fingerprints, are being held at the Dade County morgue until claimed by the next of kin.

/s/ J. D. Blanco,
Chief

Enclosures: Copy of surveillance log
            Copy of flight record,
            surveillance aircraft
            Copy of USMC enlistment
            fingerprints, Ripley Forte
            Copy of fingerprints raised
            from cadaver

"So much for our chances of handing over Ripley Forte to the Russians," said the chief of staff as President Turnbull closed the file.

"Don't you think they'd believe the report?" asked the secretary of state.

The president laughed grimly. "Would you, if you were Evgeniy Luchenko?"

"It's worth a try."

"No. I won't give them the satisfaction of knowing that we're so goddamned inept that the U.S. defense forces aren't equal to the task of apprehending a single individual in international air space, let alone on its own soil. . . ."

When the meeting finally broke up without result half an hour later, Vice-President David D. Castle dropped behind and casually mentioned that, while the president had been reading aloud, his attention had been engaged by the larger question of what they could do to quench those raging Siberian fires.

"You're forgiven, David," said the president. "After all, what does the life of one man matter when compared to the survival of the nation? You keep thinking. Involve your staff. If any of you has an idea, I want you to come to me with it immediately."

"Still," said Castle, "though I was only half listening, I had the curious feeling that something had been overlooked in the pursuit of Forte. If I had the chance to examine the file more closely, I might be able to put my finger on it."

"Of course, David," said the president. "My secretary will send you over a copy this afternoon. It's interesting reading. It's a textbook case of what a man will do to save his life."

* * *

Ilse Freeman, who lingered behind after the vice-president's press conference that afternoon, thought the file was interesting, too. "Our friends will want to see it. I'll fax it to them tonight. But they probably won't believe a word of it."

"Indeed?" Castle said coldly. "And why not?"

"They're all from Missouri. They'll suspect the SEOU made it all up to cover their incompetence, or to make them look good while sticking a finger into the eyes of CIA and the FBI, or any of a dozen other good reasons."

"Well, if they won't believe it, why send it?"

"They want to see everything we can lay hands on. And I am anxious to oblige: it shows we're doing our jobs. Besides, if Forte *did* die in that crash, if there *was* a crash, we'll be able to provide corroboratory evidence to that effect."

"How?"

"You don't need to know how, David," Miss Freemann grinned, showing smoke-stained teeth. "But I can tell you this: though President Tom Traynor pretty well cleaned out our apparatus in Texas, we have plenty of willing hands to do our work in the other forty-nine states. We have access to the FBI's fingerprint files, of course, and through our connections with Havana have penetrated the Cuban community in Miami, which will give us a line on whether what is left of Forte's corpse bears the fingerprints we'll get from his FBI file. As a matter of routine, we'll question people who observed Forte's departure from Houston and his refueling stop in Orlando. If we're lucky, we can get a line on the helicopter crew that recovered the remains from the Piper 311 splash-down. When we've added it all up, we'll have a file three times as thick as the one you gave me—and one a damned sight more credible. If the two files correspond in essential details, our employers will know that Forte is really dead."

On 10 August the second file arrived in Kiev to join the first. Premier Evgeniy Luchenko's chief of staff compared them and reported to his boss. "No doubt about it, sir: Ripley Forte is dead."

"Excellent!"

"Now that Forte's death is confirmed, what shall we do about the fires, sir?"

Luchenko laughed.

22. TESTAMENT
1 AUGUST 2009

THE TRUCK ON THE RACK WAS NO STRANGER. GORDIELO Lopez had serviced it at least half a dozen times during the three years he worked at the Amoco station in El Centro, for the owner complied strictly with the manufacturer's recommendation that the vehicle be lubricated and have its oil changed every three months. In fact, he had serviced it the previous time, and he knew damned well that there hadn't been anything taped to the new oil filter when he installed it. He unscrewed the filter and inspected it under the workbench light.

Wrapped around the filter was a piece of clear plastic, and underneath it what appeared to be a $100 bill. Lopez glanced around the shop to make sure he wasn't observed, slit the plastic cover, and removed the bill. As he shoved it in the pocket of his overalls, he noted the yellow sticker fastened to the white envelope underneath. "URGENT," it said. And "Please mail at once."

For a moment Lopez thought about opening the envelope. But he decided that if he did, he might be involved in something he didn't understand, and anything he didn't understand was dangerous. It might lead to questions, and the matter of the $100 bill might come up. The best way to deal with the matter was to keep the money and throw the envelope away, or destroy it. But then, reading the address, his suspicions were aroused. What if it were a trick? What if the money were put there expressly to trap him? What if he took the money and didn't mail the letter, and the police were waiting to pounce on him, or send him back to San Luis Potosi? He agonized, changed his mind several times, spent the morning looking over his shoulder to see whether he was being watched, and finally, at lunchtime, bought a stamp and dropped the letter in the mailbox.

Thus, five days later, the letter arrived at the office of the secretary to the President of the Republic of Texas, in Austin, Texas.

The secretary read the letter hurriedly and was about to put it aside as a crank letter when he noticed the signature. The name was that of a University of Texas scientist who had disappeared without a trace way back in February, Livia dos Santos. He took the letter immediately into the office of President Traynor.

"I think you'll want to read this, sir."

"Later," said President Cherokee Tom Traynor, annoyed at the interruption. He had been considering emergency measures to ensure domestic tranquillity among his constituents, made fearful and restive by the deepening pall of smoke that was descending from the Plains states and had already cut off the sun from the northern two-thirds of Texas. According to the meteorologists, within a week the black cloud would reach the Gulf of Mexico, putting Texas, along with all the forty-nine states, in a state of perpetual twilight. Already the fallout from the roiling smoke had ruined much of the maturing wheat crop in the northern states, a catastrophe Texas had been spared because its June harvest was already complete. Even so, the poisoning of its rivers and ground water supplies, the corrosive effects of the acid rain on clothing and buildings, and the plummeting morale of Texans who could find no effective way to fight back was making his fellow countrymen increasingly desperate, and Traynor had to find some means of arresting the slide toward disorder.

"It's from Livia dos Santos," his secretary persisted.

"Who?"

"The young woman from UT who disappeared early this year."

President Traynor snatched the letter. It was dated 26 May 2009.

My dear President Traynor:

You don't know me, but I suspect by now I am listed by the Austin police as a missing person, having left my studies at UT in February to accept a research assignment at a fee too handsome for a person in my circumstances to pass by.

I was prevailed upon by one Dr. Oswaldo Edwards to engage in a three-month research assignment for what, to me, is a magnificent sum: $125,000. As it was highly secret (United States) government research, I agreed to hold myself incommunicado from the beginning of the project until its end.

Under the circumstances, I was not surprised to learn that I was part of a group of seventeen bright young research scientists from Texas, the United States, and our free-world allies. What *did* surprise me, at first, was our assignment: to brainstorm *the options available to the Soviet Union in its quest for world hegemony* now that its military and intellectual bases had been seriously impaired as a result of the nuclear explosion that wiped out Moscow and its environs on 22 July of last year. The assignment seemed to me bizarre in the extreme, until Dr. Edwards explained that, at the moment, the Soviet Union would be convening its scientists for this identical purpose. Were we to rehearse its deliberations, the United States would then be in the position of being able to counter each Russian technological—as opposed to military—offensive as it developed, for our mission was to elaborate defenses for each Russian option proposed. And we seventeen were but one team— the Young Turks, he called us—working on the project, whose results would be compared at the termination of our research.

Dr. Edwards' logic was unexceptionable. Still, one day while we were daydreaming exotic offensive fancies, it occurred to my friend Raoul von

Williams that, for all practical purposes, we could just as easily be confined in a gulag—he called it a *sharashka*—in the Soviet Union as in El Centro, where our research was taking place. We were confined. We were incommunicado. We were totally under the control of Dr. Oswaldo Edwards. We were doing work that would be invaluable to the Soviet Union, if they could somehow discover it. What if the papers we were presenting to Dr. Edwards somehow leaked? Worse, *what if Dr. Oswaldo Edwards were actually an agent of the Soviet Union?*

Chilling though the thought was, we realized its absurdity. After all, we were ensconced in an installation of Raynes Oceanic Resources, and we knew that Mrs. Jennifer Red Cloud is a woman of proven patriotism and too astute a businesswoman to allow herself to be misled by even the cleverest Soviet agent. Still, the two of us decided it would not be a bad idea to take out a little insurance.

Each day we summarized the discussions of the group in minutes that each of us wrote independently. We made copies of the reports we submitted to Dr. Edwards at our weekly meetings. And we buried the resulting documents, which filled a shoebox, night before last on the grounds of the El Centro base, since Dr. Edwards said he was satisfied that the work we had done was more than sufficient.

The box is buried under the northeast corner of Building E, in which we both had apartments.

Of course, you will realize when you read this that all seventeen of us are either in captivity or dead.

Since we had no means of communication with the outside, we devised the following stratagem: we noted from the Amoco stickers on the inside of the door of the caterer's truck that the truck received an oil change and lubrication at three-month intervals. We expected that, if we were allowed to return to our normal pursuits, we would merely reclaim this letter before the truck went into the garage, and the documents would remain buried until mold and insects destroyed them. If we were *not* released, however, the mechanic who serviced the truck would discover the $100 bill von Williams taped to the oil filter with this letter one evening, and—we hoped—mail the letter, as indeed he apparently did.

Since we have been duped—taken for suckers is really more like it—we are eager that you reclaim the minutes and reports we buried at El Centro and thwart the plans the Russians have induced us to make for the free world's destruction. We regret that the scientist's traditional arrogance coupled with childlike trust led us to our destruction, but at least, if you act with haste, the free world will not share our fate.

Sincerely,
/s/ Livia dos Santos
and Raoul von Williams

President Tom Traynor decided that the contents of the letter were too important to entrust even to the scrambler, and enplaned that afternoon for Washington, where he went into immediate conference with President Horatio Francis Turnbull.

Within hours a special FBI team was on its way to California. The Raynes Oceanic Resources installation at El Centro was cordoned off, and a thorough search made of the premises. No documents were found at the northeast corner of Building E, or indeed anywhere else on the base. It was evident, however, that earth had been excavated at the site within the past few months, according to FBI experts.

In Washington, a search was made in FBI files for Dr. Oswaldo Edwards. There was no record of a government employee by that name. If he had been an American citizen and a research scientist, he would almost certainly have received government assistance in his researches, and his name would be on record. No such record was found.

A search was made of the arid area surrounding the El Centro installation, in hope that perhaps some trace of the bodies of the scientists could be located. No trace was found.

Officials at Raynes Oceanic Resources had neither recollection nor records of dealings with anyone named Dr. Oswaldo Edwards. Of course, it was possible—certain—that the chairman, Mrs. Jennifer Red Cloud, had given permission personally, or admission to the base could never have been effected.

The caterer could tell them nothing beyond the details of the food deliveries over a period of months.

Base security had been assumed by a group of men who, on orders from Mrs. Red Cloud, relieved the base caretakers of their duties two days before the scientists arrived and turned the base back to them on 15 June. The names and signatures on the paperwork proved untraceable.

Mrs. Jennifer Red Cloud had been assassinated on 17 July at her home on Montego Bay, Jamaica.

The trail was cold.

23. RESURRECTION
28 JULY 2009

"I SHOULD HAVE LET THEM HANG YOU, YOU BASTARD," said Jennifer Red Cloud as Ripley Forte, cold and dripping from half an hour's exposure in the sea, clambered aboard the Raynes Rover and sank gratefully into the copilot's seat.

"It might have been preferable to your warm reception, at that," replied Forte, stripping off his wet suit and oxygen tanks as Mrs. Red Cloud secured the Plexiglas hatch and prepared to dive.

"Warm is a tepid way to describe my mood. Boiling would be better."

"An improvement. Last time we met, you were as cold as an undertaker's handshake."

"Appropriately so, considering I am 'dead.' So, of

course, are you, now that your plane has been blown out of the sky."

"Two souls in search of something or other," said Forte, stripping to the buff and toweling himself dry. "Any clothes aboard, or do I have to meet my maker in the altogether?"

"Under the stack of towels you'll find a set of dungarees," said Red Cloud, keeping her eyes fixed firmly on the instruments as she leveled off the undersea craft at 200 feet and set the throttle for thirty-five knots.

So far, Forte reflected, so lousy. It would take some time to unravel the sequence of events that had led not only to Red Cloud's "death" but his own. Whatever had happened, it had effectively removed them from the fight. If either surfaced now, they would blow the cover they, in collaboration with Presidents Turnbull and Traynor and a few aides, had so carefully fabricated, with nasty consequences impossible to foretell.

Had the Russians been taken in? Maybe. He had laid down a trail the Soviets could follow, and Turnbull had provided Castle with paperwork they would even now be taking pains to verify.

Forte helped himself to a cup of steaming coffee from the machine behind the cockpit's twin seats and sipped the warming liquid gratefully. "Okay, Red Cloud, what's eating you? What the hell have you got to complain about?"

"That's right—act innocent."

"I *am* innocent. Pure as the driven snow. Men are struck dumb upon learning of my virtuous character, women shield their eyes at my approach, little children press my hand to their lips."

"Well," said Red Cloud, rounding on him, "I can tell you *one* little child who won't be pressing your hand to his lips, you scheming son of a bitch, and if I ever hear that you consulted a lawyer on this subject again, I'll kill you with my own bare hands."

"Who squealed?" said Forte, suddenly chastened.

"You shouldn't be allowed out without a keeper," Red Cloud sneered. "The San Francisco law firm you consulted to assess your chances of getting custody of little Ripley, my dear oaf, has been sucking around for the past two years to represent Raynes Oceanic Resources. Naturally they came around and spilled their guts."

"I'll sue 'em!"

"Good thinking. It's the only satisfaction you're going to get."

"You won't let me see my son?"

"Of course I will—at age eighteen, when I intend to introduce him to the more unpleasant things of life, with his father topping the list."

The rest of the hour's journey to the Raynes Oceanic Resources ship, the *Maryam*, ostensibly exploring the Puerto Rico Trench for alluvial gold, was made in strained silence.

"Somehow," said Joe Mansour, "this discussion reminds me of one of those 'peace conferences' so beloved of the United States and the Soviet Union, in which fulmination, accusation, and recrimination pass for negotiation. I think," he said, turning to Jennifer Red Cloud, who was clad in a shimmering red silk gown and sitting on his left at the dinner table built for thirty diners but now accommodating only three, "that you have made abundantly clear that Ripley has neither legal nor moral right to your son, and would be well advised to tie a can on it."

The dapper little Lebanese, who wore immaculate evening dress, turned to Ripley Forte, dressed in stiff new dungarees. "As for you, Rip, while it is obvious that you yearn to possess your son—being a billionaire *does* nurture one's acquisitive instincts—I suggest you relieve your frustrations in a more positive manner, such as finding out what the Russians are really up to and then applying your—and my—considerable resources to pronging them in the eye with a sharp stick.

"And," he went on, "while you are both ruminating on my Oriental wisdom, why don't we have cognac in the drawing room?" He rose, held the chair for Jennifer Red Cloud, and led the way to the salon, where a huge plate-glass window gave an unobstructed view of Cape Town far below them and Table Bay beset by winter's tempests beyond.

The Lebanese financier had suggested that they both

lie low until the situation was sorted out at his modest
thirty-one-room digs on Table Mountain. There in South
Africa they would be safe from prying eyes, and a sufficient staff would care for their every need. Accordingly,
they boarded the *Maryam*'s tiltjet that evening and flew
directly to Cape Town. There the entourage, which included the infant Ripley Forte cordoned off from his father by four burly bodyguards and a nurse who looked as
if she spent her spare time bench-pressing steam radia-
tors, sped in a convoy of curtained limousines to Mansour's retreat.

The first day and evening had been spent in rancorous
debate, with Joe Mansour sympathizing with Jennifer
Red Cloud and despairing of his friend Ripley Forte for
his abysmal ignorance of women. It was plain as the battered nose on Forte's face that the woman was wildly in
love with the big Texan. It was just as plain that Forte,
whose breathing became noticeably stertorous whenever
Red Cloud was in the vicinity, more than reciprocated
her feelings. But pride stood like a wall between them.
Neither would admit the truth so obvious to Mansour,
and they each used the issue of their son's custody as a
bludgeon to batter the other into submission. In other
words, two highly intelligent idiots, making war when
they should have been making love.

Well, if it was war they wanted, they could at least
wage it against a common enemy. Mansour poured a generous portion of cognac into snifters the size of goldfish
bowls, raised his, and wished "Consternation to the
commissars!"

"I'll drink to that," said Forte.

"You'll have to do more than drink to it—you'll have
to do something about it."

"I'm willing," Forte said, "but I don't know where to
begin."

"Begin here." Mansour took a folded paper from his
inside pocket and handed it to Forte. "That came for you
just before dinner. Faxed from President Traynor's office
in Austin."

Forte read the letter, part of which was a facsimile of
that received by President Traynor from Livia dos
Santos posthumously. He handed it to Jennifer Red

Cloud. When she finished reading, he said: "A nice irony. We're being subjected to Soviet environmental warfare planned at Raynes Oceanic Resources by the free world's leading young scientists."

"Yes," mused Jennifer Red Cloud, "and presumably the Siberian lignite fires are only the opening shot in what will probably be an assault on many fronts."

Mansour nodded. "But notice, as unexpected and as successful as that opening shot has been, there is an underlying weakness in the Soviet method."

"If there is, I certainly don't see it," Red Cloud replied.

"Only because you take for granted that there is none. And, in fact, there probably isn't."

"Don't mind him," Forte said in an aside to Red Cloud. "He's Lebanese. Lebanese always talk in riddles, and by the time you figure out what they're saying, you've bought the rug for eight times what it's worth."

Mansour chuckled and took a sip of cognac. "I always forget that with you, my dear Ripley, I must speak in words of one syllable, preferably less. Look at it this way: the seventeen missing-presumed-dead scientists elaborated a strategy for the Russians based on their knowledge of geography, meteorology, geology, economics, medicine, psychology, and any number of other disciplines of which they were superior practitioners. We can assume that, having co-opted their talents, the Russians will follow the strategy they outlined. That strategy is based on geopolitical, medical, psychological, economic realities. Those realities are well known by others in the various fields. Perhaps fifty, even a hundred, other top scientists would be required to duplicate the experience and expertise of the vanished seventeen, but they *could* duplicate it.

"The Siberian lignite fires, which the seventeen suggested as the opening play in the game with the world as jackpot, would produce certain foreseen results. These results would force the free world to respond. The number of possible responses is limited. Some are more plausible and effective, and less expensive and provocative of a nuclear exchange—which both powers will strive to avoid—than others. The free world will, therefore, respond in one of a limited number of ways. That stimulus, in turn, will cause the Russians to react. The numbers of possible Soviet reactions, too, are limited.

"In the months the seventeen scientists spent in El Centro, they must have created many clever scenarios and ploys. The ploys available to both sides can be arranged in a tree of probability, depending on such factors as time, cost, season, resources and forces involved, and so on. While that tree cannot be duplicated precisely, its general outlines are dependent on realities of the resources available to each side. Therefore, we can construct a tree very similar to that which is already in the possession of the Russians, the one whose limbs are to furnish the firewood that, when set alight, will consume us all. Once we know what they are up to, where the next branching will take the battle, we can anticipate their actions and thwart them."

Forte and Red Cloud, for the first time that evening, were silent. Yussef Mansour's idea would not, perhaps, win the war. But at least it was an intelligent beginning, and they had no place else to start.

Forte smiled. "Sounds good. All we have to do now is find out who are the leaders in the fields the seventeen represented, get them all in one spot—by main force, if necessary—and put the heat on them to do in two weeks what the seventeen did in three months."

Mansour laughed and shook his head. "I thought you knew me better, Rip. You should know by now that I rarely discuss an action until it has already been taken. My staff has located sixty-two eminent scholars in the fields represented by the seventeen. At this moment they are on their way—at a total cost that would give you a heart attack—to a retreat formerly owned by the Dutch Reformed Church, some miles up the coast at Saldanha. We'll be leaving for Saldanha in the morning, to give them their brief."

"You're a wonder, Joe," said Forte admiringly.

"That, or a goddamned liar," said Jennifer Red Cloud. "You said that the dos Santos letter arrived just before dinner. If that's so, you couldn't possibly have had time to locate those 'sixty-two eminent scholars' and make an arrangement with them."

Joe Mansour shrugged. "Goddamned, maybe, but liar
—no. You see, this letter *did* arrive just before dinner.
It's a copy of one I received ten hours earlier, directly
from President Traynor's secretary, who costs me more
in finder's fees than I sometimes think she's worth."

24. MELTDOWN
10 AUGUST 2009

A STATISTICIAN AT THE U.S. METEOROLOGICAL SERVICE
noticed it first—and assumed the computer had gone
haywire. He punched in the figures on another machine.
The result was the same.

He reached for the telephone.

Ten minutes later the president's chief of staff, J. Jer-
rold Hatfield, picked up his phone and listened to the
figures from the secretary of the interior. He was not
only unimpressed but quite uninterested. "Listen, Virgil,
I've got better things to do than listen to a goddamned
weather report. So *what* if 'the earth's mean temperature
has risen three-tenths of a degree Fahrenheit during the
past fourteen days'? What do you expect *me* to do—give
away all my winter clothes?"

Virgil English told him he'd had worse ideas in his
time, because this was only the beginning. The mean
temperature of the earth was ascending rapidly. A month
hence it would be seven-tenths degrees higher than average.

Hatfield simmered. "So I'll turn up my air conditioning. It's Foggy Bottom in August, isn't it? What the hell
did you expect?"

English explained, in short sentences comprehensible
to a politician whose knowledge of finer points of the
language had come from listening to breakfast cereal
commercials, the implications of that rise in temperature. As he spoke, Hatfield's choler faded to pallor.
When English finished, Hatfield put down the telephone

in a daze and walked unsteadily to the Oval Office, next to his own.

"I have summoned you here today to discuss an alarming, perhaps catastrophic development," said Turnbull to the thirteen men. They were the same he had met in conference just two weeks before, when the fate of Ripley Forte had been announced, with two significant additions: the President of the Republic of Texas, the Honorable Thomas Traynor, and the president's scientific adviser, Dr. Sid Bussek. "What I have to say is too important to soften with platitudes, so I'll come right to the point: the Russians have screwed us good—and no kiss."

Groans were mixed with sighs of resignation. The Russian shaft had become so much a part of the official scene of late that some members were suggesting that they rename the Washington Monument.

"We thought—hoped, at least—that when we threw Ripley Forte to the Russian sharks they'd bank the Siberian fires. That's all it was: a hope—and one very good man lost to us. Then we consoled ourselves with the thought that the cloud of soot that's clogging every air conditioner in the country and causing detergent sales to boom was building up over the Atlantic, and a good deal of it was drifting right back to Russia. We figured that *that* unpleasant consequence would at last make them listen to reason, since they'll soon be breathing in almost as much pollution as we are. Well, gentlemen, I have the distressing duty to inform you that we have underestimated the Russians for the thousand-and-first time. They're putting the heat on us—literally. Those fires have raised the average world temperature three-tenths of a degree since they were first ignited. By this time next month, the temperature will be seven-tenths of a degree above the world mean."

One glance around the table separated the sheep from the goats. Those with scientific training blanched, the politicians tried to look wise. Explanations were in order. "Tell 'em the cheery news, Sid," President Turnbull said to his scientific adviser.

Dr. Bussek stood. He was the youngest man in the

room, a shambling, earnest jack-of-all-sciences whose long stringy hair was less a reflection of current style than of a sixteen-hour-a-day work schedule. "In brief, gentlemen, the increase in ambient temperature will, if the warming trend continues, melt the polar ice caps. There is one hell of a lot of water contained in the ice caps. Though Arctic ice and the ice sheet covering Greenland to a depth of up to two miles constitute a relatively small percentage of the world's total, it will melt first because of the blanket of soot over the northern hemisphere.

"However, if those fires are not extinguished, and the temperature continues to climb, the atmospheric heat will slop over the equator into the southern hemisphere, and then the *Antarctic* ice cap will begin to melt. As Vice-President Castle reminded us in a historic speech a few years ago, the Antarctic ice cap contains more than ninety percent of the world's fresh water—fresh water equivalent to the flow of the Mississippi for 46,000 years."

"Are you telling us, Dr. Bussek," rumbled President Traynor, seated at Turnbull's right, "that Triple Eye's Antarctic iceberg deliveries are endangered, that our fresh water supply is about to be cut?"

"On the contrary, sir. It is about to be increased, a thousandfold. Not to the shores of the Republic of Texas, however, but to the shores of the *world*. The process is not exactly straightforward, I should warn you. In the Antarctic, if the Ross and Filchner-Ronne ice shelves broke apart because of warming, their buttressing effect on the pinned ice shelves would vanish and large sections of the below-sea-level grounded ice sheet would surge into the Weddell and Ross seas, raising sea levels by as much as sixteen and a half feet."

The Senate Majority Leader, who was from Massachusetts, chuckled. "That'll give New Orleans a good bath. Some say it needs it."

"That's true, Senator," shot back Bussek, "and what about your alma mater when the Charles River tops its banks and makes a wading pool of Harvard Yard?"

"It'll need more than sixteen feet of water to drown Harvard, sonny."

"The hell with Harvard," Traynor said testily. "What about the rest of the world?"

"The outlook is far from rosy, Mr. President," Bussek said somberly. "A five-meter rise will inundate a tremendous amount of territory and, in some instances, whole countries. Bangladesh will be drowned, as will most of Holland, much of Cyprus, Greece, the Sinai Peninsula, and Egypt, for example. Whole chains of Pacific islands will be obliterated. All major Australian cities, being on the coast, will be threatened. The water will be lapping at the foundations of the very building we're meeting in. Conservatively, five and a half trillion dollars' worth of land, buildings, and facilities will be wiped out. The human loss, of course, will be incalculable."

A leaden silence fell as the politicians tried to cope with the enormity of the coming catastrophe. The gentleman from Massachusetts was particularly perturbed. Inasmuch as the bulk of his support came from port cities and coastal towns, unless he could vote the graveyard, he just might not be reelected.

"And that, as the players of gin rummy say," Bussek went on, "is just for openers. There's nothing magical about the five-meter-melt mark. Depending on how long the Siberian fires burn, we can expect a sea-level rise of something on the order of fifty feet if there is an East Antarctic ice surge. Good-bye Boston, New York City, Albany, Philadelphia, Baltimore, Washington, Miami, San Diego, Savannah, New Orleans, Galveston, Austin, and Houston. And if those fires are allowed to burn long enough, conceivably—and, gentlemen, when I say conceivably I mean *certainly*—the entire Antarctic ice cap will melt, raising the sea level 165 feet.

"When that happens, kiss the northern European plains bordering the Baltic Sea good-bye. Say a fond farewell to the Loire, Seine, Rhine, Elbe, Oder, Vistula, Dvina, Rhone, Tiber, and Po valleys, where modern civilization was born—and say it quick, because by then we'll all be dead, or scrambling to get to Denver."

"Maybe," said the chairman of the Joint Chiefs of Staff, General Moe Sill, "but while we're trekking to the Rockies, the Russians will be heading for the Urals. After all, if the Rhine and Vistula get flooded, the waters will be high enough to inundate the better part of Russia and Eastern Europe, too, flooding the Dniepr, Don, Dniestr, and Danube basins."

Dr. Bussek shook his head. "Not *will* flood—*would* flood."

"What do you mean?"

"Simply that those Eastern European rivers will be spared flooding."

"Impossible! As the Atlantic's level rises, it will raise the level of the Mediterranean, which in turn will reverse the flow through the Bosphorus. Instead of emptying the Black Sea into the Sea of Marmara and the Mediterranean, the Bosphorus will serve as a funnel to fill *up* the Black Sea, and the overflow will flood the Dniepr, Don, Dniestr and Danube basins."

"Only if we're prepared to drop a very large bomb."

"On what?"

"On the barrage the Russians started constructing two days ago across the Dardanelles, the narrow choke point between the Sea of Marmara and the Mediterranean. The fact that they started construction proves beyond a shadow of a doubt, incidentally, that they *do* intend to drown the low-lying areas of the world, that those lignite fires are part of a greater, sinister purpose."

On that happy note, President Turnbull adjourned for lunch. They would meet again at 1500 to consider the science staff's suggestions on how to cope with this new development, short of all-out war.

The next day, 11 August, scientists, engineers, economists, and administrators began to converge on Houston from every state in the Union. President Tom Traynor had volunteered the facilities of SD-1, belonging to the late Ripley Forte, as the nerve center of what would become the largest and most hurried construction project in the history of mankind. SD-1, the workshops of Sunshine Industries, 1,450 meters below the surface in Houston, offered exceptional advantages as the focus of the binational effort. It had the unparalleled computer power of a Brown-Ash Mark IX computer, a whole constellation of engineering testing equipment, laboratories and offices big enough to house a small city, invulnerability to even a direct strike by a multimegaton hydrogen bomb, and internal security so strict that, to prevent leakage of plans, all but the most senior staff had to agree to remain in the inaccessible but comfortable underground chamber until all plans were complete and their implementation begun.

Dr. Bussek assured Presidents Turnbull and Traynor that it would probably require from three to four months, even at forced draft, for the staff of Project P (for *polder*) to work out all the details. His own White House staff were optimistic that the work could be completed before the big meltdown occurred, but Bussek himself was not so sanguine.

The Americans and Texans, working under the direction of experienced polder engineers from the Netherlands—refugees from Soviet occupation—contemplated building dikes of earth and concrete around the major threatened cities in time to prevent their being engulfed by the rising ocean waters. According to their calculations, it would take at least ten months to build the dikes to fifty feet, and five years or more to the height that the oceans would rise if both polar ice caps were fully melted.

Agonizing choices had to be made—a form of urban triage. Politicians in Washington were already waging all-out war to have smaller coastal cities in their constituencies put on the must-save list. But Turnbull was adamant: only those cities over one million in population could be so listed; all others must take their turn in what would be a long, long line. The unlucky residents of those cities had two choices: to remain and hope the inevitable would never happen, or to start thinking immediately about relocating to the higher-altitude interior. Immense dislocations were bound to occur. Families would be sundered, jobs lost, savings spent, companies bankrupted, national priorities rearranged.

One imponderable was where all the enormous quantities of building material would come from; another, how to transport it. All domestic construction was, of course, ordered to cease immediately, so that cement and other materials could be stockpiled against the time when planning was completed and actual polder construction began.

The economists worried about where the money would come from to build these immense dikes around America's cities. The manpower experts worried not only about the money to train and pay the millions of workers who would be required, but where the bodies themselves would come from and what stringencies the two nations would face when they were seconded from their present jobs. Administrators grappled with finding transportation, accommodations, food, clothing, and jobs for the millions of people who would be displaced. The environmentalists worried about defacement of the landscape, the amplified ugliness of cities surrounded by bunds taller than twelve-story buildings. Psychologists were concerned about the consequences of making every coastal city a prison, in which the inmates would vent their frustrations on each other in random violence and bloodshed. Transportation experts wondered how they could preserve the flow of traffic in and out of cities without building highways on roadbeds as high as the bunds, far into interior America. Port authorities wrestled with the problem of constructing facilities that would have to be relocated on a higher level as each stage of the bund was completed.

Nobody had yet had the guts to address the biggest question of all: would it work? The Dutch engineers, who had reclaimed their country from the ocean, were convinced it would. They had done it before, and they could do it again. But the couple hundred miles of Low Country coastline hardly compared with the 12,400 miles of coastline of the United States and Texas, let alone the 88,600 miles of shoreline on which a dike would have to be built to protect the two countries completely. What the politicians and experts contemplated was a remaking of the face of America. Was it worth the struggle, when the nations' leaders knew that this was merely the opening salvo in a war-without-weaponry the Russians had launched to conquer the pitiful remainder of the world they did not yet possess?

Or should the U.S. drop the bomb—now—and get it the hell over with?

25. A STROLL IN THE SUN
3 OCTOBER 2009

"HOW DO I MICTURATE?" SAID THE VICE-PRESIDENT.

"How do you *what*?" a puzzled Captain Stanley Poldz replied.

"How do I *piss*?"

"Oh . . . Well, sir, you don't," said Poldz, commander of the supply ship *James Madison*, "unless you're looking to get a shoe full of it. Actually, of course, since there's no gravity up here, it's liable to migrate up through your suit and slosh around in your helmet."

"Why the hell wasn't I told before I suited up?"

"You were, Mr. Castle, but I guess the warning slipped off the glaze you got in your eyes in the second hour of your briefing. Don't worry, though—unless you grow to like it out there, you probably won't be gone more than an hour."

"An hour?"

"That's how much oxygen your main tank's carrying."

David D. Castle shrugged as best he could in the confines of the space suit and allowed the crew to screw on his helmet. He should have been excited, he realized, first time in space and all that. But by now, at a rough calculation, some twelve thousand Americans had preceded him, and manned space flights were so commonplace that even the local press at Cape Canaveral nowadays gave the event no more than a paragraph. Anyway, his mind was on the information he had to impart to Deputy Premier Anatoliy Badalovich.

Castle had rehearsed his brief with President Horatio Francis Turnbull personally. His command of the information, the circumspection that had become second nature as a result of a lifetime as a double agent, and his lawyerly sense of language's nuances made him confident that he would perform the mission in his usual elegant and exemplary fashion.

"Docking in ninety seconds," said Poldz. His attention was held by the monitor which showed the Soviet spaceship closing. The operation, which had been carried out countless times in the fitful bursts of cooperation that characterized the Russian and American conquest of space, was entirely automatic. The link-up would last only as long as Castle's brief colloquy in space with the Russian—whose identity Poldz couldn't even guess—required, after which Poldz' ship would proceed to its scheduled three-hour supply rendezvous with American Scientific Space Station Number Four.

Over Poldz' shoulder, Castle watched the approaching Russian ship and suddenly felt dead tired, even though the trip was less than half over. First there had been the flurry of conferences at the White House the past forty-eight hours, then the decision to negotiate, the call to Moscow on the hotline, the flight to Canaveral, the thundering takeoff of the *James Madison*, the tedious briefing, the long wait until the two ships' orbits were synchronized, and finally the elaborate suiting up. He could sleep for the next stage of the trip, but he'd have to be strapped in again to his seat on the final descent. He marveled that some men actually found space travel pleasurable.

A loud *clank* and shudder signaled that the mating of the two ships was achieved. Normally, the communicating doors would now be undogged and the smiling crews would exchange Russian vodka and American beefsteak, or perhaps a Russian Orthodox icon and the latest American porno cassette. On this trip, however, there would be no personal contact at all. Neither crew had been told the identity of the man their passenger would meet in space. For all they knew, in fact, it could be a woman.

"Open overhead hatch!" Poldz ordered.

A patch of blinding sunlight appeared overhead.

"Permission to disembark," said Castle.

"Permission granted," replied Poldz.

Castle pulled down the helmet's sun visor and tapped the control on the panel in the suit over his left wrist, which disengaged the electromagnet that held his steel-shod shoes to the cabin floor. He flexed his knees, pushed off gently, and floated straight through the hatch into the sky. He edged his thrust lever forward, held it there two seconds as his instructor had briefed him, cut it back to neutral, and coasted. The distance between him and his ship lengthened to five or six hundred meters before his umbilical suddenly went taut, and he spun around in the sky like a burnt-out firewheel. He hit the attitude-stabilizer switch. His jets sputtered like a leaky steam valve, and his motion relative to the mother ship was arrested. Beyond the *James Madison*, from the north pole to well below the equator, the earth was swathed in a solid mantle of black smoke.

Now he saw a dim white spot rocketing toward him from the Salyut 1183. The white spot grew into a blob that finally resolved itself into a bloated space suit that wobbled cumbersomely around the American as the Russian maneuvered his jets to bring himself alongside Castle. He stretched out his hand. Castle missed it and grabbed his foot, bringing the gyrating figure to a halt.

Castle unreeled his communications line and plugged his jack in the box at the base of the other man's helmet, who in turn plugged into Castle's circuit. Immediately, on the inside surface of the visor in Castle's helmet was projected the image of Deputy Premier Anatoliy Badalovich, smiling broadly. "Greetings, Deputy Premier Badalovich," Castle said, "from President Horatio Francis Turnbull and myself, and from the peace-loving peoples of the United States to those of the Soviet Union."

"And so forth and so on," said Badalovich in almost unaccented English. "We can omit the hypocrisies, I believe, Mr. Vice-President, since only the two of us are here to listen to them—which in itself is an interesting commentary on 'progress.'"

"Come again?"

"Well, after all, we had to come all this way, hundreds of miles above the earth's surface, merely to be sure that we are not overheard by somebody's electronic ears. If it weren't for 'progress,' this conversation would have taken place along some forest path or in a meadow with cowbells tinkling in the distance."

"Where we'd still have to be wearing these suits in

order to be able to see each other without being asphyxiated, thanks to the damnable smoke you Russians have made to blanket the earth."

"I beg to correct you, sir," Badalovich said indignantly. "The fire, which not at all incidentally destroyed our wheat crop for the entire year, reducing the proletariat to a diet of potatoes and cabbage, was started by the renegade Ripley Forte. It is the United States and Texas, of which he was a dual citizen, who bear responsibility for this heinous crime. He—"

"He paid for his 'crime' with his life," rejoined Castle. "And since we're skipping the hypocrisies, maybe you'll be good enough to stop pretending that it was Ripley Forte who started those fires. Our intelligence—so-called—finally figured out that you orchestrated the whole operation. Forte learned, or rather was *allowed* to learn, of the massive diversion of Australian wheat to Russia via Bangladesh and other ports. He tracked down the shipments, discovered that some wound up in the Crimea, the most accessible area in the Soviet Union to infiltration. Forte, being Forte, infiltrated, just as you planned he would. And when he got there—with astonishing ease—he was allowed to abstract samples of a chemical being extracted from domestic wheat, the deficit of which the Soviet Union made up for with imports of Australian wheat. The Soviet Union intended to contaminate the American water supply with that chemical, beta-3, in order to render the American people impotent through euphoria. And to make sure nobody missed the point, you engineered the defection of Valentin Shishlin, the vault of whose KGB courier plane conveniently happened to contain comprehensive plans for dosing the American watersheds with beta-3."

"Fascinating!" Badalovich commented. "Is there more?"

"Plenty. The burning of the wheat fields, which you knew Forte would consider—as indeed it was—the only way to eliminate the beta-3 menace, was merely a cover for the Russian leadership to set fire to its own lignite mines."

"Come, come!" chided Badalovich. "If it was fire in the mines we wanted, we could have set fire to them ourselves—openly, for are they not on our own Russian soil?"

"And risked nuclear bombing by the United States for polluting the atmosphere over the western hemisphere, with distressing and perhaps fatal consequences for much of its population? No, you couldn't chance that. So you stage-managed Forte's foray and lighted the lignite fires under cover of his wheat field conflagrations."

"Is there any proof of this absurd scenario?" scoffed Badalovich. "Or am I to believe it as coming from an honest, incorruptible American?"

David D. Castle laughed sardonically. "Unfortunately, in our continuing conflict, we've never been as successful in penetrating the Soviet Union as you have been in honeycombing the United States with agents, turncoats, and outright traitors. Still, while we don't have agents, we have brains. And satellites. Putting them both together, we observed that while you were frantically buying wheat in Australia, your own storehouses were bursting from the surplus of two consecutive years of good harvest. So, why should you buy? The answer: to set in train the sequence of events that would allow you to fire your lignite mines with impunity."

Badalovich sighed. "Very well. Since we are up here alone with the stars, you may as well know you are entirely correct. The KGB *did* concoct the scheme to get Ripley Forte's unwitting cooperation. The KGB *did* do all the nasty things of which you've accused us. And the fires still burn, and they'll continue to burn. But not, as you poor Americans believe, to run up your laundry bills or make your eyes water or poison your crops with acid rain or put millions in the hospital with bronchial complaints. We're doing it to—"

"—melt the polar ice caps and drown the American continent."

"You *know*?"

"Of *course* we know. We've known for some time."

"But—but—" sputtered the deputy premier, "we have had no reports to that effect."

"Yes, sometimes the peril to America is so great that we manage to keep our big mouths shut. We've known for weeks. And we're doing something about it, too."

"What, pray tell?"

Castle mentioned entirely spurious scientific committees that had been formed to discover technical solutions to the coming rise in the level of the oceans. They would deliver their report within two months. Meanwhile, select committees of Congress were discussing the best manner to raise the immense sums that would be required for passive defense of the nation. Groups of experts were considering how to relocate displaced populations. Other groups . . .

"Lies," Anatoliy Badalovich said complacently. "All lies. We have your establishment penetrated. To the KGB, the United States officialdom resembles a thoroughly ripened Swiss cheese. No such discussions on a scale that would be effective could possibly take place without our knowledge. Your great coastal cities are going to drown. And you Americans are going to go broke, meanwhile, doing too little too late to remedy the situation. Your whole history assures us of this fact: World War I, Pearl Harbor, Korea—you've always avoided pressing problems until destruction was almost inevitable."

"True. But we won eventually."

"Not this time, my dear Mr. Vice-President. This catastrophe will overwhelm you. When your economy is completely shattered, your people in distress, and large-scale rioting begins in the streets, you will welcome the order Soviet occupying troops will bring. You'll react as if you were all given a huge dose of beta-3."

David D. Castle was silent. The bluff had not worked. But then, with those arch-bluffers the Russians, it hadn't been expected to work. Everything he'd said so far was mere buildup.

"Lies, as you say," Castle said resignedly.

"Aha! You admit it."

"We hoped you'd see the futility of pursuing this madness of polluting the world and come to reason."

"We pollute the world first. America the Soft will give up. America the Fat always does when the going gets tough—Viet Nam being proof, if proof were needed. Only when you have thrown in the towel will reason assert itself—*Marxist* reason."

It was time for the trump. Castle played it.

"I realize your impatience to rule the world," he said, "but I'm afraid we can't allow you to destroy it in order to satisfy a national whim."

"Indeed? And how do you propose to stop us?"

"Actually, stopping you is easier than you think. Our scientists have not put all our eggs in one basket. We have a fallback position, and we are prepared to take it."

"Threats from Americans are not only ridiculous but tedious. I recall that, back in the last century, Iran tweaked your noses, and you responded with fire-eating declarations. But what did you do? Nothing. The pathetic little Nicaraguan people spat upon the foot of the helpless giant, and he removed the foot instead of stomping the life out of the Sandinista clique. We invaded Afghanistan, and you bombed us with pious platitudes. You are a gutless people, waiting to be swept aside by the tides of history. You will die as cowards always do—miserably."

"You took the words right out of my mouth."

"I beg your pardon?"

"I was just about to tell you how *you* will die—you and your people, unless you extinguish the fires in your Siberian lignite mines immediately."

"Indeed?" Deputy Premier Badalovich chuckled. "Come—frighten me."

"I will do my best, Comrade," Castle said evenly. "Our scientists have developed a great many biological agents during our decades of uneasy peace. One of them is a strain of anthrax for which there is no known cure. A vaccine or even a serum against this strain could be devised and manufactured. The process would, however, take two or three years. You do not have that leisure because we have been sowing that bacillus by 'weather' satellite the length and breadth of the Soviet Union for more than six weeks."

"I thought we were going to be frank, Mr. Vice-President," Badalovich said sadly. "And here you are trying to pull my leg again. I am not a biologist, still less a microbiologist, but we, too, have our laboratories, and I have read many reports on our progress. The incubation period of *Bacillus anthracis* is, as I recall, two to three days. It is highly infectious. Its symptoms appear very quickly. I have the pleasure to report that we have not had a single case of anthrax in many months in the Soviet Union."

"We know that. We do not kill people without warning. As for the warning—I have just given it. If you do not take it, if you do not put out those fires within two days, this is what will happen: we have other satellites aloft, dozens of them, with a capacity of twenty-five tons each. They are programmed to distribute an aerosol over the Soviet Union. That aerosol consists of various chlorofluorocarbons that, as you are well aware, destroy the ozone layer. With the ozone layer stripped from above the Soviet Union, the sun's ultraviolet light will penetrate the earth's atmosphere with its full intensity. Normally, the worst you could expect is a much higher rate of skin cancer. However, no one will be around for that slow-killing disease to develop. The ultraviolet light will break down the protein coating our scientists have wrapped up the bacillus in to keep it inactive indefinitely. Uncounted trillions of anthrax bacilli will be liberated, to be picked up by the wind and blown across the Soviet Union, to be inhaled by every single Russian with soon-fatal results."

Badalovich thought for a moment, then spoke: "Your bacteriological warfare will not be so effective as you imagine, Vice-President Castle. Smoke will absorb the ultraviolet radiation fully as effectively as the ozone layer. Should you actually deploy the chlorofluorocarbons you threaten us with," he said triumphantly, "we will simply ignite coal and lignite mines in European Russia, thus covering the entire nation with a blanket of smoke."

"Exactly. And without sun, photosynthesis will cease entirely. Your forests will wither and die, and seeds of next year's crop will lie ungerminated. You will have a choice: cancer, anthrax, or starvation."

Badalovich's jaw sagged. In a complete reversal of form, the Americans had opted for the clever and devious instead of brute force. They had introduced a Trojan horse into the Marxist camp. If what Castle had just told him was true, and the Politburo refused to close down the fires, the great Russian people would become extinct.

He thought fast. What could he say that would give the American vice-president—the Soviet Union's top agent—the opportunity to indicate whether his threat was real or bogus? He had to be careful—very careful. He didn't dare risk exposing his agent, but neither did he take the threat of Russian genocide lightly.

He realized that Castle didn't dare to give him a negative wag of the finger of his gloved hand, indicating that his threat was not to be believed, for the American spaceship crew, like the Russian, would undoubtedly be filming the meeting in space and the gesture would be detected. Nor could Castle indicate by a wink or other facial gesture that he was anything but deadly serious, for the Americans would, like the Russians, be videotaping the meeting by means of optical-fiber surveillance of their "private" circuit.

In the end, before his own facial expressions gave away his thoughts, he yanked his jack from Castle's box and abruptly signaled to Salyut 1183 to reel him in.

Castle hovered in space for a minute or two, wondering whether analysis of the tapes would somehow expose him. The strain of not knowing was too much for him. As he radioed to the *James Madison* to haul on the umbilical, first mist, then an acrid yellow liquid began to fill his helmet.

26. SIXTY-TWO CERTIFIED SAVANTS
6 OCTOBER 2009

RIPLEY FORTE HAD MADE A SCIENCE OF MOVING BILlion-ton icebergs from the Antarctic to Texas. On the other hand, persuading sixty-two world-famous savants to move in the same direction, even to yoke them to the same wagon, proved impossible.

From the first days in August, when Forte took possession of the former Dutch Reformed Church retreat in Saldanha and received the scientists who were bused up from the Cape Town International Airport, they had been nothing but a headache. Most were from the free world—Canada, the United States, Japan, Australia, and South Africa, but fifteen were refugees from various communist countries—England, France, Poland, Brazil, Italy, and Israel. The mixture didn't work.

The refugees complained about their cell-like quarters, the food, the cold wet wind off the South Atlantic, the occasional snake, the omnipresent blacks. They belly-ached about their companions, assignments, health, and pay. As for the free-world scientists, they were unhappy with the refugees for complaining so much.

Forte tried organizing the scientists by discipline, putting all the biological scientists, for instance, into one study group, allowing them to elect their own chairman who would suggest lines of inquiry. Four days were spent in rancorous politicking for the top job, the chairman elected being a relative nonentity from Columbia University whose inoffensiveness was the one qualification upon which all could agree. His suggestions for lines of research for biological warfare were similarly inoffensive, and weeks were lost before Forte summarily deposed him.

Simultaneously, Forte disbanded the study groups. He observed that they spent most of their time drinking coffee, talking about women, boasting of their previous scientific achievements, buttering up each other against the time when one academic hand could wash the other, dozing, and playing practical jokes like connecting the chairman's chair to the nearest electrical outlet and dosing each other's drinks with exotic bacteria that produced what came to be called the Saldanha Samba.

By September each savant was confined to an individual carrel for at least four hours each day. Forte made it clear that unless a scientist produced, he would be invited to leave. As they were all being paid handsomely on a daily basis, the pace of research picked up. By the middle of the month, the spate of papers turned into a torrent; by the end, to a trickle. At that point, Forte shut off the faucet and told his sixty-two savants to relax and enjoy the beach while he, Joe Mansour and Jennifer Red Cloud examined their contributions to the art of war.

"Here's a cute one," said Mansour, picking up a thin sheaf from the stack of papers on the desk in his study overlooking the sea. "The abstract says that it would be practical to destroy the western hemisphere's oxygen supply, and notes that even without the deleterious effects of the blanket of smoke covering it, the oxygen–carbon dioxide ratio is already out of balance. As an example, he notes that as early as the 1970s, California was consuming six percent more oxygen than it produced through the respiratory processes of green vegetation. Most of the deficit was due to combustion of hydrocarbons in automobiles, for industrial power, and essentials like air conditioning and heating swimming pools."

"That explains why I was breathless all those years I've been living in San Francisco," said Red Cloud. "I always knew it couldn't be the men."

"Maybe it was," Ripley Forte said sourly. "Maybe they used it all up running away from your hostile takeover bids." He was still seething from Red Cloud's continuing refusal to allow him to see their son. Ripley Jr. was almost six months old, and Forte had seen him exactly once. He had pleaded, he had threatened, he had sulked, and he had bargained, all to no avail. He had tried everything but threatening her bodily harm, and by now even that prospect had emerged from the shadows, beckoning.

"Maybe," Red Cloud conceded. "Or maybe you used it all up yourself, huffing and puffing when I kicked you out of the company with such childish ease."

"You're both wrong," Mansour said equably. He had been in the middle of too many exchanges like this during the past two months to take them seriously. "As a matter of fact, the author of this little gem says that the deficit, now nearer twenty percent, is compensated by winds off the Pacific."

"Then how are the Russians going to destroy our oxygen supply?" Red Cloud asked.

"Well, you see, the Pacific supplies only a fraction of total American needs. Most comes from our own trees and grasses and other green plants. But not all. A substantial proportion is brought from the southern hemisphere by means of atmospheric mixing. And the oxygen in the southern hemisphere is largely produced by the Amazon forests."

"Is he suggesting that the Russians, who already control Brazil, are going to cut down a couple of million square miles of trees in order to asphyxiate us?" Red Cloud said, unbelieving.

"That he is. At least, that is one of the substrategies. The Russians could shut down investment in Brazil's troubled industries, causing them to collapse completely. Its 180 million people would be forced, willy-nilly, back to the land, of which not nearly enough already under agricultural production exists. In order to survive, they'd have to cut down the Amazon to plant their crops. With the Amazon greenery gone, they'd get a crop or two out of the thin lateritic soil and the next growing season die by the tens of millions. And the consequent loss of Brazil's oxygen would so reduce that of the United States that our people—*your* people, that is—would suffer progressive breathing difficulty, asthma, respiratory infections, heart trouble, lowered productivity due to diminished energy, diminished mental capacity due to a lack of oxygen on which the brain depends. The United States would become a nation of zombies.

"And that's only the *long-range* scenario. The Russians could make it come to pass within a single year by spraying defoliants over the rain forest. Or they could start fires in their coal and oil reserves to consume the oxygen that is now exported north on the winds. Or they could—"

"Spare us," said Forte. "We get the idea. And so, apparently, does the author of *this* paper, one Stanislaus Pec. He has come up with the same idea, but his is even more sneaky. Noting that chlorophyll a—$C_{55}H_{72}O_5N_4Mg$— the most abundant form of the pigment—contains a single atom of magnesium, he has come up with a cheaply manufactured chemical that, if sprayed across the forest, will combine with that magnesium atom, breaking down the chlorophyll. The result will be instant death for all foliage so affected, for the chlorophyll is the engine that runs photosynthesis. Without it, the plants themselves will be unable to breathe, metabolism will cease, and good-bye Brazil."

"Good-bye Brazil, hello Russia," said Red Cloud, plucking a study from the stack before her. "Chaim Rosenberg here believes in youth. In fact, he believes in it so fervently that he suggests every Russian get a piece of it."

"Youth?" queried Mansour.

"Sort of. He suggests we sow the atmosphere with an aerosol the length and breadth of Russia. The aerosol would contain a human analogue of the juvenile hormone used in pesticides to promote rapid growth of the young in such species as grasshoppers. The growth of their soft tissues is so rapid that the insect is compressed in the shell or carapace that normally it would moult at the end of each stage. Its accelerated growth causes the juvenile hopper to be crushed by its own shell."

"Humans don't have shells," Forte pointed out.

"I can think of *some* old crabs that do," she said archly. "Anyway, shells aren't the operative mechanism with humans. Dropping human juvenile hormone on Russia would cause early maturation. The six-month-old baby would have the body of a six-*year*-old, but its mental powers would naturally not progress at the same rate. Ten-month-old babies eating like twenty-year-olds, while not providing any productive capacity to the national economy, would soon bankrupt the nation. Furthermore, the hormone would accelerate the aging of adults. The ten-year-old would have the body of a centenarian. Russia would become a nation of instant geriatrics. No soldier would be up to the task of so much as lifting a rifle or doing a single push-up. What do you think?"

"Jolly as all get-out," Forte said. "And what happens if the wind blows the aerosol back on the U.S.?"

"Well," she replied, "in your case—not a thing. You've never acted your age anyway. . . ."

There were more than a hundred other papers repre-

senting the fruits of brilliant scientific minds turned to
barbarous mischief. Magnetic forces of ley lines could
react with the sperm of humans who drank water con-
taminated with the extract of the spikes of the forking
larkspur, so that the weakest instead of the strongest
sperm fertilized the egg. This reproductive misadventure
would produce a race of monsters.

One such monster must have thought of culturing a
H_2S-producing variant of the microorganism that causes
red tides, then releasing them from cargo submarines by
the ton. Prevailing winds would blow the organisms toward American beaches on both coasts, and the hydrogen sulphide–permeated atmosphere would depopulate
both East and West coasts.

Enzymes, viruses, mutants, inorganic catalysts,
deeds in the night and other unpleasantness chemical,
biological, nuclear, and psychological filled the three
stacks of studies that Joe Mansour had procured at such
cost. But they didn't tell Ripley Forte what the Russians
were going to do next.

"Well, Joe," he said when they had made a comprehensive review of the possibilities, "where's that 'tree of
probability' you told us about?"

Mansour looked uncomfortable. "I don't know about
the tree, but there's certainly plenty of manure here to
make it grow. I hate to admit it, but maybe science isn't
the answer."

"It's not the science but the scientists," Red Cloud
put in, "who are the problem. It seems that dear David's
man Dr. Oswaldo Edwards picked off the seventeen
most competent of them and left us only the culls."

"What we've got," Forte said, "is this: a lot of wild
ideas, some of which the Russians may already have
planned for us. None of them are what we really want."

"Which is?" said Red Cloud.

"Something strictly defensive. Something nongenoci-
dal. You'll notice that nearly all the suggestions so far
proposed involve mass extermination. Despite Stalin's
demonstration that it can be done, and though I have no
great love for the Russians, I still don't see the humanity,
much less the wisdom, of wiping them out wholesale.
Personally, I think we've been on the wrong track."

Mansour looked up. "What's the right one?"

"Psychological. They've defrauded the free world—not to mention this innocent babe in the Chittagong and Sevastopol operations—so often that they've forgotten they're susceptible to a good con, just like everybody else."

"I'm inclined to agree," said Mansour. "Back in the 1930s, Hitler so mesmerized both friend and enemy with his aura of invincibility that he rolled right over Europe even though he had only a fraction of the manpower of the Allies, and fewer aircraft and tanks than the French alone. It was all applied psychology, and it was the fact that he suckered us—not that he was a mass murderer, not that he came so close to winning—that I believe is the basis for our hatred of him. Still, he was a very shrewd individual, and he had the political, military, and propaganda machine to work with."

"None of which you or your vaunted 'experts' possess," said Red Cloud acidly. "All you've achieved in this convocation of savants is to collect a lot of silly ideas unworthy of being dignified by being put in writing." She pushed the pile of papers away. "Why don't you just admit failure, like the men you're supposed to be?"

"Because all the cards haven't been played yet," said Forte.

"Nor will they, considering you're not playing with a full deck."

Forte glowered but said nothing.

Red Cloud, unaccustomed to having the last word, laughed. "What a pathetic object you are. You inhabit a dream world, a world in which the great Ripley Forte can accomplish any prodigy, no matter how outlandish."

"I've accomplished a few," said Forte evenly. "I brought in the *Alamo* when everybody, you among them, said it couldn't be done."

Red Cloud reddened. "It was scarcely an individual effort, as I recall. Besides, bringing the Soviet Union to heel is a feat several orders of magnitude more difficult than simply bringing an iceberg to port. No—I am being, as usual, too charitable. It is, in a word, impossible." She pushed her chair back and got up to go. "I'm afraid I can't waste any more time on these children's games, so you'll forgive me if I leave you. It's time to feed young Ripley."

She was halfway to the door when Forte spoke. "Want to bet?"

"What—that I'll feed him?" she said over her shoulder.

"No. That I'll bring the Russians to heel."

"*You?*"

"Me." -

"Like a shot. What do you want to bet?"

Forte leaned back in his chair and inspected his jagged fingernails. "You've got Raynes Oceanic Resources back. That makes you maybe the richest working woman in the world. How would you like to be the richest *person* in the world excepting, maybe, Joe Mansour here?"

"State your proposition," said Red Cloud. Her nostrils dilated, her eyes flashed, as she heard the clarion call to a new battle of wits with Ripley Forte.

"If I don't make Russia sue for peace, within the next six weeks, say, you get Forte Ocean Industries—every last share. I'll go further: I promise you every single dollar I otherwise possess, in corporate and personal assets. If I lose, you get it all."

"Put it in writing."

"Gladly. But first, let me tell you what you're gambling."

"Raynes Oceanic Resources? I'd bet twenty corporations just like it on your proposition."

"Well," said Forte slowly, "Raynes Oceanic Resources, of course. But since Forte Ocean Industries just happens to be about twenty times the size of Raynes, and growing fast, you'll have to sweeten the pot to get yourself a deal."

"Name it."

"Ripley Junior. Whoever wins gets custody of the boy. No visiting privileges for the loser. No contact whatever until he's twenty-one."

"You *are* a bastard!" she flared.

Forte leaned back in his chair and roared with laughter. "See?" he said, turning to Joe Mansour, who had watched the exchange without changing expression. "She imagines she's a captain of industry. Hell, she's nothing but a petticoat in a lumberjack's world. She's all fired up to lose her cozy little company—which she didn't do a lick of work to get—first as a result of my half brother Ned's death, then as a free gift from a Russian mole—but when it comes to risking something in which she's made a personal investment, she folds up like a card table. The typical female—all whine, no spine." He got up and gathered his papers together.

Red Cloud stood transfixed, trembling with rage and frustration. He'd struck the most sensitive nerve. She had always been proud of her ability to get the better of men in a man's world, and had proved her toughness and business acumen repeatedly. As for Forte's boast that he, single-handed, could bring the Russians to the bargaining table, it was just too absurd. Were he to so much as show his face abroad, if the Americans didn't kill him, the Russians would. On the other hand, the mere thought of losing young Ripley to that ape, his father, was more than she could bear. She would die before taking the one chance in a billion that the Texas windbag could do what he claimed.

Forte walked toward the door. As he passed her, he patted her patronizingly on the backside. "See you later, *Captain*," he sneered.

It was the sneer that did it.

"Write up the goddamned agreement!" she snarled back at him. "Have it on my desk in an hour." And she walked through the open door, slamming it behind her with all the strength she could muster.

Forte, suddenly sober, looked at the closed door. Then he turned back to the table and resumed his chair.

"I hope you know what the hell you're doing," Mansour said doubtfully, flicking imaginary lint from the sleeve of his dinner jacket.

"So do I," said Forte. "But you can't say she didn't have fair warning. I *told* her all the cards hadn't been played." He picked up a paper from the pile in front of him. Written by a distinguished Hungarian scientist, it was only five pages long. "For a minute there I even toyed with the idea of dealing this one from the top of the deck."

"Now," said Mansour, "*that* would have been a novelty. . . ."

Three days later Forte flew from Saldanha down to Mansour's palace—Mansour himself called it a "cottage"—on Table Mountain. Waiting for him were the chiefs of the atomic energy commissions of the Benipic countries—Bangladesh, Egypt, Nigeria, India, Pakistan, Indonesia, and China. Yussef Mansour had sent an urgent personal invitation to each of them, and backed it up with an honorarium—half of it paid when they stepped aboard the private plane he had laid on for each —that would enable them to live in sybaritic ease the rest of their lives.

"You carry the weight of the world's future on your shoulders," Forte told the six men and one woman assembled in the conference room. "What I am going to ask of you will, no doubt, shock and disturb you. It is nothing less than a declaration of war against our common enemy, the Soviet Union, by nuclear means.

"I realize that the specter of a worldwide nuclear conflagration appalls you. Well, it appalls me, too. But I can think of no other way out of our dilemma. You know what will happen if the burning of Russian lignite continues unabated. Bangladesh will be drowned. So will Calcutta, Bombay, Madras, Mangalore, Surat, Alexandria, Cairo, Djakarta, Surabaya, Port Harcourt, Lagos, Shanghai, Hong Kong, Canton, Tsingtao, Amoy, Hangchow, Ningpo—well, the list is long. Too long, your leaders have been forced to conclude, to even think about evacuating your coastal populations and moving them to higher ground. The process, if carried to completion in the United States, will wreck its economy. For your countries even to attempt such wholesale relocation of your endangered fellow citizens will cause confusion, stampede, revolution. It must not be allowed."

"But there must be alternatives," said Philomen Dutt, the saturnine Indian scientist.

"There are—many. For weeks we've had the best scientific minds in the free world grappling with the problem. Dozens of counterstrategies have been proposed. All of them are unworkable. All, I should say, but one."

He outlined it in detail. His listeners were skeptical. They discussed the implications of the plan far into the night. By morning they had to accede. There was, they reluctantly decided, no other way.

27. MISH-MISH PASHA
8 OCTOBER 2009

"HIS EXCELLENCY, PROFESSOR MISH-MISH PASHA, THE Ambassador of the Union of Soviet Socialist Republics," announced the president's aide, ushering in a small, dapper Azerbaijani who resembled the diplomat out of the late nineteenth century he wished he had been, instead of a messenger boy delivering ultimata from the Kremlin. He was dressed in morning coat and spats, and wore a pince-nez. He was one of those people whose faces suggest those of a dog; Professor Mish-mish Pasha's was that of a Shetland sheep dog—long-nosed, skin of apricot hue, with soulful eyes and hairy ears that came to a point.

Ambassador Mish-mish Pasha bowed from the waist to President Horatio Francis Turnbull, who enveloped the Russian's small manicured hand in his practiced grip and exerted his own brand of political pressure. He liked the ambassador, who came from a more civilized time, but didn't want him to go away with the idea that Turnbull was soft on communism.

"Long time no see, Mish-mish," Turnbull said cordially. "How are all the Kremlin's gremlins?"

"Deeply concerned, Mr. President, which is to say, in layman's language, that from time to time they're thinking about that spaced-out meeting between your representative and ours."

"If you don't have to deliver their answer standing up,

I'll know we're not going to have to start shooting just yet."

Professor Mish-mish sat down. He crossed his legs, shot his cuffs, and smiled. "The news from Kiev is good, Mr. President. We are prepared to accede to your request, even though it will require a great national effort to put out the fires ignited by the late renegade Mr. Ripley Forte."

"That's good."

"Of course, since we live in the real world, we cannot but anticipate that our heroic sacrifices will be met by equally significant sacrifices on your side."

"That's not so good."

"Nevertheless, it is necessary."

"Tell me more about the sacrifices you want us to make," Turnbull said warily.

"It's like this, Mr. President: the national effort that the Soviet Union will have to undertake to extinguish those hundreds of fires is one fraught with difficulties. Civilians will be unwilling to do—not to mention incapable of doing—this dangerous work. Therefore, we must draft our soldiers. Our experts expect many to perish from burns, smoke inhalation, falls, and other misadventures. That is a grievous human toll that the Soviet Union can ill afford. Moreover, from the defense standpoint, our armed forces will be weakened by this diversion of skilled manpower. That will leave us at a strategic disadvantage. For this reason, we expect that the United States will cut back its fighting strength commensurately."

"Sounds reasonable," said Turnbull. "We'll disband national guard and reserve units equal to the numbers of your firefighters for the duration."

Mish-mish shook his head. "I'm afraid that won't do, Mr. President. I'm instructed to hand you this list of units to be demobilized and this list of capitalist war materiel that must be destroyed." He took two sheaves of papers from his pocket and handed them across the desk to Turnbull.

Turnbull riffled through them with growing incredulity. "You can't be serious—whole divisions, air wings, aircraft carriers?"

Mish-mish returned a sickly grin. "Perhaps there is some small room for negotiation and compromise, sir, but I have been instructed that these reductions in your armed services must precede any Soviet effort to bank the fires the capitalist criminal Ripley Forte set. It's a matter of equity, a matter of Soviet national security."

"Bullshit! It's blackmail."

"That, too," conceded Mish-mish. "But cannot all diplomatic initiatives be called blackmail, in the final analysis? You do this, or we'll do that. If you don't do this, we won't do that. It's all a matter of semantics. But there is one fact that all the semantics in the world won't alter: it's dark outside." He gestured to the windows of the Oval Office.

It was indeed like 6:30 P.M. of a bleak mid-December day, even though as they spoke the hour of 11 A.M. was striking on the Oval Office grandfather clock. The little light that filtered in from the outside came from the street lights on Pennsylvania Avenue and the security lights that surrounded the White House, which had long since become as soot-encrusted as a smokehouse chimney. In the Oval Office the air was filtered, but outside everyone but the destitute or unheeding wore gauze masks. Aid stations on downtown street corners administered oxygen to those who suddenly keeled over from breathing the foul air. And the scream of ambulance sirens had become so commonplace that nobody noticed them anymore, as new victims of respiratory ailments were hauled away to District hospitals.

President Turnbull made some rapid mental calculations as he considered the Kremlin's proposal. The force reductions the Russians demanded would temporarily cripple America's armed services. But the manpower wouldn't just evaporate. Though demobilization would rob them of their tight organization and fighting edge, these could be retrieved within weeks—months at the outside. Junking of planes and ships was another matter altogether. It took six months to build a modern aircraft, six years to build a man-of-war. The destruction of the materiel on the Kremlin's list would put America's armed forces effectively out of action long enough for Russia to launch and win a conventional war.

And in the end, what would be accomplished? The Russians would put out the fires in Siberia and unleash another offensive conceived by the seventeen missing scientists—and they'd all be right back where they started. Meanwhile, in SD-1 in Houston work was nearing completion on plans for the evacuation to the interior of millions of inhabitants of the Atlantic and Pacific coasts. Also nearly complete were plans for the largest construction job in history: the building of dikes around America's major low-lying coastal cities. That effort would stalemate Russia's smoke offensive. And once the Soviets saw it wouldn't work, they'd go on to something else, which the Americans, in turn, would thwart.

But there remained the problem of cost. America could win each battle, Turnbull was convinced, but each response would be prohibitively expensive in manpower, materiel, and mental stress. If he could somehow moderate the Russian demands, they might be something the United States could live with.

Professor Mish-mish observed President Turnbull as these thoughts churned through his mind. He knew the Americans far better than most knew themselves. When he had heard of Vice-President Castle's threat to Deputy Premier Badalovich to kill the Soviet people with anthrax, he had a hearty laugh, a distant echo of the hilarity in the Kremlin that had greeted Castle's ultimatum. The Russian leaders were all students of American psychology and history. They knew Americans would never, *never* resort to such draconian measures, even if their national existence depended on it. Throughout history other nations might, would, and regularly did use all the weapons in their arsenals, no matter how barbarous, to ensure national survival. But biting this particular bullet was way beyond the capacity of the American people and their leaders. The ACLU-human-rights mentality prevailed, a self-abasing death wish. The American conscience felt comfortable in battling to the death the genocidal frenzy of other nations, but shrank from using the enemy's methods against him, and so sparing American lives. So Mish-mish waited, secure in the conviction that, having called the American bluff, the Russians could rest easy. If the Americans had indeed sowed anthrax over Russia, which he seriously doubted, they would never activate it. Mish-mish was not a gambling man, but he was willing to bet money on it.

When the negotiations concluded ten days later, the Russians proved to have been remarkably flexible. To the surprise of the American negotiators, the Russians agreed to a reduction in America's armed forces by one-third and the retirement and mothballing, rather than outright destruction, of the long list of American war machines. To be sure, once these steps had been taken, it would give the Russian armed forces an indisputable three-month advantage in any war they cared to launch. But the disorganization and decimation of the Russian army after the Moscow blast had not yet been repaired, and Turnbull seriously doubted whether the Soviet Union was in any position to consider further military conquest in the near future. It was far more likely that it would continue measures short of war and hope to wear the United States down. The only posture the United States could now adopt was that of a watchful defense.

"Well, we did it," exulted the secretary of state.

"That we did," agreed Turnbull. "But what, exactly, did we do?"

28. SWITCH HITTER
18 OCTOBER 2009

"I DON'T KNOW WHO YOU ARE, BUDDY," SAID THE SECUR-ity man at the kiosk guarding the elevator shaft of SD-1, "but you're sure as hell not Ripley Forte. Mr. Forte's dead."

"Yeah," Forte said, "I guess I must look that way, after flying all night from halfway around the world. But appearances deceive. I'm not only alive, I'm Ripley Forte. Get Mark Medina, and he'll tell you the same thing."

"Mr. Medina's in Washington."

"How about his chief of administration, Jean Schlessinger?"

The guard reached for the telephone.

Five minutes later Jean emerged from the elevator, took one look at Forte, and fainted dead away. She came to with Forte sponging her lips with a handkerchief soaked in bourbon from the guardhouse bottle. "Mr. Forte," she murmured weakly, looking up with a puzzled frown. "They said you were dead."

"Wishful thinking."

She licked her lips and sat up. "But that airplane crash—and the body." She shuddered.

"Phony—as I hope you'll assure the gentleman here who's itching to draw his forty-four and bag himself an imposter."

"It's all right, Cecil. This *is* Mr. Forte," Mrs. Schlessinger said. "You'll have to forgive Mr. Allen, Mr. Forte," she went on as Forte helped her to her feet, "but he's a bit loopy on the subject of security."

"The only way to be," Ripley assured her. "In SD-1 we can't take any chances on a spy or saboteur sneaking in to do his dirty work. Shall we?" He gestured toward the open elevator doors.

It was months since Forte had descended the 1,450 meters to the laboratories and workshops of Sunshine Industries, which his father Gwillam had hollowed out of an ancient salt dome nearly thirty years before. In that time, face-liftings and shifts in research and production priorities had periodically transformed the underground facilities. One of the constants had been the manufacture of such weapons as the most recent development, the Jim Bowie rail gun, named for the famed Texas knife fighter who could chop up an enemy with as much deadly certainty as his modern namesake.

The subterranean barracks that were to house the 3,000-man work force should nuclear war rage aboveground had been enlarged to accommodate the extra 1,400 economists, engineers, draftsmen, transportation and housing experts drafted into service to plan dikes around the major coastal cities and the evacuation of those left unprotected. They commandeered the laboratories for working space, ripped out all the weapons-testing equipment, and installed desks, drawing boards, and filing cabinets. They produced tons of detailed plans each week, ready to be shipped to the appropriate sites for execution the moment the president gave them the go-ahead.

For the sake of security—after all, the future of the United States and the free world rested on the implementation of the plans—every room in which plans were drawn up was heavily guarded, with admission only on a need-to-know basis, except for Mark Medina and a few of his top administrators. To minimize damage from possible fires, high-pressure sprinkler systems had been installed. And outside each of the twenty-odd locked storerooms where the completed plans were stored were stationed two armed guards, around the clock.

As sole owner of SD-1 and employer of Mark Medina and the others in the SD-1 hierarchy, Ripley Forte had the responsibility, now that he had risen from the dead, to assure himself that the installation was indeed impervious to penetration by the enemy. But to Denton Fulda, the government's chief of security, Forte's concern bordered on paranoia.

"I understand your reservations, Mr. Forte," the sandy-haired young man said respectfully, "but I think, when you have had a look around, you'll agree that no precaution has been neglected."

"Maybe," said Forte. "But you haven't had as much experience with the Russians as I have. They're the trickiest people on earth. Half of the Soviet Union spends its waking hours figuring out new ways to diddle us—and the other half spies on them to make sure they're doing their job."

"Well, it's all wasted effort as far as SD-1 is concerned," Fulda assured him. "Every man down here has been screened to a fare-thee-well. Lie detectors, voice stress analysis, pupillary-contraction monitoring, muscle-tension examination—we used them all on every man and woman you see down here. We've run deep-background checks, and everyone with even so much as a citation for spitting on the sidewalk was excluded. Once down here nobody has been permitted to leave, even to attend the marriage or funeral of a loved one.

Even the three who died since the project got under way are still here—refrigerated. Nobody except Mark Medina—and your own self, of course—has permission to enter and leave. Only when the project plans are complete and delivered to competent authorities for execution will anybody be permitted to see the sky again. There are no phones or radios from SD-1 to the outside ... So you'll see that the installation is hermetically sealed. Safe as houses, as the Brits say."

"Look at the Brits' houses, with Russians quartered in the best of them, and maybe you'll pick another simile," Forte said. "What about physical penetration—the enemy digging a shaft into SD-1?"

"Impossible. Every wall surface contains hundreds of sensors. Computers filter out the background noise— earth shifts, traffic overhead, and so on; a gopher trying to tunnel in would trip every alarm in SD-1."

Forte was impressed and said so. But he wanted to see for himself and so was taken on a grand tour of the project. It lasted the better part of the day. At its conclusion, he pronounced himself satisfied, except for one small detail.

"The storerooms?" said Fulda. "But they are locked and guarded by two guards at all times."

"And the walls?"

"Walls?" Fulda said blankly.

"The storerooms are sandwiched between working spaces, aren't they?"

"Yes, sir. That's been done to minimize transportation of documents. Each department has its own storeroom, adjacent to its work spaces."

"And no connection between work and storage spaces?"

"No, sir. The storerooms are four walls, ceiling and floor, with a single combination-locked door—guarded day and night."

"And who guards the walls?"

"I'm afraid I don't follow, Mr. Forte."

"Isn't it conceivable that a saboteur has, just for the sake of argument, foxed your security investigators? That he had managed to obtain office space next to one of the storerooms? That he has access to tools? That he has surreptitiously bored a hole through one of the adjacent walls? That he will now be in a position to pour a flammable fluid into that hole, so that it will be soaked up by paper inside the storeroom? That, at a time of his choosing, he will ignite that flammable fluid and thus destroy a room full of documents? That these documents and plans are inextricably integrated with those stored elsewhere in SD-1? That, in short, one determined man might wreck the entire project and jeopardize the existence of Texas and the United States?"

Denton Fulda was overwhelmed. Forte's logic was impeccable, even if his argument did rest upon the presence of a saboteur in SD-1. The investigation of each man and woman had been too intensive, too exhaustive, for a foreign agent to slip through the net. But Fulda was too experienced in security work to trust anybody, including himself, one hundred percent. Human nature was little understood and even less predictable. Brainwashing, psychological preparation, a sudden inexplicable change of allegiance, spite, mental aberration—any of these could inspire even the most thoroughly cleared worker in SD-1 to commit the arson Ripley Forte feared. And it had taken an outsider to demonstrate, almost offhandedly, that he, Denton Fulda, had been remiss in the execution of his job.

He drew himself up and looked Ripley Forte in the eye. "I guess the best thing for me to do, under the circumstances, is to put my responsibilities in the hands of someone better qualified. I'll have my resignation on the desk of—"

Forte laughed and put his arm around the younger man's shoulders. "Let's not do anything drastic—not until we see if we can handle the problem in another way."

"What do you mean?"

"Simply that you're probably right in believing that SD-1 is clean. And if it *is* clean up to now, maybe we can guarantee that it remains that way."

"How?"

"When I was in Johannesburg a couple of weeks ago, I was shown an interesting device. It looks like an ordinary felt pen. But it's actually a mass of sensors and a miniaturized transmitter. It can detect vibration, such as that given off by an electric drill. It can detect a change in air quality, such as would be apparent if gasoline or other flammable were introduced into a closed chamber. It detects heat through an infrared sensor. In short, any change in the status quo causes the device to transmit an alarm, which is picked up and identified as to source by its particular wavelength. The receiver is installed in the security operations room. Even a tiptoeing mouse will set bells ringing."

Fulda tried to be calm. "Do you think we could get some of those sensors?"

"Well," said Forte, "I can always try."

Three days later President Horatio Francis Turnbull was awakened from a sound sleep at three-thirty in the morning by his military aide, Major General Habib T. Noonie.

"What time is it?" said Turnbull, rolling over on his back and rubbing sleep-swollen eyes.

"I let you sleep as long as possible while the members of the National Security Board were called. They've all arrived, and they're waiting for you in the conference room."

"What the hell's going on?" demanded the president, sliding out of his bed and reaching for his dressing gown.

"Fire in SD-1, sir."

It was more a postmortem than a conference. The National Security Board could do little more than listen to the report forwarded by President Tom Traynor of the catastrophe that had occurred in SD-1 two hours earlier.

According to President Traynor, each of the twenty-odd storerooms containing plans and other documents relating to the evacuation of the coastal regions and construction of dikes around the major cities had been burned out, suddenly, simultaneously, and completely. Nothing but ashes remained of the months of work by thousands of the nation's top experts. Fortunately, there had been no human casualties.

"Sabotage?" asked President Turnbull of President Traynor, on the videophone.

"Without question," the Texan said grimly. "I've personally questioned SD-1's chief security officer, one Denton Fulda, and got the story firsthand. You're not going to like this."

"I'm sure I won't. What happened?"

"Ripley Forte showed up a few days ago, and—"

"The hell you say! Why wasn't I informed? He was supposed to lie low in South Africa until we got this Russian winter sorted out."

"I didn't know myself," said Traynor. "He just appeared out of nowhere, and Fulda let him in—owner, patriotic American, and all that. I'd have done the same, of course."

"You're not telling me that *Forte* had a hand in this?"

"Up to the armpit. He engineered the whole scheme. He persuaded Fulda that security for the storerooms was slack and volunteered a 'sensor' he had seen demonstrated in South Africa to tighten it up. Two days later a whole box of so-called sensors arrived by air, along with the 'console' that monitored them. Fulda and Forte personally planted sensors in all four walls of each storeroom, plus a couple right in among the boxes of documents themselves."

"The sensors were sabotaged."

"Hell, no! There *were* no sensors. What Forte led Fulda to believe were sensors were actually nothing but simple thermite pencil incendiary bombs, set to go off at midnight."

"Jesus! But those document storage places were protected by sprinkler systems. Surely—"

"Forte knew all about them, of course. Sometime before midnight he turned off the valves regulating the water flow to the sprinklers, then stripped the threads so they couldn't be turned on again. By the time we got water flowing half an hour later, nothing was left but gray ash."

It was bad, very bad, but it could have been worse. The Russians, Turnbull felt sure, had never known about the existence of the standby plans the Americans would put into force should they continue to make smoke. Therefore, the fire wouldn't affect their actions one way or the other.

The timing of the fire in SD-1 seemed suggestive, but of what, no one could say. Six days before, American surveillance satellites had observed a slackening of smoke from Siberia's lignite mines; two days later all fires had apparently been extinguished. Besides the filth, acid rain, widespread respiratory ailments, erosion of buildings and monuments, general depression of the populace as a result of the eternal night, and the prospect of a massive and expensive clean-up, no irreparable harm had been done. Indeed, some defense savings had been effected by demobilizing units and mothballing ships and planes. As for the sea level, it had risen scarcely four feet, and in the absence of the Siberian fires would now stabilize at about six feet higher than normal before natural weather patterns removed the excess in the form of snow, once again building up Antarctic ice. Many coastal homes had been flooded, and even parts of some cities were underwater. Still, the damage was nothing like what it could have been.

"What about Forte?" asked President Turnbull. "What in the hell inspired him to do such a crazy thing?"

"Your guess is as good as anybody's."

"Have you tried asking him?"

Tom Traynor's lips were pulled down in a scowl. "Can't. He's disappeared. We got belated word that a fisherman saw him on a speedboat roaring out of the Houston Ship Channel into the Gulf of Mexico. Air traffic control reports that no helicopter or tiltprop plane that could have snatched him from the sea was operating in the area at that time. No larger vessels, either. That leaves a submarine. We believe that he left the way he came, in one of those new titanium-hulled South African pig boats. If so, by now it's submerged so deep we'll never be able to locate it threading through the thermoclines."

"The goddamned madman had better stay there," Turnbull said, "because the next time he turns up, I'm going to feed him to the fishes for sure."

"Amen," said President Tom Traynor.

The satellites in polar orbit that had confirmed the quenching of the Siberian lignite fires were the first to detect the new menace: hot water.

"What the hell do you mean—hot water?" grumbled the president, buttonholed by General Noonie as he was sitting down to lunch. He was in a pleasant mood for a change. During the two weeks that had elapsed since the Russians put out the fires, the skies had begun to clear. Not enough for the sun to shine through, but at least enough to give promise that one day soon they would see real daylight. And now his aide had come rushing up to him, burbling something about hot water.

"Calm down, Habib T.," he said, "and say something coherent."

"Hot water, sir. Billions of tons of it an hour. It's pouring out of every nuclear generating plant in every single Benipic country."

"Is that bad?"

"Bad? Well, sir, for one thing, the superheated water is killing all the fish in rivers and seas for dozens of miles around."

"Never did like boiled fish," commented President Turnbull, eyeing the platter of steak on the table.

He didn't get to eat it. General Noonie dragged him off, protesting, to the conference room, where five of his National Security Board had already arrived.

"What's the hassle?" he asked. "Why are you getting so stirred up over a little hot water?"

Dr. Sid Bussek, his scientific adviser, told him.

The hot water that was pouring out of more than a thousand reactors into the southern seas was sending immense clouds of roiling steam into the atmosphere. The clouds that formed as a result would act as an insulating blanket, just as the smoke had done in the northern hemisphere: the greenhouse effect all over again. The heated troposphere would cause the Antarctic ice cap to melt—but faster than before, since the heat and cloud cover were that much closer to the South Polar regions.

"Well," said the exasperated president, "get the presidents of the Benipic countries on the line and tell them to shut down those reactors, pronto!"

"We've tried that. Everybody has the same story:

that the operating staffs have barricaded themselves in the plants with enough food and water for six months."

"Then call out the Strategic Air Command and bomb the bastards out!"

"I'm afraid that won't do, sir," demurred his scientific adviser. "If we attacked the nuclear stations, by air or by land, the nuclear reactions, now controlled, would go wild. We'd have meltdown, and the consequences of that . . . Well, you know the consequences as well as I do."

"Then what the hell *can* we do?"

His staff looked back at him blankly. They had no answers. With new infusions of terrestrial heat, the oceans would continue to rise. Unless contained, they would obliterate both American coasts.

And the plans designed to protect the vulnerable cities and their populations had been destroyed by Ripley Forte.

29. ALARUMS AND EXCURSIONS 27 OCTOBER 2009

DAVID D. CASTLE SIGHED WITH CONTENTMENT. THE SUN was hot, but vagrant clouds conveniently interposed themselves just when the heat threatened to become unbearable. The breeze off Montego Bay was brisk, giving his skin a pleasant tingle when he emerged from periodic dips in the sea. His heart was serene, since the cares of office, never unbearable for a vice-president, weighed lightly on his capable shoulders.

He lay in the sun on a white beach towel the size of a squash court while pleasant thoughts gently nudged each other for pride of place. The current political crisis would wreck President Horatio Francis Turnbull's political career no matter what the outcome: he had the unenviable choice of letting half the population's homes and industries drown, or saving them at the cost of bankrupting the country by building dikes and making millions homeless. He, David D. Castle, would without question become the next president; no other worthy contender was even on the horizon. His Russian mentors were ecstatic at his unprecedented success as a mole: he expected promotion to lieutenant general in the KGB any month now, and when he became president, he didn't see how the Kremlin could refuse him Marshal of the Soviet Union rank. The only worm in the golden apple from the tree of fortune—his irritating, irreverent, stumpy-legged, arrogant, cigarette-smoking, stable-scented control, Ilse Freemann—was safely several hundred miles distant, in Washington, D.C., where she could not possibly disturb his peace of mind.

Her voice, as sharp-edged as a scalpel, cut into his reflections. "A little more meat on those bones and you'd be fit game for a real woman like me," she greeted him.

He sat up with a start and opened his eyes. At first he saw only a silhouette, as she was between him and the sun. That was a mercy, for as she sank to her knees by his side, he had a full view of her bosom slopping around the sides of a too-tight white bathing suit, skin corpse-gray where it wasn't mottled, her blizzard-blown hair, thick glasses the size of a scuba-diver's goggles, and to-bacco tar–stained teeth behind a hideous grin that was meant to be coy. "What—what—?"

"*To* what, I guess you mean."

"To what?" said the stunned Castle, fearing that at any moment she might rise, favoring him with an unobstructed view of her gnarled, lumpy, thick-ankled legs.

"'To what do I owe this unexpected pleasure?' you were about to say."

"Oh, yes."

"To our leaders, God bless 'em. They told me to track you down and brief you immediately. I *think* 'brief' was the word they used." She let her eyes slide down his body suggestively.

Castle felt his skin crawling. He wished he could join

it. "Brief me on what?" he said quickly, before her innuendo got out of hand and onto his thigh.

"New policy," she said, dragging her eyes away with visible reluctance. "They want the United States to redouble its efforts to apprehend—*really* apprehend this time—Ripley Forte."

"Why the sudden interest in Forte?"

"Because our people in the Kremlin are convinced that Forte is behind the runaway nuclear reactors in the Benipic nations."

"I'm afraid I don't understand. If anything, I'd think the Russians would want to give him a medal. After all, if Forte *is* behind all that hot water being dumped into the oceans, he'll only be doing what the Soviet Union itself has been doing for months—heating up the atmosphere. Why the sudden concern?"

Ilse Freemann didn't know, but she wasn't the sort to parade her ignorance. "It ought to be obvious to you, but since it isn't, there's no use in my spreading the Kremlin's secrets around. All you really need to know is that you have orders directly from Premier Luchenko, through me. You're to get your sweet little tail back to Washington at once, and while you're on your way, think of some good reasons why Forte must persuade—it's obvious that the United States itself has been unable to do so—the competent authorities to stop these hot-water emissions. I have been instructed to tell you, furthermore, that this mission is of the highest priority you'll ever receive. If you succeed, you will receive the Order of Lenin."

"And if I fail? Remember, I'm only vice-president. If the president himself and all his cabinet, plus the President of Texas, can't find and turn Ripley Forte around, how the hell can *I* be expected to? The order is unreasonable."

"Unreasonable or not, those are your orders. You must do your very best on this one."

David D. Castle grimaced, shrugged, and started to get up.

Ilse Freemann put a thick-fingered hand on his chest and playfully pushed him back. "I don't suppose half an hour's delay will mean the end of the world."

But it would mean the end of *me*, Castle thought desperately as he parried her thrust and struggled to his feet. She rose with him, stepped in hard against him, grabbed his wrist and pressed his hand against her steatopygic bottom. He removed it. "Orders are orders," he said sternly.

In a guard kiosk overlooking the beach from the fringe of palms in the distance, Lieutenant Colonel South turned to the gunnery sergeant who was tracking the couple walking up the beach with a parabolic dish mounted on a heavy metal tripod. "Still coming in okay?"

The gunny lifted one earphone, made a thumb-and-index-finger sign, and grinned. "Clear as a bell, Colonel. How about the video?"

"With this baby," he replied, patting the black 2000-mm lens approximately the size of a drain pipe attached to his videorecorder, "I guess I could pick up the warts on the old biddy's ass. We'll track them to the house, and after that the inside team will take over. But I don't suppose they'll have much to say to each other when they know the servants might be listening. . . ."

30. EXCURSIONS
1 NOVEMBER 2009

THE VISIT WAS UNPRECEDENTED. FOR THE FIRST TIME IN American diplomatic history, a foreign chief of state arrived uninvited, unheralded, and unwanted. Also unreceived, for President Horatio Francis Turnbull was closeted at his Camp David retreat with his advisers grappling with the sudden crisis of hot-water emissions from 1023 nuclear generating facilities in the world's poor nations.

"What the hell's he doing here?" growled Turnbull when his aide arrived with a message from the secretary of state announcing Premier Evgeniy Luchenko's unexpected excursion to Washington.

General Noonie had a pretty good idea. Ripley Forte had gone over to the enemy, presumably in furtherance of the grand Soviet strategy laid down by the seventeen American scientists. Noonie could only speculate on the inducements the Soviets must have offered the second richest man in the world and Russian-hater, Forte, to turn his coat, but they must have been spectacular. As for the strategy itself, it was simple enough: the Russians started the fires in Siberia, waited until the United States realized that it would be ruined if they continued to burn, then offered to extinguish them—for a price. Having done so, traitor Ripley Forte, presumably a loose gun, then contrived the dumping of uncounted billions of tons of hot water into the seas, accelerating the ice-cap melt. The Russians would, of course, disclaim all responsibility, for if they admitted it the desperate Americans might drop The Bomb. Nevertheless, the premier had come to let the Americans know that the Soviet Union, and *only* the Soviet Union, could stop Forte, but of course there would be a small charge. . . .

"It seems that's my fate: to get a charge out of the Russians," Turnbull said when he had urged General Noonie to tell him the worst.

"We can, at least, stall," said the other. "After all, we had no official—not even *un*official—notification of Luchenko's visit. It's against all protocol. We can say you had an urgent meeting scheduled—which is the simple truth. We can let him cool his heels—"

"While he warms our coasts. No, Noonie, we've got to get this issue resolved, and resolved fast. The fair-and-warmer boys tell me that the ambient temperature is ascending at the rate of nearly a tenth of a degree every day. They can't predict precisely when it will happen, but they *do* know that at a certain point whole damned chunks of the Antarctic continent will suddenly slip into the sea, raising the sea level by up to ten meters at a crack. We can't let that happen. We've got to talk to the Russians right away—tomorrow at the latest."

But he didn't. The strain of the crisis had sapped the chief executive's vitality, and he was caught by a sudden autumn shower during his postprandial walk around the grounds. That afternoon President Turnbull began to suffer from a scratchy throat, and his temperature shot up to 101 degrees. By nightfall his voice was gone. His medical adviser filled him full of antibiotics, administered a brimming hot rum toddy, and told him to get a good night's sleep.

He got three.

By noon on the fourth, Premier Luchenko was pacing the floor at the Soviet Embassy on 16th Street like an old con in solitary. "It's an affront!" he shouted, crimson-necked, to Ambassador Mish-mish Pasha. "It's an insult, an outrage! I am not some piddling ambassador he can push around. I am the Premier of the Soviet Union, and I will not be treated like a lackey. *Do* something!"

"What do you suggest, sir?" replied Mish-mish mildly. "I have a Ph.D. in political science, not an M.D. in internal medicine. The State Department and the Executive Office both claim he is in bed with a bad cold."

"Lies—all lies! It's a diplomatic illness if I ever saw one. He's got to see us, I tell you." His voice was almost plaintive. "Every passing day increases the danger."

Mish-mish didn't know what Luchenko was talking about, but he hadn't achieved ambassadorial rank by asking leading questions of his superiors. Like Major General Habib T. Noonie, he had assumed that Luchenko had come here to strike while the water was hot, perhaps demanding that the Americans demobilize their armed forces entirely as the price for his ordering the spigots shut. But Luchenko's agitation belied such a theory. The premier would have been confident. He would have gloated at the delay, knowing that each passing day would increase the Americans' discomfiture, allowing him to raise the ante commensurately when payday finally came. But no, Luchenko was acting like the American president should have been. Mish-mish was at a loss to explain this strange role reversal, thank God an ambassador wasn't required to do so. The job of messenger boy had its merits. "They're bluffing," Mish-mish said, falling back on a cliché that, applied to the Americans, had never failed him yet.

"But what if they *aren't*?" said Luchenko miserably.

"Ah," said Mish-mish, returning an inscrutable look, signifying exactly nothing.

The meeting between President Horatio Francis Turnbull and Premier Evgeniy Luchenko took place on 5 November. No interpreters were present, since Luchenko spoke fluent English, and the room in which the meeting took place had been twice swept—first by KGB men who planted their own pinhead-sized surveillance devices, then by NSA security men, who removed them. Whatever the chiefs of state said would be between them.

"Congratulations on your recovery, Mr. President," Luchenko said with a tight smile.

Turnbull blew his nose. "Nasty, these between-season colds," he said.

"But not as nasty as all-season heat."

"True. But you know as well as I that I can't control what Ripley Forte does. We have an all-points alert out on him. He's to be shot on sight."

"Like the last time you shot him?"

President Turnbull shrugged. "We're big boys, Evgeniy. You know we're not going to kill an honored, valuable citizen just because Russia wants him dead. Sure, we screwed you people a little, but then, you're not exactly virgins, are you?"

The Russian glared at him.

"Anyway," the president continued, "*this* time *we* want him dead, and dead he shall be as soon as we can find him. But you didn't come here to talk about Ripley Forte."

"On the contrary, that was my purpose."

It was Turnbull's turn to be perplexed. Once the Russians discovered that Ripley Forte was alive, he had expected them to raise diplomatic hell. But the issue wasn't the kind of thing that would inspire an impromptu and secret visit of the Russian premier to America. "Better explain that."

Luchenko chose his words very carefully. Whatever he said, it must not contain a hint of his real purpose. He knew he could get only so much mileage out of Ripley

Forte, so he had to pursue a different tack. He decided
that the man-of-reason approach would work best.
"Look here, Mr. President. Those Siberian fires were a
bad mistake. They were set without my permission, and
I was systematically deceived as to the difficulties involved in putting them out. Once I found out the truth,
of course, I ordered troops personally loyal to me to extinguish them. Then I conducted an investigation,
rounded up the culprits, and had them all shot. A very
useful practice, which you would be well advised to
adopt."

"We give them a fair trial here, *then* shoot them. But
I'm glad you are man enough to admit the mistake."
Turnbull was more at sea than ever. What Luchenko had
told him was a lie of course, but why did he *admit* to
such a monstrous act, especially when he knew that any
American president, under the circumstances, would immediately use the admission as an excuse to reactivate
the nation's armed forces?

"Yes," Luchenko said, "I admit the mistake. I declare, our informal agreement committing you to a scal-
ing-down of your armed forces to be null and void."

Jesus! thought Turnbull. What the hell is going *on*
here? Next thing old Luchenko would volunteer to
demob his *own* military forces.

"And to prove my good faith," the Russian continued,
"I shall unilaterally mothball an equivalent number of my
ships and planes, and cut our land forces by one-third,
beginning at once."

"Fine. Fine," mumbled the stunned president.

"With one proviso."

Here it comes, thought Turnbull.

"That you arrest Ripley Forte and shut down those
nuclear reactors. You see," he went on hurriedly, "our
environmentalists fear for the fishing industry on which
we largely depend for our protein. They fear disrupted
rain patterns that could cause drought in the world
wheatlands and torrential downpours over the Sahara.
They fear that the progressive heating of tropical waters
could make veritable steambaths of the tropical lands,
killing hundreds of millions of people in Asia, Africa, and
South America."

Bullshit! thought Turnbull. They feared something, all right, but environmental and humanitarian considerations didn't bring Luchenko hotfooting to Washington. But if not that, then what *was* it he feared? Why did the Soviets, who had heated up the atmosphere to begin with to blackmail the Americans, suddenly cool to the idea? How did Luchenko's determination to nail Ripley Forte square with Turnbull's conviction that Forte was working for the Russians? None of this made sense. He couldn't understand Luchenko's sudden about-face.

What Turnbull *did* understand was Luchenko's desperation. It was obvious that the rugged old bullet-headed marshal wanted that hot-water tap turned off and that he was willing to pay considerably more than the concessions he offered. Turnbull decided to see how far he could push the wily Russian.

"What if I were to tell you I don't have the slightest influence on Ripley Forte?"

"I wouldn't believe you, naturally."

"What if I were to tell you that I'm convinced that Forte is actually working for *you*?"

Luchenko's jaw dropped in incredulity. Then he laughed, a short, sharp, disagreeable sound, like a dog worrying a rag doll. He had misjudged Turnbull. The American had some political sense after all. Turnbull would now take an extreme position on the side of the angels, denying any connection with Forte, until he, Luchenko, granted sufficient concessions to make the exchange worthwhile to the Americans. Well, the situation was too desperate for such a traditional political minuet. He had to get those emissions stopped, and stopped right now.

"Your approach might have worked with Mish-mish, and on any other occasion, perhaps even from me you might have wrung certain advantages. I am, after all, a reasonable man. But the situation of the moment does not permit us such luxuries as bargaining like a pair of Armenian rug merchants. I must have your answer, at once, and without equivocation: will you turn over Ripley Forte and make to cease those hot-water emissions, in return for the concessions I offered, and even perhaps others that can be negotiated?"

Turnbull would dearly have loved to be able to say yes. The opportunity to wring out Luchenko, squeeze him down to the last destroyer, airplane, and paratrooper, was one that would never come again. But it was impossible. He'd already done his best to lay hands on Forte, but the cagey bastard was hiding on a sub among the thermals somewhere in the millions of square miles of open ocean. He'd surface only when *he* wanted to. Turnbull would have to convince Luchenko of this unpalatable truth and go on from there.

He tried...and tried...and tried. And failed. Through a lavish lunch brought in after three hours of nonstop discussion he attemped to convince Luchenko of his sincerity. But the Russian's natural suspicion of Americans, coupled with Turnbull's admission that the previous assassination attempt on Forte was rigged, made the Russian rocky soil on which to plant that fragile flower, the Unvarnished Truth.

Luchenko wiped his lips, drank a glass of water, and pushed himself back from the table. "I'm sorry, Mr. President," he said, "but you force me to unpleasant alternatives. If you do not get those emissions stopped within forty-eight hours, I will be forced to order the activation of Reserve Plan B-1, by which a radio signal from Kiev will cause the release of some twelve hundred canisters of nerve gas secretly planted throughout the United States over the past fifteen years. The gas will penetrate every known type of gas mask, including ours. Fewer than a million people, mainly in remote areas, will survive."

President Turnbull was grim. "You may do that, Mr. Premier, but meanwhile, you should remember just where you happen to be sitting. Before you leave this room—if that's your final word—to put your genocidal scheme into effect, I shall order satellites loaded with anthrax, tetanus, plague, and other exotic diseases medical science hasn't even heard of aloft to dump their cargoes on Russia. This time I won't be bluffing, and after your threat to wipe out the American people, you'd better believe me."

The two men glared at each other across the remains of their lunch. Neither was bluffing now, and both knew it. Still, neither knew where to go from here. They had each threatened the other's nation with wholesale death. Both realized that there was absolutely no guarantee, at this stage of the game, that the other might not do it. For several minutes they remained mute, trying to think of some way to resolve the impasse.

The telephone rang.

President Turnbull picked it up. "I told you I didn't want to be disturbed for *anything*."

"Yes, sir," said General Noonie. "But I *know* you'll want to talk with the party I've got on the other line."

"Who the devil is it?"

"Ripley Forte."

31. SNOWBLITZ
5 NOVEMBER 2009

"MR. PRESIDENT, THIS IS RIPLEY FORTE."

President Turnbull had a number of things to say to Forte, but decided they could wait. "Speak your piece," he said through clenched teeth.

"I understand Premier Luchenko is in Washington, out for my blood."

"And any other parts of your anatomy he can lay his hands on."

"Have you seen him yet, may I ask, sir?"

"You may, and I have. He's right here."

"In that case, would you please put this call on the speakerphone?"

President Turnbull shrugged and flicked the switch that made Forte's call audible to the Soviet Premier.

"Welcome to the Land of the Free, Mr. Premier," said Forte. "My informants tell me you'd like to see me."

"Preferably dead," replied Premier Evgeniy Luchenko. "But not until you order your minions to stop their criminal dumping of hot waters into the oceans."

"Why the concern?" Forte said innocently. "The

emissions are merely heating up the atmosphere—like
your Siberian lignite fires. We—"

"The renegades who committed that crime against the
Soviet Union have been rounded up and shot. The fires
have been extinguished and further harm to the world
environment averted. If, that is, you can be made to see
reason and instruct your cohorts to cease the flow of hot
water."

"I see," said Forte. "You've come to Washington to
plead for the world environment."

"That is correct. I must admit, to be perfectly candid,
that injurious consequences to our national interests may
result if these emissions are not halted."

"Such as?"

"Mainly the killing of marine life on which our nutri-
tion heavily depends, the drastic alteration of rain patterns—making deserts of our wheatlands and seas of our
deserts, and the heating of tropical lands to the point
where tens of millions will die from heat exhaustion."

"Is that all?"

"Is that *all*? My God, man, isn't that enough?"

Forte didn't answer for a moment. Finally he said:
"How about snowblitz?"

Premier Luchenko glanced at President Turnbull out
of the corner of his eye. His brow had wrinkled interrogatively. Unless he was a better actor than Luchenko
thought he was, Turnbull was completely in the dark.
"Showbiz?"

"Nice try, Mr. Premier. In your discussion with President Turnbull about the main consequences of the hot-
water emissions, did you happen to mention snowblitz?"

"I'm afraid I don't know what you're talking about."

"Yes, what the hell *are* you talking about, Forte?"
Turnbull broke in angrily.

"The weather, what people always talk about, but
never do anything about—until the Russians came along
with their fires in Siberia. That injection of particulate
matter and carbon dioxide into the air, as you are well
aware, disrupted the earth's temperature balance. It produced the greenhouse effect, heating the atmosphere,
which caused melting of the snowcap and a rise in the

sea level. But the Russians, in possession of the calculations of our seventeen missing scientists, knew they could stoke the fires only so long. If you recall, Mr. President, they finally desisted on what turned out to be very easy terms. That was uncharacteristic: Russians *never* offer easy terms."

"I've already explained that, Mr. President," Luchenko said hastily. "It was a conspiracy. We shot the conspirators. We want only good relations with the United States."

President Turnbull smiled. "Sure you do, Evgeniy. Anything else, Forte?"

"So why did they stop? Because they had already wrung all the concessions out of you they were able to get. Also, their principal aim had been achieved: the imminent implementation of a plan to relocate coastal populations and dike the major American seaports. That was their *real* objective, for it would bankrupt the United States and make its conquest by Russia a mere formality."

"I see what you're driving at, Forte, but why should they stop at all? Why didn't they keep the home fires burning, turn up the heat a notch, hurry us into making mistakes?"

"They didn't dare. They feared the snowblitz."

A snowblitz, Forte explained, paradoxically was the end result of *too* much global heating, and the Russians had to quench their fires before they reached that point, or the Soviet Union would be submerged beneath the advancing glaciers of a sudden new ice age.

The heating of the atmosphere did indeed melt the ice cap, raising the ocean's levels. The hotter air over the oceans also caused greater evaporation from the sea and denser cloud cover. The ice cap's weight kept enormous quantities of ice submerged below sea level; when the ice cap melted, raising the sea level, that submerged ice would also surge into the open sea, cooling it.

At the same time, the clouds of water vapor would provide an albedo effect, reflecting the sun's warming rays back into the sky. The earth would cool rapidly. Precipitation from the clouds would, even in temperate climates, come down as snow. The white ground covering would reflect much of the sunlight that did penetrate the cloud cover back into the sky, and the earth's surface would grow still colder. The combination of albedo from clouds and from increased snow cover and ice-surge cooling could, his scientists calculated, snowball and trigger an instantaneous ice age—"instantaneous" in the geologic sense. It might take a hundred or even a thousand years, as it did during a similar abrupt cooling 89,000 years ago, as the result of volcanic eruptions that enveloped the earth in clouds of dense ash. Europe suffered a brief but severe snowblitz 75,000 years ago when Indonesia's Mount Toba blew its top, dispersing up to 480 cubic miles of debris into the atmosphere. Even such recent and minor volcanic eruptions as Tambora in 1815, Krakatoa in 1883, and Agung in 1963 had led to large-scale, though not catastrophic, cooling.

President Horatio Francis Turnbull felt a warming surge of relief. Ripley Forte was no traitor, after all. He had somehow duplicated the researches of the seventeen missing scientists, saw through the Russian's schemes, and turned the tables on them. If they persisted in their enmity and their subversive attacks on the United States, he threatened Russia with a new ice age. Since Russia was much farther north than the United States, it would be the first to be covered with ice along, unfortunately, with Canada and Alaska. But Forte knew they wouldn't allow that to happen. They'd bargain furiously, they'd bluff and storm, but in the end the Soviets would have to capitulate.

Turnbull could see it now: the complete dissolution of the Red Army, Navy, and Air Force. The extirpation of the KGB. The liberation of all the lands that had fallen under Russian subjection. A new, revivified Europe. A world under the humane guidance of the United States. A world in which American democracy would be universal.

"Forte," intoned Turnbull, "the free world is in your debt. But the contest is not entirely won yet. You'll have to keep control of those nuclear plants and their hot-water emissions until we can disarm the Soviet Union and put a U.S. army of occupation in place. Once our democratic institutions are firmly established, then you and your men can reap the rewards of a grateful world."

"I'm afraid we're going to have to adopt a slightly different scenario, sir."

"Well," Turnbull said grandly. "I leave it to you to work out the details. The main thing is, we have won."

"No, sir," said Forte, "nobody's won anything yet. It doesn't take much imagination to guess what was going on between you and Premier Luchenko before I called."

"We were discussing our differences, of course."

"Discussing your differences, or threatening to wipe each other out because of them?"

"I believe Premier Luchenko *did* advocate certain typically barbarous measures to ensure that the Soviet Union got its way. I, on behalf of the American national interest, naturally had to point out that, if he even *thought* about implementing any such horrors, we'd reluctantly but certainly wipe his nose, but good."

"Premier Luchenko?" Forte said softly.

"Yes," Luchenko agreed, "there were intimations of violence. On our side, of course, they were only suggested as purely defensive measures to counter American aggression."

"Sure," said Forte. "Now, gentlemen, I'll tell you the way we're going to resolve this situation, without firing a shot, without dropping a single bomb or bacillus. We're going to have us a little congress."

Turnbull and Luchenko regarded each other uneasily.

"As you recall," Forte went on, "Europe was in a hell of a mess after a generation of Napoleon's adventures—just as the world is in a hell of a mess today because of sixty years of conflict between Russian ambitions to rule it all and American attempts to have everybody become nice little Americans. Europe resolved its problems for almost a hundred years at the Congress of Vienna in 1814–15. We're going to solve the *world's* problems starting next week at a congress between the only two powers that can make binding decisions: the United States and the Soviet Union. And just to make sure that you conferees take the matter seriously, I'm going to keep the hot water flowing until agreement is reached."

Premier Luchenko's heart bounded. The very thing! Once the conference began in Kiev, the KGB could keep track of the secret deliberations of the Americans and by means of indirection, subversion, blackmail, and threats manage events that would make the Union of Soviet Socialist Republics, finally, the only remaining world power.

President Turnbull's heart bounded. The news media would give saturation coverage to the congress taking place in Washington, D.C. World opinion, thus informed, would demand that the Russians yield to the demonstrated capacity of the American leadership to achieve a democratic government, prosperity, and tranquillity for its citizens. The United States would, at last, be king of the hill.

Ripley Forte broke into their reflections. "The rules are simple: each side is to bring to the congress the delegation it sees fit. One man or five, five or five thousand. Ideally, each delegation will include the experts who provide the factual background and analysis on which policy is founded, as well as the deliberative bodies that discuss policy, judges who determine the policy's constitutionality, and the executives who are empowered to carry it out. Is that agreeable to you both?"

"It is," said the president, echoing the premier.

"Then all that remains is to decide the venue for the Russo-American Conference, to begin on November ninth."

"Kiev, of course," said Luchenko.

"Washington, of course," said Turnbull. "After all, it is the capital of the world."

"It seems that we have a tie, gentlemen," said Forte. "As I have not yet voted, I shall cast my ballot . . . against Washington."

Dammit, thought Turnbull furiously. The man's a dirty communist after all.

"I shall cast my ballot," Forte went on, "against Kiev, as well. For the sake of strictly impartial deliberations, the congress will convene in neutral territory: Houston, the Republic of Texas."

32. THE CONGRESS OF HOUSTON
14 NOVEMBER 2009

THE RED ARMY WENT ON FULL ALERT ON THE EVENING of 7 November, when the first aircraft bearing the lowest-ranking members of the Soviet delegation—representatives of the Supreme Soviet—took off for Houston. The aircraft was escorted by long-range Il-51 Fanfire bombers, which had orders to disperse and fire their nuclear-tipped cruise missiles at major American cities at the first confirmed sighting of hostile interceptors. In the event, no opposition to their passage was encountered, and the bomber escort refueled at Houston International Airport and returned to the USSR for another batch of bureaucrats. By 9 November the airspace between the Soviet Union and the Republic of Texas was as busy as the aerial corridor between Washington and New York City as more, and steadily higher-ranking, delegates arrived in Houston.

They were met by squadrons of KGB men, dispatched the day after Ripley Forte's fateful conversation with the American president, to ensure that the convention-center hotel to which they had been assigned was bug-free and totally secure. The Russian secret police contingent was given complete control of the two adjacent hotels and allowed to carry whatever weapons they considered necessary. After all, this was Houston, where even schoolboys carried magnums—and not of champagne. The KGB brought over one planeload of cooks and more than a dozen loaded with Russian food, water, and liquor, to preclude any attempts by the Texans to poison them. Behind police lines that prevented the approach of the curious closer than three city blocks, they made each hotel a citadel. They established machine-gun positions at each entrance, a complex system of identification cards and passwords, walking armed patrols on every corridor, and a sophisticated optical cable communications system, with signal scramblers to make it immune to the inevitable American attempts at surveillance.

Even these ample precautions did not seem sufficient to the nervous Russians. They were, after all, surrounded by more than two million hostile citizens of Houston, whom the Russians twice in a single decade had tried and failed to exterminate. KGB Security Chief Igor Gabalan demanded that all Texans be cleared within the radius of a mile from Sam I and Sam II—the Sam Houston and Sam Rayburn hotels. President Tom Traynor refused. The Russian shuttle flights abruptly ceased. President Turnbull interceded with Ripley Forte, who was in daily contact by radiotelephone from his subterranean hiding place. Forte prevailed upon Traynor to do the Russian bidding. The flights resumed.

Forte had told Premier Luchenko that the Soviet delegation could consist of one man—or five thousand. By the time the airlift over the pole was completed, more than six thousand Russian bureaucrats were installed in unaccustomed luxury in Sam I and Sam II. Such a convergence of Soviet leaders upon a single city was unprecedented. The Russians were unanimous in opposing such a concentration of power, but it had been unavoidable. Premier Luchenko did not dare enter into binding decisions with the United States in Houston, leaving Deputy Premier Badalovich in Russia to disavow them, seize the Party apparatus, and become premier in his stead. The same logic applied right down the line, from ministers of state, party chiefs, KGB functionaries, marshals, and admirals to the leaders of autonomous republics, *krays* and *oblasts* who, while they would not be called upon for opinion or decision, would at least be unable to engineer a palace coup. The temporary administrators left behind were third- and fourth-rate men, who would be too busy spying on their counterparts and foiling their power plays to attempt any themselves.

The American delegation, housed in the Howard

Hughes and Chester Nimitz hotels some blocks away, was less numerous but equally high powered. Led by the President of the United States, it comprised his cabinet and undersecretaries, the members of both houses of Congress, senior officers of the National Security Agency and the CIA, and the senior flag officers of the armed forces, not quite seven hundred in all. Conspicuously absent were state governors and members of the judiciary.

Of the more than thirteen thousand delegates, security men, aides, and flunkies, only twenty-three actually mattered. They were the sixteen men of the Presidium of the USSR, and the American president and six of his closest advisers. Their respective entourages were present merely to rubber-stamp agreements reached by the leadership. Indeed, with the hot-water emissions making the seas boil and black clouds form over deserts where rain had not fallen in eons, there was no time for lengthy deliberations. What the twenty-three men decided would become the fate of their respective nations, the fate of the world.

"Gentlemen," said President Tom Traynor, conference host and self-appointed moderator to the twenty-three men seated around the oval mahogany table, "we are here today not to talk about peace in our time but to make large-scale war impossible.

"They are not the same thing. Peace will not come until man's fundamental aggressive instincts are curbed. When that happens, his defenses against a hostile environment will have atrophied, and he will be an endangered species awaiting only the coup de grace of those—rats or roaches, ants or amoeba—that were here millions of years before us, and have survived and prospered only by unremitting warfare against a thousand enemies. What we must seek here are not absolute solutions. We haven't the leisure to wander in the dreamland where all men are brothers, where violence has ceased, where love is the only conqueror. We've got to work with what we are: lazy, selfish, stupid, mean men; but men, also, with intelligence, vision, courage, reason, and hope.

"I ask you, then, to consider ways to ensure that this

world of ours endures—not a utopian forever—but simply, say, for another hundred years, without us killing each other by the tens of millions over inflexible, doctrinaire ideologies. There are some fairly obvious solutions. History has precedents, and I pray that you invoke them. I pray, moreover, that you do so with some speed, for I am advised by my scientific staff, as I presume you have been by your own, that unless a decision that we can all live with is reached in seven or eight days, the heating of the atmosphere will have irreversible effects: first will come the drowning of coastal cities around the world, and within seven or eight months a gigantic sheet of ice will form at the North Pole and the resulting glacier will begin its inexorable descent across the face of Russia, across Europe, down to the Pyrenees.

"Mr. Premier," he said, turning to Marshal Evgeniy Luchenko, on the left side of the table, appropriately, "since you are our guest, you have the floor."

Marshal Luchenko cleared his throat and launched into a set speech on which his staff had labored through the night. It contained numerous references to the virtues of Marxist-Leninist socialism, the dignity of workers of the world, the peace-loving intentions of the Soviet people, and the necessity for the Americans to demonstrate their goodwill by a progressive reduction in their armed forces over a period of five years, which the Russians would match missile for missile, division for division, man-of-war for man-of-war.

"Very generous of you, Marshal Luchenko," President Turnbull said dryly when the premier had finished his two-hour speech. "The trouble is, with twice the number of missiles, divisions, and capital ships that the free world possesses, a step-by-step reduction will eliminate all our armed forces and leave the Soviet Union with enough firepower to conquer those countries it does not already possess."

"You see?" Luchenko said resignedly to President Traynor. "The United States insists on keeping its aggressive imperialist power intact. To construct a peaceful world, we need hammers and sickles, not bullets and bayonets."

Traynor raised an eyebrow toward President Turn-bull.

"Understanding—that's what we need," said Turn-ball, speaking without notes. "We need trade, exchange of students, a common planning policy for the underde-veloped countries and a common budget to implement it, a free press, free elections, free speech. Only when we can achieve these goals will suspicion and enmity be-tween our two great countries be dispelled."

"Fine," commented President Traynor, "but it seems to me you're talking about ends, not means. What's the first step? What do we do next week?"

"We begin with free elections, of course," President Turnbull said grandly. "Let all the men and women as-sembled here in Houston submit their resignations, and free elections be held. The voice of the people will deter-mine which leaders and policies will prevail."

Premier Luchenko with difficulty kept his lips in a straight line. If this man of the people thought *he*, a mili-tary man who had fought and conspired his way to the top, was going to submit to the judgment of a nation of peasants, factory workers and petty bureaucrats, he was much mistaken. But the soft answer, he had read, con-founded the enemy. He had one at hand: "Yes, Mr. Presi-dent, what you say is very sound indeed. But even in the United States the electoral process requires months. We have but seven days."

They flew.

If anything, by week's end the Russians and Ameri-cans were farther apart than they had been the first day. Their positions hardened with a repetition of demands, a refusal to concede that to get they had to give. At bot-tom, the Russians were convinced that only if the Ameri-cans joined the march of the proletariat toward the beckoning horizon of universal communism would the world be saved. The Americans, in turn, believed that if the Russians embraced a system of representative gov-ernment based on the American model, as all reasonable men had to concede was only just, mankind's problems would be washed away in that great democratic solvent —cooperation, goodwill, and fraternity. The passage of days weighed upon them. Each morning the lines in the faces of the twenty-two men—one Russian delegate had been hospitalized by a heart attack—deepened. Their voices became hoarse, their expressions taut. Hands that lit cigarettes trembled. The seventh day came and went.

On the eighth day President Tom Traynor, who had abstained from the discussions, brought the meeting to order and announced that the time for deliberation had come to an end. "Since you cannot decide among your-selves how to avoid war, gentlemen, a decision must be made for you."

"By *you*?" said Premier Luchenko.

President Traynor shook his head. "No. I seldom make decisions I lack the power to enforce."

"Then who?" asked President Turnbull.

"The man who controls the destiny of us all—Ripley Forte." He nodded to an aide, and behind him the large wall television screen was illuminated. Traynor moved his chair to one side and addressed the empty screen. "Have you heard it all, Rip?"

"Enough," came a voice from the screen, and the craggy face of Ripley Forte came into view. He was wearing a turtleneck sweater and stood before the peri-scope on the quarterdeck of a submarine. "Believe me, I wish you gentlemen had been able to sort out your na-tional differences in a reasonable and imaginative fash-ion. Since you didn't, I'm afraid I've got to do it for you."

Premier Luchenko reddened and shot to his feet. "I cannot speak for the President of the United States, but if you think the Premier of the Soviet Union will accept dictation from a criminal renegade like yourself, you are mistaken. I shall return to the Soviet Union immediately, and we shall resolve our dispute in the traditional way."

"The forum of war?" said Forte.

"If necessary."

"You've already lost, Mr. Premier. If you'll step to the window, you will observe that the building is surrounded by tanks and heavy artillery. Technicians of the Texas Army have laser-zapped your transmitters. Communica-tions between your delegation and Kiev have been severed. The same is true of communications between Houston and Washington."

"This is an outrage!" shouted President Turnbull, joining Luchenko and the others at the plate-glass window overlooking the street fourteen stories below. He had naturally expected that Forte, being a dual-national Texican-American, would side with him and force Russia into unilateral disarmament.

"Call it power politics," said Forte, unmoved. "You boys are playing with big toys, and unless I take drastic measures, everybody's going to die before his time—including you."

"And precisely what do you propose to do?" said Turnbull, livid at the thought of being betrayed by a man he thought his friend—a Texican, at that. "Hold us for ransom?"

"Not me."

"Then what?"

"The two delegations are going to be put aboard their respective aircraft and fly out of here to Kiev and Washington."

Luchenko and Turnbull looked at each other, bewildered.

"I don't understand," said Turnbull, speaking for both.

"Unless your official biographers lie more than usual, you both studied classical history. Do you recall how the Greeks and Romans made hostile tribes behave?"

Luchenko and Turnbull looked at each other and paled.

"That's right," said Forte grimly. "You're each other's hostages. The Russians will go to the banks of the Potomac and administer Russia from the White House and Capitol Hill. The Americans will go to Kiev and run the United States from the banks of the Dniepr. Somehow, I have the feeling that the chances of either of you declaring war, when you yourselves will be among the first to be atomized, will be pretty slim."

Once Forte's dictum spread through the American and Russian delegations, second thoughts about the attractions of the political life began to sink in.

American senators, congressmen, and cabinet members would no longer have the luxury of large and compliant staffs, chauffeured automobiles, foreign junkets, the fawning attentions of lobbyists, and inflated salaries—what was worth buying in Russia, after all? Their staffs, Forte promised, would consist of a single Russian each. The president would have more, but not enough to crowd a commodious coat closet. Living conditions would be Spartan. They would be surrounded by Russians, who would quickly reward any sign of hostility against Russia by the armed forces the Americans commanded in the United States. But as diluted as their authority would undoubtedly become, life as an American politician, even in Russia, was more attractive to most of them than actually working for a living.

The Russians headed for Washington had different concerns. To be sure, their standard of living would vastly improve. Also, though senior KGB officials would be among them, the secret police would no longer be able, on a whim, to cause them to disappear into the far reaches of Siberia. On the other hand, the one great benefit of holding office in Russia was the status it conferred, the ability to command the attention and the obedience of the masses. In Washington, that perquisite would be missing. They would be so many faceless clerks.

Lacking the machinery of command, both the style and substance of Russian and American national leadership would undergo a profound metamorphosis. Public servants in both countries, shorn of their propaganda machines and their power to coerce through pork barrel and security apparatus, would shrink to more human dimensions. An officeholder would be chosen by the consonance of his public policy with the will of his electorate; lacking the power of patronage and a public relations staff, he would be turned out of office when seen to violate promises to constituents.

The behavior of military leaders, too, would be modified. No longer surrounded by yes-men eager for promotion, they would concentrate on their nation's defenses. But observing those of the enemy daily and at close hand, the respective forces would tend toward parity as each sought to imitate the other. Eventually the futility of attempting to gain decisive superiority over the enemy would become apparent, and mutual agreement—or mutual exhaustion—would presage a wholesale and mutual disarmament.

By then the nationalism that had been responsible for the slaughter of millions since Napoleonic times would have come to a natural end: the Brownian Movement, whose fortunes Ripley Forte had closely followed, convinced him of that. With the national executive and national legislature absent from direct control of each nation's daily affairs, the states in America and the republics in the Soviet Union would at long last reclaim the sovereignty their peoples craved. Latvians, Lithuanians, Estonians, Georgians, Ukranians, Uzbeks, Khirgizians, Moldavians, Azerbaijanis, Armenians, and dozens of other Soviet cultural and linguistic minorities, which nearly a century of forced association had failed to homogenize into a "Russian" people, would vote with their feet and secede from central control. The Russian army would crumble. Remnants would, very probably, form militias responsive to their own ethnic interests, but the day of a Soviet juggernaut steamrolling over Europe and Asia would be gone.

A similar parochialism would overtake the United States, too. Certain common concerns—telecommunications, trunk roads, water resources—would doubtless be best administered by the dwindling national bureaucracy. But everything else—taxation, budgets, urban policy, public health, mines, education, family planning, commerce, agriculture—would become again the province of the states, as the Founding Fathers had envisioned, or even smaller political entities, where the people's will would be applied firsthand, by-passing an expensive, cumbersome, self-aggrandizing, and, especially, growing, national beaucracy.

The millennium, Forte realized, was not in the offing. Regional rivalries could—doubtless would—lead to strife and bloodshed. But the desire of every citizen to control his fate to the greatest extent possible would militate against once more allowing big brother in faraway Washington or Kiev to make life-and-death decisions in his name. Forte's solution would make war a restricted, regional, modest affair rather than an international disaster. People would gravitate toward that state or city which most closely represented the kind of life they wanted for themselves and their families. Who could tell? Perhaps it would be a happier world.

The American and Russian leaders, who in seven days had not agreed on anything, at last agreed on something: they might lose the battle to maintain their ranks and privileges, but they would fight to the last breath to win the war against Ripley Forte's brave new order.

33. MR. PRESIDENT CASTLE 17 NOVEMBER 2009

DINNER ON THE STARLIGHT ROOF OF THE SAM HOUSTON Hotel was for four: the two chiefs of state and their deputies, Vice-President Castle and Deputy Premier Anatoliy Badalovich. It was arranged at the suggestion of Premier Evgeniy Luchenko, who hoped that some last-minute entente between the two leaders could produce a common front that would wreck Ripley Forte's plans.

"We don't have much time, considering that tomorrow our delegations must begin to leave Houston for their new homes," Luchenko pointed out to President Turnbull as the soup plates were removed. He waited until the four waiters had brought the entree, poured the wine, and left the room before continuing. "But if we can reach an agreement tonight, I believe we can still maintain control of events in our respective countries."

"I doubt it," said Turnbull. He was ten years Luchenko's senior, and at his age, optimism was a sometime thing.

"I admit it won't be easy, with Forte's people—read the Republic of Texas Intelligence Agency—monitoring the radio traffic between the two countries," Luchenko persisted, "but it will be possible. We will establish back channels. Once the Presidium and I are in Washington, we will make contact with our KGB and GRU operatives who already have penetrated your government agencies. They will then relay our decisions to the respective departments in Kiev for action. If necessary, we will activate our network of sleepers for backup. Our predicament, in the last analysis, is not one of geography but of communications."

"Your suggestion has merit," said President Turnbull, examining his steak with a conspicuous lack of relish. Since they had arrived in Texas, scarcely a meal they had been served didn't have steak as the main course. "It does, at least, for you Russians, who have spent years building up your espionage apparatus in the United States. But what about us? You know damned well that we've never had more than a handful of low-grade, scared-green part-time spies in Russia, most of them triples and most of them atomized in the Moscow holocaust. What do *we* use for a back channel?"

"Yes, there's that," Luchenko conceded. He had methodically cut up his steak into bite-sized portions, and now he impaled one on the end of his fork. With it as a foundation, with his knife he constructed a little edifice of mashed potatoes, peas and carrots, topped by a sprig of parsley. He popped it into his mouth and closed his eyes in rapture as he slowly masticated it. "The Texans have no culture," he said, "and so, of course, their yogurt is without taste, but they do know how to broil a steak.... However, I can suggest a way out of your dilemma."

"Kill Forte?"

"That would be the optimum solution, but what I had in mind was for you, once established in Kiev, to use *our* KGB-GRU apparatus for relaying communications."

"Employ the fox to carry the grapes? Oh, yes, that would be the epitome of political wisdom."

"Can you think of another way?"

Turnbull couldn't. There probably *wasn't* another way. Forte had outsmarted them all, and there just wasn't any way out of the Texas trap they had walked into. He controlled the nuclear plants spewing hot water into the world's oceans. The plants were vulnerable to attack, but only at the risk of meltdown and heat emissions immeasurably worse. The men barricaded within them had provisions for at least six months. Unless the American and Russian leadership acceded to Forte's demands and switched headquarters, the whole northern hemisphere would be drowned by flood, then crushed beneath a mile-thick sheet of ice. If they tried to avoid their fate by delaying tactics, Forte would surely inform the world of the consequences of their leaders' acts, and they would be torn to pieces by their own wrathful constituents. No—the leaders of Russia and the United States now assembled in Houston could do only what Forte demanded and hope for the best.

And, speaking for himself, why not? Turnbull had spent a lifetime in politics. Already twice elected to the presidency, he had nowhere to go but out. He was jaded, and he was tired. Why *not* give Forte's crazy idea a chance? Whatever happened could surely be no worse than World War III, which he and Luchenko had been on the verge of starting when Ripley Forte intervened.

Turnbull recognized that he, who had stood for election a dozen times, understood the popular mind better than Luchenko, who had the tunnel vision of the military mind. Luchenko seemed to believe that his regime, even headquartered in Washington, would go on indefinitely. The American president knew better. The Russian people, liberated from the suffocating hand of Big Brother, would erupt like a dormant volcano, sending hot streams of repressed energy in a hundred directions, seeking unexplored paths of political, artistic, scientific, and personal expression. Inertia and fear would continue to rule for a week, a month, a year. But when the Russian people saw the state no longer capable of exercising day-to-day control, they would explode like a hand grenade. And God help anyone who tried to pick up the pieces and reconstitute the monolithic state.

And the Americans? They would probably react much like the Russians. Freed from the top-heavy bureaucracy in Washington, freed from the necessity of paying taxes for idle welfare recipients, pork-barrel construction projects, protection money to uneconomic industries, subsidies to millionaire farmers, millions of paper-shuffling federal employees, and unwieldy and (now) unnecessary armed forces, they would concentrate their attention, resources, and vigor on making for themselves and their families a better life, which has always been the main concern of Americans.

"No," Turnbull said finally, "I can think of no other way to avert our fate than to kill Ripley Forte. But I won't consent to such a barbarity for two very good reasons: first, it's murder, and while an American president may declare war that will kill millions of his people, he cannot consent to the killing of a single individual."

"Hypocrisy!" retorted Luchenko.

"True—and also an irony. Still, it's a fact. Besides, Ripley Forte may, in his own warped and devious way, be doing the world a favor."

"That's nonsense. But you mentioned *two* reasons."

"Yes, in addition to the moral, there's the practical one: before you can kill him, you have to find him."

"Indeed. But remember, Forte is a citizen of the United States as well as Texas. He'd answer an appeal from his president for a personal meeting to discuss his proposal."

"Whereupon I'd have him shot, I suppose?"

"No, no," said the Russian premier, "the *KGB* would. That way both our consciences would be clear, and we'd have achieved a nice division of responsibility."

Turnbull shook his head emphatically. "No."

"Is there nothing that I can say which will make you change your mind, no political compromises we can reach, no inducements I can offer?"

"None."

Premier Evgeniy Luchenko sighed and regarded the older man with compassion. Turnbull was obviously a decent, honorable man, but decent, honorable men can rarely make the distasteful decisions and perilous compromises that are the daily bread of a successful leader. After a lifetime of teething on the flabby American body politic, in which statesmen died in bed rather than in prison cells or on the gallows as was customary elsewhere, Turnbull still had not learned to bite the bullet. Of course Turnbull, according to the secret report provided by Castle, was dying of cancer, even though he *looked* healthy enough. He probably wanted more than anything else, even than the security of his country, an undisturbed mind and the applause of his people ringing in his ears as he lay down for that final, forever sleep.

Luchenko wished Turnbull's end could come thus peacefully, but a Russian premier had the interests of the Russian people to consider. He reached into the breast pocket of his dinner jacket, adorned only by the Order of Lenin, and drew out a black lizard-skin wallet. From it he took a photograph and laid it beside Turnbull's plate.

Turnbull picked it up and examined it. It was the usual family photograph. Seated in the center was Marshal Evgeniy Luchenko, with a port list from the row upon row of ribbons decorating his uniform jacket. His expression was suitably authoritative. That of the plain woman whose hand rested on his shoulder was resigned, those of the two teenage sons on either side, sullen. "Your family?"

"Yes," said Luchenko. "I love them very much. And I'd kill them with my own hands if the survival of the Soviet Union demanded it. Yet you won't even order the dispatch of a criminal troublemaker to save our two countries."

President Turnbull handed the photo back. "I guess you've just defined the difference between Russians and Americans."

Luchenko tucked the photograph back in his wallet and returned it to his pocket. "One of them, Mr. President. The other is that we Russians plan far ahead, take into consideration every misadventure that might befall us, and take steps to cover each and every contingency."

"Then you anticipated my reply."

"I feared it."

"And you plan to murder Ripley Forte."

"We plan to, and we will—for the good of both our countries."

"I must warn you, Premier Luchenko, that I will communicate your intentions to Ripley Forte. I will also order our security forces to take whatever precautions necessary to protect him."

Luchenko shook his head sadly. "As Julius Caesar said when he crossed the Rubicon, 'The dice are cast.'"

"'The die *is* cast,'" Turnbull corrected him. "Singular, you know."

"That's even better," said Luchenko, "considering we do not share your American enthusiasm for a pluralistic society..."

Half an hour later, having failed to reach a consensus, the diners said their good-byes.

Premier Luchenko walked swiftly back to his hotel suite, where he found his personal physicians awaiting him. Without a word, they stripped off his dinner jacket, handed it, wallet and all, to a waiting KGB man for immediate incineration, and led him to the bathroom. Their own protected by rubber gloves, they bathed both the premier's hands thoroughly in isopropyl alcohol, followed by scrubbing in strong soap and water. Only when they took a swabbing of the surface of Luchenko's right fingertips and tested it to make sure that all traces of the vasodilator and fibrillator with which the photograph had been impregnated was removed did they peel off the transparent collodion that covered Luchenko's fingers and swab them with acetone to remove all traces of the protective layer.

The next morning, at 0130, President Horatio Francis Turnbull died peacefully in his sleep. Doctors summoned to the bedside at dawn were unanimous in attributing the president's death to a massive heart attack, a finding supported by a subsequent autopsy.

At noon the chief justice of the U.S. Supreme Court arrived from Washington to swear in David D. Castle as the forty-fifth President of the United States.

34. TO THE WINNER...
17 NOVEMBER 2009

THE SOUTH AFRICAN SUBMARINE *NATAL* WAS CRUISING, not in the South Atlantic, where the Russians had concentrated their search, or in the Gulf of Mexico off the coast of the Republic of Texas where the Americans were convinced it must be, but in the mid-Pacific south of Hawaii. It was there that Ripley Forte received a message from President Tom Traynor that at one last dinner meeting, which ended an hour before, the leaders and their deputies had reluctantly decided to accept Ripley Forte's terms. The transfer of the Russian seat of government to Washington, D.C., and of the American to Kiev, would begin on the morrow.

Ripley Forte pushed his chair back from the desk in his stateroom and read the message again, savoring every word. The accord meant that, henceforth, the life of every living human being was going to be different— radically so. The individual would have to accept a greater share of responsibility for his own actions rather than depend on a distant, faceless civil servant to decide his destiny. Without Big Brother to lean on, the family, the clan, the community would again become the foci of moral and physical development and support. Change in that direction would be rapid but not cataclysmic, for the restraining hand of big government would relax its grip only reluctantly. The weak, inept, and slothful would doubtless suffer the slow extinction Darwin predicted for the unfit as a result of the continuing competition between individuals to reproduce their kind. On the other hand, a new order would challenge the resourceful and inventive to feats of creation that might even rival the fecundity of Renaissance Italy. The world didn't know it yet, but it was in for heady times.

And so was Ripley Forte.

He folded the radiogram, stuck it in his shirt pocket, and left the tiny room that had a hundred fathoms of blue water for a ceiling. His compartment was in the fo'c'sle among the men and petty officers, while Jennifer Red Cloud, at her insistence, had been quartered with her nanny and their son aft, near the twin water-jets that propelled the ship silently through the depths. He walked down the low narrow passageway, squeezing past crewmen, through the mess hall, past the exercise compartment and missile tubes, to officers' country. It was the first time he had been beyond the wardroom since the voyage began weeks before. He knocked at the door that bore a neatly lettered card: "MRS. RED CLOUD."

From within came her voice, dull and listless. "Who is it?"

"Forte."

The pause was so long that Forte thought she hadn't heard. He was about to repeat himself when the door was unlocked, and she slipped through the opening into the passageway, closing the door behind her. Inside, somebody shot the bolt home. His son was in there, and Forte wanted nothing more in the world than to see him, but a great calm had descended upon him: he would not only see young Ripley but *possess* him from now on. "Let's go to the wardroom," he said.

He expected protest, but she merely nodded, and preceded him down the passageway. From behind, she looked the same—voluptuous, with long straight legs whose smooth contours it would take more than a pair of tailored gray flannel slacks to conceal, straight black hair to her narrow waist. But as she passed him, he noticed that her face was wan, the eyes brilliant but sunken, as one who is running a fever, the jaw tense. Her Indian intuition, he was sure, had already conveyed the bad news.

Forte held a chair in a corner of the wardroom at one of half a dozen tables bolted to the deck. Two officers who saw them enter—the two Americans who had until this moment remained the length of the ship apart—hastily finished their coffee and left. Forte and Red Cloud were alone.

He went to the coffeemaker and filled two thick white mugs. He put them on the table and sat down facing her. "I've missed you, Red."

"You don't need to lie," she said dispiritedly. "You only miss Ripley, and you've come to tell me that he no longer belongs to me, haven't you?"

Forte extracted the radiogram from his pocket and laid it on the table in front of her.

She read it and, like Forte, read it again. "This could be a fake," she said, looking up. Her eyes didn't quite focus. "I wouldn't put it past you bribing a radioman to fake it."

"You know I didn't," Forte said softly.

"Yes, I guess I do. You want Ripley, don't you?"

"Wasn't that our agreement?"

"It hasn't happened yet," she said, her voice tense, her eyes fearful. "The Russians and Americans are still in Houston. They aren't going to let you push them around so easily. They're just leading you on. Just because they agreed doesn't mean they'll do what they promised. After all, they're *politicians*."

Forte sipped his coffee. "Give up, Red. I've won, and I've come for the boy."

"You can't have him."

He cocked an eyebrow at her.

"We were just *talking*," she said, her voice rising. "We never did sign any agreement. You don't have a legal leg to stand on."

"No, but I have your word. Are you going to tell me you'd lie about a thing like this?"

"The 'thing' you're talking about happens to be my *son*, and—"

"—and mine."

"—and I'd not only lie for him, but I'd steal, turn traitor, burn, *kill* for him," she shouted. "Do you understand?"

"I'm beginning to."

"A child needs a mother," she went on plaintively. "Very well, I concede that he needs a father, too, but before everything else, a mother."

Forte drank his coffee and said nothing.

"Admit it," she persisted. "He's not one year old yet. He *needs* a mother."

"You said that. And as a matter of fact, I agree."

"You do?" For the first time a hint of a smile illuminated her eyes.

"That's right. I plan to *get* a mother for him. That should take care of your objections."

Jennifer Red Cloud was speechless. She had stupidly walked into another of Ripley Forte's nasty little traps. She had cut the ground out from under herself. Now she'd have to retreat to the narrow legalistic ledge she had impetuously abandoned. She'd look foolish, but she'd be safe. "I won't give him up."

"I'm not asking you to, you idiot," Forte said with some exasperation. "Don't you know a proposal when you hear one? I'm asking you to marry me. You're a businesswoman, and it's good business—you get two Fortes for the price of one. You also get two guys who love you more than— than—"

"More than you can say?" said Jennifer Red Cloud. Her expression suddenly softened. Her hand reached out tremulously to caress the edge of his jaw.

"Yes."

"Well, dammit, if you can't *say* how much, you inarticulate ape," she whispered, "maybe you can show me...."

35. *SPIROCHAETUM ENCAUSTUM*
18 NOVEMBER 2009

HE WAS BACK IN NICARAGUA, LEADING HIS MARINE recon platoon through the steamy, matted jungle, when the point man raised his rifle to his shoulder, muzzle pointed in the direction of march, indicating that he had sighted the enemy ahead. Forte sent out flankers, motioned his men to disperse and take cover, and in a crouching run slithered through the underbrush to the side of the point man. Putting binoculars to his eyes, he could discern cami-clad Sandinistas fanning out ahead of them in an enveloping movement, at least a company on either side. Were the Nicaraguan troops guessing that the Marines were ahead, or had they been spotted?

Through a gap in the overhead cover he found his answer: high above them circled an OK-77 reconnaissance aircraft. The foliage was too dense for visual observation, but he knew that his men's body heat could easily be detected by the spotter aircraft's infrared sensors. The only course to follow now was to get out— fast. Facing back along the trail, he raised his arm over his head and dropped it to the horizontal, indicating advance to the rear—Marines *never* retreat. Then he pumped his arm up and down twice to signal "double time," and was following his point man at an easy lope when the first mortar shell went off with a tremendous roar. A moment later he was caught in a veritable rain of deafening explosions . . . and an insistent banging at the door awakened Ripley Forte from feverish sleep.

He rolled over on his back and looked at the glowing hands of his watch. One-forty-five A.M. The knocking continued.

"Bug off!" Forte shouted, but the thuds on the door only redoubled.

Forte examined the sleeping form next to him and sighed. It would take the thunder of Armageddon to rouse Jennifer Red Cloud from her sex-saturated stupor. He leaned over and kissed her on the small of the back. She stirred and moaned softly. "Don't go away," he said, reaching for his trousers.

Outside an agitated Yussef Mansour awaited him. That made it important: Mansour was the kind of man whose pulse rate would rise about two beats per minute by being thrown in a pit of horned vipers.

"The president is dead," Mansour said without preamble.

"When—how?"

"The doctors believe it was about six hours ago, one-thirty Houston time. His aide went in with a wake-up call, and—"

"The cause?"

"Heart failure."

Forte's eyes narrowed. "I know thirty ways to induce a heart attack, and half of them can't be detected by the best pathologists."

"No arguments. He died a couple of hours after dinner. And guess who he dined with?"

Forte shook his head.

"Premier Evgeniy Luchenko... and Deputy Premier Anatoliy Badalovich... and Vice-President David D. Castle..."

"And?"

"That's the complete list," said the diminutive Lebanese, who as usual, despite the lateness of the hour, was attired in impeccable Savile Row suiting, as if he were about to take an evening stroll along the Champs Élysées instead of down the dimly lit corridor of the South African submarine *Natal*, preceding Ripley Forte to the deserted wardroom for a council of war.

"That means big trouble," said Mansour, accepting a cup of oolong tea from Godolphin, his gentleman's gentleman, who poured Forte a cup of coffee and silently disappeared. "With the KGB chasing you, you were so hot that it took total immersion in the Pacific Ocean at five hundred fathoms to cool you off. But when *President* Castle sics the FBI, the CIA, and the Boy Scouts of America on you, as well, there won't be anywhere to hide."

"They don't cut any ice in Texas," Forte reminded him.

"True," admitted Mansour. "You'll be safe there—for a while. But once the word gets out in Washington and Kiev that you're there, things will heat up. Castle will discover reasons why you must be apprehended and brought to justice, and the Russians who give him his orders will back him to the hilt. Economic pressure and the threat of military measures will force President Traynor to hand you over to the wolves."

Forte pursed his lips. "When we brainstormed this exchange-of-hostages scenario, how long did we give the central governments to hang on, before local control made them superfluous?"

"Six, maybe eight months. If you're thinking we can stay down in this submarine until that happens, though, forget it. I happened to be discussing the matter with the captain only yesterday. The sub can cruise for two more years without nuclear fuel rod replacement, but provisions aboard, especially oxygen and carbon-dioxide scrubbing chemicals, will last for only another forty to fifty days. . . ."

The two men kicked the problem around until the sun rose from the empty sea above them, and then went to see the captain, who had been instructed by the South African navy's chief of staff to assist Mr. Mansour, the nation's largest businessman and defense industrialist, in any way possible. Ten minutes later the *Natal* was headed southeast at flank speed for Cape Horn, en route to Galveston, Texas.

In the darkest hours of 29 November, the undersea craft cruised at ten knots the final hundred kilometers from deep water in the Gulf of Mexico, up the submarine trench that Forte Ocean Industries had scooped out of the shallow bottom to accommodate the giant icebergs towed to Texas from the Antarctic, and into Matagorda Bay. At 0330 Forte and Jennifer Red Cloud, now Mrs. Ripley Forte after a marriage ceremony performed by the *Natal*'s çaptain, disembarked from the submarine, along with Joe Mansour, in a FOI helicopter. Half an hour later they were descending the elevator shaft to the Houston–Kiev subway terminus at SD-2.

The underground city was considerably larger than when Forte had last been there. More than 18,000 men had been involved in the construction of the underground railway, and their numbers, in addition to mountains of materials that had been brought down a new supply shaft, required not only sizable housing and recreational spaces but extensive electrical generation, transportation, security—no man would be allowed to leave until the tunnel was completed—water and food supply, and warehouse space.

After a vertiginous but controlled drop of more than

half a mile, the elevator braked to a stop, and the steel doors *whoosh*ed open. Mark Medina stood there, beaming.

"God—you're a sight for sore eyes," said the white-haired *hidalgo*, clutching Forte in a rib-cracking embrace.

"Wrong identity, but right sentiment—which I fully reciprocate." Forte smiled, peeling himself loose. "Shake hands with our new partner, Mrs. Forte," he said, stepping aside for Jennifer, who was clad in a tight-fitting orange flight suit.

"Shake hands, hell!" said Medina, grabbing her and squashing his white handlebar moustache flat on her face.

Jennifer sighed in mock chagrin. "'Marry in haste, repent at leisure,'" she quoted. "I *knew* I should have waited!"

"Well, you're going to wait a long time for the next kiss from this old goat," Forte said severely. "If I ever see him nosing around, I'll file for divorce, and make him put his money where his mouth was."

"Married a week, and jealous already," Jennifer said airily. "I thought you were the modern, understanding type. But it seems you're the typical male-chauvinist spoilsport, after all."

"Right on the button," replied Forte. "However, the sport I intend to spoil is your erstwhile fiancé, David D. Castle."

"With a little help from the staff, of course," qualified Medina. "Right this way." And he shepherded his flock of three toward the conference room.

With words and pictures, he and his staff gave the Fortes and Joe Mansour an up-to-date situation report. The project, as outlined in a coded radio message sent by Forte from the submarine nearly two weeks before, was not only on track, but slightly ahead of schedule.

Forte's secret weapon was a small bacterium with a big name: *Spirochaetum encaustum*. It had been simple to manufacture, since it doubled its numbers every nineteen minutes. The genetically engineered bacterium had been produced in a small plant isolated from the rest of the underground SD-2 complex by three separate enclosures and armed guards at the single entrance. As each five-gallon batch was finished, it was put in an airtight steel drum and connected with a supply of liquid nutrient just sufficient to sustain the bacteria's life. The waste products, mainly carbon dioxide, were subjected to 3,000-degree temperatures to kill any bacteria that might escape.

"When liberated on target," Medina said, "they will be combined with an aerosol to provide even, fast, and wide distribution. The beauty of the beast is that it's self-limiting: when it does its work, totally consumes its food supply, it dies of starvation."

"Yes, that's what's been worrying me," said Forte. "We can't take any chances with that damned stuff. If it got loose, that would be—"

"The end of civilization as we know it?" Jennifer smiled.

Mark Medina shook his head sadly. "The end of civilization—period. That's why we've been backstopping the *Spirochaetum encaustum* project with the so-called SE-slay. This is essentially a species-specific alkaloid that can be distributed, like the *Spirochaetum encaustum*, as an aerosol or applied to surfaces as a liquid. The bacterium, running out of food, is attracted to SE-slay, whose chemical composition mimics the nutrients that it must have. It gets set for a feast and gets a bellyful of lead."

"Figuratively," said Mansour.

"No—literally," Medina corrected him. "The lethal component happens to be lead. Once the bacterium is killed, its corpse is lead-impregnated. Considering the considerable bulk of food the trillions of bacteria will have ingested, the clean-up is going to be a large problem. We're working on it, but it will take a couple of months before we come up with an airtight plan."

"We can't wait," said Forte. "We'll go with what we have. We *do* have enough SE-slay, I hope?"

"Plenty. And, as I say, more than enough *Spirochaetum encaustum* to wipe out both our targets."

"And the Houston-to-Kiev Railroad?"

"Finished up six days ago. We've made two full-speed trial runs. It's working fine."

"That leaves the troops."

"No problem. We have 2,400 picked men, all veterans of the Texas Army special forces—1,600 for Kiev, 800 for Washington. They're all briefed, equipped, and ready to go."

Forte nodded. "We move the first day of December."

36. *TABULA RASA*
1 DECEMBER 2009

IT WAS LIKE CRUISING IN THE MOTIONLESS REALM OF THE fourth dimension.

Now that the maglev train had reached its terminal velocity of 488 miles per hour, all sensation of movement ceased. The only sound was the faint whisper of the slipstream as the bullet-nosed train hurtled through the tunnel along its single welded rail. No engineer sat in the cab of the automated train: there was no cab—and no stops until the train reached Kiev. At hundred-mile intervals along the route were sizable service chambers crammed with spare parts, communications and air-scrubbing equipment, bags of ceramic mix, bottles of compressed air, an ample reservoir of fresh water, and a small dormitory for maintenance workers. But the passengers on the thirty-two-car train saw none of this, for the train had no windows. It had no seats, either, but three ranks of bunks ranged on either side of a narrow aisle, separated from each other by the space just deep enough to accommodate a muscular young man.

The subsurface transport vibrated gently with the thrum of the powerful linear motors. The men slept, for they would need all their energy on arrival at Kiev. In the command center Ripley Forte, Texas Army Chief of Staff Artur Machado, and their assistants reviewed their tactics over outspread maps and mugs of steaming coffee. The plan was quite simple: the dispersion of the *Spirochaetum encaustum* from various points upwind of the new Soviet capital and the simultaneous deployment of SE-slay in a wide band outside the perimeter of the bacteria's release. Spreading the two substances presented no problems; the only difficulties Forte and Machado anticipated were the interception of some of his teams by Soviet security forces. But they relied on the Russian army uniforms the men wore, the excellent forged documentation each carried, and the ability to improvise of the Russian-speaking "officers" who led them, to disarm all suspicion until it was too late to halt the operation. Six hours out of Houston, they folded their maps and retired to their bunks. Forte, serenely confident that the decapitation of the Russian hydra would proceed as scheduled, slept the sleep of the just.

At 0110 they glided into the brightly lit but cavernous station 220 meters below the Soviet capital. With a minimum of talk and confusion, the men formed up into companies on the platform. The company commanders briefed once again—in Russian—their platoon and squad leaders. General Machado glanced at his watch. At exactly 0200 he lifted his hand, and the troops went their various ways.

The low-ceilinged Kiev station platform was nearly as long as a football field, and wider. The muster points had been marked with stenciled unit designations on the pavement and, to further diminish the risks of confusion, each unit was mustered closest to the access tunnel through which it would deploy. Now the platform emptied of Texan soldiers bundled up in Red Army winter uniforms and carrying spray canisters on their backs, the various units marching to their assigned stations down tunnels that radiated from the station like spokes on a wheel. Because satellite weather reports relayed from Houston to the subsurface transport indicated that the cold wind now sending shivers through Kiev came from the northeast, those tunnels to the southwest resounded only with the tread of boots from the SE-slay teams, which would have completely to encircle the city, while their mates transporting the *Spirochaetum encaustum* had merely to release their voracious bacteria from the northeast downwind upon the sleeping city.

Two hours and twenty minutes later all units were in position. Those along the northeast arc of the inner circle, the SE-slay teams, mounted steel ladders to assembly stations within five feet of the surface and stealthily bored small holes, large enough only to admit a periscope, to ground level. Then, assuring themselves that they were in a rural area as the map showed, with no visible sign of man nor beast, they quickly extended the manshaft up to the surface and poured out upon the countryside, lightly dusted with snow. The snow was a piece of luck—too light to impede their progress, heavy enough for them to use their tracks to find their way back to the assembly point. Squad by squad they proceeded toward their dispersal points. In case of challenge or interception by Soviet authorities, the Russian-speaking officers had written authorization directly from "the Red Army chief of staff" for this test of an aerosol-dispersed anti-influenza vaccine. If the story and their credentials still failed to convince the Russians, the Texans had the firepower to deal with any small patrol they might encounter.

At the same moment the teams were emerging from the earth, other SE-slay teams surfaced like moles along a twenty-eight-mile perimeter well outside the city limits of Kiev. At this dark and forbidding hour, they encountered few humans—a drunk wandering along a frozen road, an old woman returning from a trip to the privy, two men in a decrepit truck having ignition problems. The squads passed through the countryside without exciting the smallest notice, even by the two stranded men; apparently they were used to seeing Red Army units on night maneuvers.

Immediately upon emerging from the ground, the unit leaders of the SE-slay teams switched on their hand-held homing devices, spread their twelve men out in a line of approximately one hundred meters, and moved at quickstep toward the adjacent shafthead, guided by the signal from the transmitter placed there by their fellow squad leaders. This allowed each of the SE-slay teams to cover the maximum swath of ground without retracing their steps. As they walked rapidly forward, the men opened the nozzles of their spray tanks, which poured out a thick mist behind them.

Twenty minutes later, along the arc of the inner circle, the *Spirochaetum encaustum* teams released their aerosol, which within minutes crept like a thin fog into Kiev. There the destruction began, and continued at an accelerating pace as the Texas soldiers returned to their manshafts, replaced the sod, and plugged up the holes through which they had gained the surface. By 0540 all Texas army troops had returned to Kiev station, mission accomplished, without having been intercepted or incurring a single casualty. By 0615 all hands reboarded the maglev and were rocketing back toward Houston, twelve and a half hours away. Kiev station, its function fulfilled, was totally deserted, and would remain so until and unless a further Russian threat materialized. Considering the sweeping destruction, it would take generations before the city was restored to its former eminence—if ever.

While the 1,600 men of Machado's army were occupied in the environs of Kiev, a Texas army of 800, in civilian garb, had invaded Washington, D.C., where dusk had just fallen. Their task was easier: they needed only a dozen men to deploy the *Spirochaetum encaustum* at key points around the city—near the White House, the Congress, the Pentagon, the Central Intelligence Agency, the State Department, and other repositories of the nation's millions of tons of paper. Two-man teams, in tanker trucks equipped with spray nozzles, ringed the city with SE-slay, by saturating the ten-lane pavement the entire length of the Beltway girdling Washington. The rest of the men were armed with spray tanks and the cover story that they were neutralizing a possibly toxic spill. They laid down wide bands of SE-slay around the Library of Congress, the Folger Shakespeare Library, the National Archives, the National Institutes of Health, the public libraries, the Smithsonian Institution, the National Gallery of Art, Georgetown and George Washington universities, and various other centers of useful knowledge. Law libraries were studiously excepted. It took less than an hour before they completed their work, climbed in cars, and drove to outlying airports where chartered planes were waiting to convey them—having aroused little suspicion, and no opposition at all—back to Texas.

In both Kiev and Washington, the moment the *Spirochaetum encaustum* came into contact with a printed page, bacterial action began—on the ink. The bacterium was an ink-ravenous beast, and consumed the stuff with the zest of King Henry VIII attacking a leg of mutton. As it gorged, it proliferated, doubling its population by a factor of fifteen every hour. The exponential increase of the *Spirochaetum encaustum* quickly and simultaneously blanketed the two cities, except for those enclaves spared by the application of SE-slay around them. Newspapers turned white before their readers' eyes as the bacteria did their work. Billboards went blank. The labels on ketchup bottles disappeared. Maps vanished, collectors' valued first editions in private libraries became so much waste paper, love letters faded even as they were being read by eager young maidens. Washington suddenly became an illiterate's paradise.

And at the hundreds of govenment agencies, the bacterium was busy drinking oceans of ink on mountains of law books, speeches, memoranda, reports, scrolls, pamphlets, drafts, transcripts, text and reference books, tax and police records, weapons specifications, and court decisions that stretched back beyond the Revolutionary War. And of course, money... There was so much printed matter that it took the night of 1 December and most of the next day for the fulminating bacteria to complete their work. But in the end, save in the protected zones, not a single letter, printed or written by hand, remained in Washington—and none at all in Kiev.

The two world capitals had become white cities. Government abruptly ceased, for how can central governments exist without papers to shuffle? Willy-nilly, local control of the people's destinies, without regard or recourse to Big Brother in Washington or Kiev, had become a sudden reality. For the first time in three hundred years in the United States—and a thousand years in Russia—men were free to pursue their own bent without interference from ideologues, demagogues, and tyrants intent upon shackling the masses for their own enrichment, prestige, and comfort. The profession of politician became suddenly obsolete: the fat cats would now have to scratch out their living like everybody else.

ABOUT THE AUTHOR

For 30 years Daniel da Cruz has lived and worked—as a diplomat, teacher, businessman, and journalist—in Europe, Asia, and Africa.

He spent six World War II years as a U.S. Marine volunteer, serving ashore, afloat (in 1941 aboard the *Texas*), and aloft in the three war theaters. A *magna cum laude* graduate of Georgetown University's School of Foreign Service, da Cruz has been variously a census enumerator, magazine editor and editorial consultant, judo master—he holds a second degree Black Belt of the Kodokan Judo Institute, Tokyo—taxi driver, farmer, public relations officer for an oil company, salesman, foreign correspondent, publishers' representative, vice-president of a New York advertising agency, slaughter-house skinner, captain of a Texas security organization, American Embassy press attaché in Baghdad, copper miner and Adjunct Professor of Anthropology at Miami University.

Da Cruz has published many books, among them an American history text, a monograph on Amerindian linguistics, and three suspense novels for Ballantine Books, the most recent of which, *The Captive City*, was awarded a special "Edgar." He has written five other science-fiction novels, *The Grotto of the Formigans* (Del Rey, 1980), *The Ayes of Texas* (Del Rey, 1982), *Texas on the Rocks* (Del Rey, 1986), *F-Cubed* (Del Rey, 1987), and *Mixed Doubles* (Del Rey, 1989).